PERFECT IMPERFECTIONS

MARIAH ANKENMAN

ISBN: 979-8-9881-7376-2 (ebook edition)

ISBN: 979-8-9881-7377-9 (paperback edition)

Edited by P.K.

Cover Design by Getcovers

❀ Created with Vellum

DEDICATION

To the little girl who thought she was broken because her brain told her scary things: someday you will lose to the dark voice and some days you will win.
Keep fighting!

CONTENT WARNING

Perfect Imperfections is a fun, open door steamy romance with a happy ending, but there may be some on page depictions that may be triggering for some readers. On page sex/Past spousal and parental abandonment/Discussion of car accidents resulting in deaths/Discussions of substance abuse/On page OCD compulsion and rituals. Please read with care.

CHAPTER 1

*P*enguin poop smelled divine. Other people might not think so, but to Ellie Clark, the slightly sour stench filled her heart with purpose. It had a lot to do with the cute little tuxedo-wearing creatures who produced said feces. As the keeper for the penguins at the Sunlight Zoo in Park County, Colorado, those tiny creatures were her responsibility, and she loved them.

Animals had always occupied a special place in Ellie's heart. They didn't judge or pity her for her compulsions and rituals. Never commented on how weird it was when she locked her door three times before she went to bed. Sure, they didn't comment on anything because they technically couldn't speak—except for Bill, the parrot who could say "hello" "welcome to the zoo" and "you're fabulous, Doll-face." The last phrase being taught to him by her best friend and co-worker Cam, who said if the bird was going to be squawking all day long, he might as well say something positive.

"Hey, Doll-face, what's the bird word?"

Speaking of Cam. Ellie smiled as her fellow keeper

entered the back room of the aviary building where they housed all the food and supplies for the birds living here. The eleven-hundred square foot building was home to various species of birds. They had macaws, tawny frog mouths, a variety of ducks, finches, and warmer climate aviary animals, Bill the parrot, and, of course, a dozen African Black-Footed penguins. She and Cam were the head keepers of the exhibit, and the women loved the animals as if they were their own feathery little babies.

"Hi, Cam." She waved a gloved hand at her tall, red-headed friend. "Everyone seems in good spirits today."

"Bingo's looking good?"

Bingo was an approximately eight-year-old male penguin they'd gotten from an animal rescue team in Key West. They had found the poor guy washed up on the beach, his right flipper torn almost in half. No one knew how it happened or how he'd strayed so far from the southern shoreline of Africa —the penguin's natural habitat—but they had fixed him up as best as humanly possible and sent to the Sunlight Zoo. While they could release some animals back into the wild, Bingo could never survive on his own with his damaged flipper. Here, he didn't have to hunt his own food. Which suited the tiny bird just fine. Unfortunately, Bingo had recently developed arthritis. Both she and Cam worried about the little guy.

"He seems to be doing better today." Opening the large industrial fridge beside her, Ellie grabbed the bucket of sardines she'd prepared when she first came in this morning. "Killian checked him out about an hour ago and seemed pleased with his progress with the new therapy."

Doctor Stephan Killian and his husband Rob were the Zoo's on-staff veterinarians. The two men were excellent doctors who loved animals more than anyone Ellie knew. They were also very nice people who never made her feel awkward or weird about her OCD. Most people at the zoo were like that—most of the people who worked directly with animals, that is. It could be something to do with their shared ability to connect better with the furry, feathered, and scaled community than the homo-sapiens one.

Cam crossed the dark gray cement floor, grabbing a microphone headset from the rack on the wall, and set about checking the device before clipping it to the brown-corded belt on her khaki shorts.

"Good. His waddle was worrying me last week." Her friend fiddled with the earpiece before tossing her mass of riotous red curls over a shoulder and affixing it to her ear. She adjusted the small mic connected to the headpiece before continuing. "I think you should sneak him an extra sardine today."

As she checked the penguins' food—for the second time— she smiled and shook her head. "You know I can't do that. Killian said he needed to shave off a few ounces. The extra weight is bad for his joints."

Cam stuck out her bottom lip. "But he's hungry."

No, Bingo got plenty of food, just like every animal at Sunlight Zoo. The old penguin was a con artist, and Cam had a soft heart when it came to the fancy flights of feathered friends in their care. Her friend loved the animals as much as Ellie did, but she wasn't above sneaking them treats. Nothing harmful, of course, Cam would never cause harm to... anything. The woman was sweet as caramel apple pie. But all the birds knew she'd give them an extra fish if they turned those dark eyes on her.

"You're a sucker."

Full lips turned up into a wide grin. "Damn right. I can't resist a dapper."

One of their jokes. They called the penguins dappers since the two-foot birds appeared to be wearing formalwear.

"Speaking of dappers…"

Ellie set the bucket of fish down on the metal counter and reached up to the cabinet on the wall to grab the vitamins she'd slip into the sardines' mouth seconds before the penguins ate them. A handy trick they used to get the extra supplements to the animals who needed them. She grabbed the small bottle, counting out the seven she would need and slipping them into her front pocket.

"Are you ready for speed dating?"

The cap she'd been trying to screw back onto the bottle flew across the room at her friend's question. Cam chuckled, jogging over to where the bit of plastic clattered to the floor and grabbed it.

"I take it that's a no?"

Squeezing the lidless bottle in her palm, she tried to breathe as her pulse raced out of control. "You signed me up? I told you I didn't want to do it."

"And I told you, you need to get back out there," the tall woman said as she walked over to Ellie, cap extended in her hand. "It's been, what, a year since Jeff the dickhead?"

A year and a half, but who cared? She didn't need to *get back out there*. She liked it in here. In her world where there were animals and Cam, and house-buying shows she could binge, alone. Without anyone commenting on how she'd never own a home with her mountain of student debt. What more did a woman need?

An orgasm?

Okay, yes, but that's what the internet was for. A woman could buy all sorts of fun toys to get her where she needed to go. No man required.

"I'm fine, Cam. I don't need a guy."

"Doll-face," Cam laughed. "No one *needs* a guy, but they're kind of fun to have around every now and then. Trust me."

She did trust Cam, but guys were always falling all over

themselves around her friend. With her long legs, generous curves, beautiful copper red hair contrasted by her ice-blue eyes and her smooth, pale skin so flawless it looked photoshopped, the woman could have her pick of guys. Not that Ellie was hideous. Her five-foot two stature wouldn't win her any modeling contracts any time soon. The brown spots scattered on her fair skin looked more like sunspots than cute freckles, and her brown eyes and hair were what one date called *forgettable*. But she could manage *cute* when she tried.

Trying was exhausting, which was why she so rarely put in the effort. Her bestie, however, was a romantic at heart. Always on the lookout for that happily ever after. She was always trying new dating apps and gimmicks to find "Mr. Right." Meanwhile, all Ellie wanted was to have one date where the guy didn't look at her like she was an alien from Neptune for tapping her straw three times before drinking.

"Just don't do it, sweetie."

Her mother's words rang in her head like the clanging of a bell tower. A very loud and very wrong bell tower. If controlling her OCD was that simple, she would have stopped years ago and not spent thousands on therapy to get to where she was today.

Able to live with her OCD rather than letting it control her.

"Yeah, maybe," she agreed with her friend. "But speed dating?"

"Well, you suck at Tinder, so I had to think of something else."

"All the guys on that app just wanted to have sex."

Cam's mouth opened, an incredulous gleam filling her eyes. "Of course, they wanted sex! Most people do, not all, but the people on that app are looking for hookups."

But she didn't want a hookup. Ellie wanted someone to

laugh with, to feel comfortable enough around to be herself and not worry about her compulsions. And, yeah, okay, some hot sex would be nice too, but that just wasn't in the cards for her. As evidenced by her last few disastrous attempts at a relationship. She wasn't meant for love, and she was fine with that. If only her friend would agree.

"Cam, I don't know. I really don't want to—"

"Look," Cam cut her off with a wave of a hand. "I know this whole...opening up to people thing is hard for you. I get it. I mean, I don't *get* it, but I understand it's difficult, but I just want you to be happy. I know there's some great guy out there who can make you happy and he would be so damn lucky to have you."

And that was another reason they were friends. Cam accepted her. Sure, her bestie tried to push her boundaries every now and then, get Ellie to "live a little" as she said. Her friend only wanted what was best for her and that's why she let Cam talk her into stepping out of her comfort zone.

"Just come to this one night and if it's a bust, I promise to put the matchmaking on the backburner. Okay?"

She nodded with a sigh. "I'll think about it, okay?"

"Yay!" Cam squealed, grabbing Ellie and pulling her in for a hug. A slightly awkward hug since her friend was significantly taller than her. She let out a small squeak as her face was smothered against her best friend's very generous chest. This was not the first time Cam's boobs had suffocated her face. Pretty much every enthusiastic hug was like this. Cam gave Ellie a lot of enthusiastic hugs. Because she was awesome like that.

"Enough mushy stuff. It's time to feed the penguins."

Cam released her, a huge grin gracing her beautiful face. "All right, let's get out there and feed the high society."

Ellie made her way through the back room to the door leading out into the penguin enclosure with Cam following close behind. The birds had an inside area closed off to the public, but they preferred the outside enclosure with the faux rock and large pool designed to replicate their natural habitat. As always, a sizeable crowd had gathered to watch penguin feeding time. Cam turned her mic on and welcomed the group, giving a brief explanation of the African Black-Footed penguins and their diets.

As her friend and coworker addressed the crowd, Ellie scanned the tiny aquatic birds. The two-foot tall, adorable animals waddled about. They hurried toward her as they realized they were about to be fed. Her gaze sought Bingo, brow furrowing until she spotted the older penguin at the back of the oncoming huddled mass. A smile turned up her lips as the slightly overweight bird waddled over to her, his gait much better than it had been a week ago.

"You're still not getting any sympathy fish from me, Bingo," she said under her breath.

Sometimes she thought animals could understand humans better than anyone realized because the moment she uttered the words, Bingo let out a loud, pitiful bray. The Black-Footed penguins had a distinct donkey-like bray call, which gave them the moniker "jackass penguin" in the animal sciences.

"Oh fine, but if you go over your goal weight this week, Dr. Killian is going to be mad." She was just as big a pushover as Cam. Chuckling, she slipped Bingo an extra fish when he reached her outstretched hand.

The crowed ooed and ahhed over the little birds, calling out for the midday meal, but Ellie barely heard them. Feeding hungry animals was a laborious task. She had to keep the chum bucket out of reach. A challenge even when you considered the tiny stature of the penguins. They were extremely clever and motivated. Once, she had a couple team up on her. Sunny had lain down beside her, and his mate

Daisy hopped up on him. The penguin tower made Daisy just tall enough to jump up and dive headfirst into the bucket. Since then, Ellie kept the sardines high above her head during feeding time. Hurt her arm, but it kept the cute creatures from eating too much and getting a bellyache.

As she mentally counted who had been fed, while also discreetly slipping the vitamins from her pocket into the fish and making sure the proper penguin received it, movement from outside the exhibit caught her eye.

A quick glance up revealed a large school group of what looked to be elementary students. Not uncommon. School groups visited the zoo all the time and feeding times were popular educational experiences. What disturbed Ellie was what she witnessed happening at the edge of the group.

Her chest tightened as she saw three large boys taunting and holding a notebook above the head of a small girl. Having been on the tiny side her entire life, she couldn't help but flash back to some very similar experiences. The small girl with short blonde hair jumped in the air trying to grab the notebook, but the biggest kid held it high above her head, laughing.

Kids can be real jerks.

Temper flaring, Ellie wondered where the teacher and chaperones were. Why was no one helping the young girl? She looked so small, couldn't be more than seven or eight.

One of the penguins, Apollo, brayed, demanding her attention. She reached into the bucket for the last sardine, passing it off to the cute but ornery bird. Mr. Impatient nipped her finger in return.

"Ouch!" Silly bird thought his name meant he was a god and must have his every wish granted right this very moment. "Calm down, Apollo. You got your lunch."

He nuzzled her hand in apology before hopping off the edge of the fake rock, making a perfectly splash-less dive into the pool below. And just like that, all was forgiven. She could never be mad at these wonderful creatures. They filled her with such joy. Zoo keeping may not pay much in cash, but it sure filled her heart with happiness.

The rest of the brood, realizing chow time was done, either followed Apollo or waddled off to sun themselves on the rocks, preening and posing for the dozens of camera flashes aimed their way. Little divas.

As Cam finished her speech, calling for questions from the crowd, Ellie found her gaze returning to the group of boys and the small girl. She'd hoped someone had discovered the inappropriate behavior and intervened, but to her dismay, no one had noticed. Her breath caught as she saw the teasing had gotten worse. The taunts had increased from holding the book out of reach to the three boys tossing it back and forth in a cruel game of keep away. Tears pricked at the back of her eyes.

Where the hell are the adults?

Her mind raced. What to do? She could shout out to the boys to stop, but she wasn't big on reprimanding other peoples' children, plus the zoo frowned on their employees yelling at the guests. She could try to signal the school-teacher, but it was almost impossible to tell who that was in the enormous crowd gathered. There was no way for her to intervene herself. A pool of water and a metal railing separated her from the group of children. But she had to do something!

Seriously, could no one see the poor girl needed help?

Mind racing a million miles a minute, all the worst-case scenarios flashed through Ellie's mind like a macabre movie. The girl could fall and break her arm or tumble over the rail into the water. Her throat closed as anxiety coursed through her body, tightening every muscle. She hated this, hated that her stupid brain did this. Why? Why did she have to envision

9

these horrible things? Pulse racing, she tried remembering what Dr. Mitchell, her therapist, taught her.

Nothing bad was going to happen. The little girl would be fine—emotionally scarred maybe, but she was safe, the zoo was safe—nothing would hurt her. The crazy images flashing through Ellie's mind were just her brain sending an error message. It wouldn't come true. Nothing was going to—

At that moment, time stopped. As if in slow motion, she watched as the fear in her mind became real. Watched as the small girl jumped for the notebook one boy was holding while another boy snuck up and pushed her from behind. The push catapulted the small child into the air. Tiny arms flailed as the child fell headfirst over the metal railing straight into the cold, musky water of the penguin pool. Shouts and screams filled the air. People panicked. Some ran, calling out for help, others stood there, mouths hanging open in shock.

The penguins, confused by this interloper to their habitat, scattered. The ones in the water swam fast and far, the birds on land waddled back to their huts safely tucked away in the stone façade wall.

Ellie didn't even think twice. With all the chaos raging around her, she did the one thing she knew had to be done. Without a pause, or breath, she tossed the empty chum bucket aside and dove in after the girl.

CHAPTER 2

*T*he frigid water enveloped her, shocking Ellie's system. They kept the pool at fourteen degrees Fahrenheit to mimic the Benguela current the penguins were used to in the wild. But Ellie wasn't a penguin and the icy water stung like a thousand needles piercing her skin.

Holy crap!

Inside she screamed, but outside she needed to keep her cool—ha!—and find the little girl. Luckily penguins were not aggressive creatures. Sure, they'd nip at your hand if you got in their space, but they really couldn't do much damage to a human. Icy cold water, however? Now that could harm a person.

She dove, spotting a small flailing body at the bottom of the pool. The water only reached a depth of eight feet, but the tiny girl, bogged down by her shoes and clothes, had sunk like a stone. Ellie kicked her legs, stretching her arms as far as those short limbs would go. Her hands slogged through the resistance of the water and finally made purchase with one frail arm.

With an iron grip, she tugged, pulling the terrified girl

through the water to her. With one arm wrapped around the child's chest, she shifted, pointing up and kicking her legs with all the strength she had left in her body. They rocketed toward the surface, breaking through the freezing water into the life-giving bliss of air.

"We have a code red. We need medical and security personnel here now!"

She could hear Cam shouting into her walkie-talkie as she pulled herself and the girl out of the water onto the hard ground. People were screaming and yelling, but all Ellie cared about were the hacking coughs and muffled sobs of the young girl held securely in her arms.

"It's okay, sweetie. I've got you. You're going to be all right."

The small girl coughed, spewing water from her mouth and nose. A hoarse cry left her blue lips. Her skin was ice cold and pale white. Ellie tightened her arms around the child, rubbing her back, knowing as cold as she was right now the tiny thing had to be feeling the effects of the icy water much worse.

"Cam, I need a towel!"

Her friend ran back into the aviary, long legs sprinting. In mere seconds, she was at Ellie's side, wrapping a soft, cotton towel around the child clinging to her.

"What the hell happened?" her friend asked, face calm, but gaze wild with panic.

Tucking the towel around the shivering girl, she spoke softly, "Some ass— not nice boys were teasing her and pushed her over the railing into the water."

Her friend's blue eyes turned colder than the water Ellie had just been submerged in.

"Little jerks!"

"Mrs. James sa-says it's not nice to ca-call people jer-jerk," the girl said between shivers and more hacking coughs.

Ellie's heart squeezed. Where the hell were the medics? "You're absolutely right, sweetie. It's not nice to call people names, but it's also not nice to tease and push. Those boys shouldn't have been mean to you."

"Is Mrs. James your teacher?" Cam asked, bending her head down to smile at the girl.

Her tiny wet blonde head nodded. *Mrs. James.* Good to know. Now Ellie knew who to rip a new one for not paying attention to her students.

"Charlotte! Charlotte!"

Speaking of. The woman frantically waving her arms on the other side of the pool, terrified expression on her face must be the teacher in question.

"Charlotte? Is that your name?" After one more cough, the tiny head nodded. "Hi, Charlotte. I'm Ellie and this is Cam."

"Hey, kiddo. Is that lady screaming your name your mommy?"

Charlotte gave them a hesitant smile and shook her head. "No. That's Mrs. James. I don't have a mommy."

Ellie wiped at the water dripping down her cheek. A tear might have leaked out to join the wetness of her appearance at the sweet girl's matter-of-fact statement. No mother and being bullied? Couldn't life give the poor kid a break?

Nope, because life could be a real asshole to people. She knew that as much as the next person.

"You want to handle the teacher?" she asked Cam. "I'll stay with Charlotte until the medics get here and—"

Her words were cut off as the screaming sound of the Zoo's emergency vehicle overpowered the noisy crowd. Vehicle was a generous term. The thing was just an extra-outfitted golf cart used to transport injured people to the front gate for an ambulance ride. A man and a woman in

EMT uniforms jumped off the cart as it slammed to a stop in front of the birdhouse.

"About damn time," Cam grumbled, standing. "I'll go let them in."

As her friend went to show the EMTs through the back of the aviary to the outside exhibit, Ellie tried to keep Charlotte talking. She took some biology classes in her undergrad program, but it was mostly concerning animal biology, not human. One thing she knew was never to let a person in danger of hypothermia go to sleep. She couldn't say if little Charlotte had been in the water long enough for that, but she wasn't taking any chances.

"So, Charlotte, do you like penguins?"

Nice question, Ellie. The girl just had a traumatic experience dealing with the animals and here you are shoving it in her face.

Crap. This was why she had no social life. Tact, thy name was not Ellie.

"They're okay. I like elephants the mostest, but Daddy says I can't have one. He says they're too big to fit in our backyard."

Oh, thank goodness she had a dad. Ellie couldn't take it if the poor girl had no one.

"He's right. Elephants need a lot of room. In fact, the elephant enclosure we have here is only one area for our elephants to play in. They have an entire yard behind the big gray fence that only special people can see."

The little girl pulled her head away from Ellie's chest, bright green eyes big and round. "I'm special. My daddy always says so!"

Sounded like a great dad. She wondered if super dad knew about his daughter's bully troubles.

"I bet you are. Maybe I can work something out and we can find a time for you to have a visit to their special yard."

14

Charlotte squealed with delight. The smile on her little face warming Ellie's heart.

"Really?"

"I'll talk to my boss."

She was sure Tammy would say yes. This entire incident was going to be a PR nightmare. Thank goodness it happened in the penguin enclosure where the birds were relatively harmless and not somewhere like the tiger exhibit. If anyone fell into a predator exhibit, the DART team would have to be called and there was always the possibility the animals would have to be put down. Tragic, but human life trumped animal. Something not everyone agreed on and that had brought up many fierce debates among everyone in the zoology and animal rights field.

Her thoughts were interrupted as the sounds of heavy boots hitting the cement reached her ears. Suddenly, two EMTs crouched by her side. She glanced up to see Cam standing behind the two emergency personnel, a worried smile on her face. The male EMT unzipped the large bag he carried, pulling out supplies, including—thank goodness—an emergency blanket. As he opened it, taking the towel from around Charlotte and replacing it with the shiny PET film around the small girl's shoulders.

"Hey there, my name is Jayla, and that's Jay," the female EMT nodded to the man, then winked. "No relation."

That got a chuckle out of Charlotte.

"What's your name?"

"Charlotte Green."

"Well, Charlotte Green, would you like to come with me so we can check you out and make sure you're okay?"

Tiny hands clutched Ellie's wet shirt, digging in with a fierceness that wrapped around her heart. Charlotte nuzzled her face into Ellie's chest, refusing to move from the safety of her lap. Emotions clogged her throat. She'd never been good with people. She was crap with them, to be honest. Her anxiety and compulsions either got on their nerves or freaked them out. Which was why she preferred animals. If it wasn't for Cam forcing her to be social every now and then, she might never leave the house other than for work.

Charlotte clutching her as if she never wanted to let Ellie go was foreign to her. She didn't understand the small child's fierce attachment. It could be because Ellie saved her or because she held the draw of a promised elephant encounter. Whatever the reason, Ellie found herself suddenly very smitten and protective of the girl.

"Somebody's got a fan," Cam chuckled.

The feeling was mutual. The kid was quickly easing her way into Ellie's heart. She was so small and precious. How could she not? "Can you do the exam while she sits in my lap?"

She wanted Charlotte to get the medical care to make sure she was all right, but she didn't want the little girl more stressed than necessary. Poor thing had a tough enough day as it was.

Jayla glanced at her partner, who nodded with a shrug. "We can do most of it right here. Is that okay with you, Charlotte?"

The tiny head bobbed up and down, her grip easing on Ellie's shirt.

"I'm going to use this light to check your eyes, okay?"

Charlotte nodded. "That's an otoscope," the girl announced proudly.

Her eyebrows rose. Someone was certainly smart. She shared a shocked look with Jayla.

"That's right, Charlotte. Now, can you follow my finger with just your eyes?"

Charlotte sat like a perfect angel in her lap as the EMTs ran through their list of checks. Halfway through the examination, some commotion beyond the enclosure caught her eye. Tammy, the Zoo's general manager, had arrived along with a few other department heads. She watched as Tammy identified the teacher—or more likely knew who Mrs. James was thanks to a radio call from Cam—and pulled the harried woman aside to talk.

"Crap, I mean dang," Cam corrected with a quick glance at Charlotte. "We're going to have to fill out so much paperwork for this."

"Am I going to be in trouble for falling in the water?"

Ellie glared at her friend, who winced at the softly uttered question. Pasting on what she hoped was a comforting smile, she glanced down at the sweet child in her lap. "No, sweetie. You did nothing wrong. Though those boys will have to face the consequences of what they did. It's not nice to push."

"One time I pushed Molly when she wouldn't share the trucks and Daddy grounded me from TV for a whole day!"

Hopefully, the boys would get a more severe punishment than loss of television privileges. Today's incident could have been so much worse. If it hadn't happened during penguin feeding time, no one would have been out here. Sure, the zoo staff around was always around, but no one would have been in the enclosure, near the pool. Charlotte could have drowned before anyone had time to jump in and—

No!

She had to stop thinking like that. It didn't happen that way.

"Ma'am, are you okay?"

Jay glanced at her neck, where she could feel her pulse racing a mile a minute. His gloved hands reached out to grab her wrist, checking her heart rate.

"I'm fine."

"You're sure?" Worried eyes called her bluff.

"Yes." Just your run-of-the-mill anxiety caused by the

ever-present daily battle she fought with her OCD. No biggie. She took a few deep breaths, reminding herself everything was fine now, and no one had died. The pounding in her chest slowed, heart rate returning to normal even as her anxiety stuck around. She knew from experience it would be there for a while. "I'm good."

He glanced over at her once more with doubt but nodded. "Okay, we should really give you an exam too, since you were in the water as well."

Wasn't the first time she'd jumped in there. She didn't do it often, but once Bingo had cramped up mid-swim and she jumped in to save the poor old guy. Turned out he'd been fine, and she'd just freaked out a little. Luckily, it had happened after closing time, so no one had borne witness to her ridiculousness.

"Okay, guys, let's set up over here. I want to get the rescue team in the shot."

Her head snapped up at the deep, professional sounding voice calling out orders. She groaned in unison with Cam as she glanced across the pool to see News Channel 4's special reporter and crew setting up their equipment.

"Oh man, and now the vultures descend."

Her friend had it wrong. Equating reporters to scavenger birds was insulting. Vultures were beautiful, useful creatures. Reporters were…well, Ellie didn't much care for the media, and she hated giving interviews.

"You don't think Tammy's going to make me talk to them, do you?"

Her friend let out a snort of a laugh. "Are you kidding? Tammy's about to blow her lid right now over this whole thing."

The director looked steamed as she marched her way over to the news crew.

"If she can't shut them down, she's going to offer you up

on a silver platter as the hero of the day. Anything to make the zoo look good and non-culpable for this…incident."

She wanted the zoo to look good. This was her job, and she'd like to keep it. If people thought the zoo was dangerous, they might stop coming. Then they'd lose funding and cut jobs, and not only would Ellie be out on her butt, but more importantly, where would all the animals go? So yes, she could understand painting her the hero, but did that mean she had to give an interview?

She watched as Tammy talked to the reporter, nodding her head, and turning with a big smile on her face to point at —*crap*—Ellie.

Noooooooo. Dammit!

Looked like she was going to be giving an interview. Her stomach turned over, mouth going dry despite the two mouthfuls of water she'd spit out hauling Charlotte out of the pool. Ugh! She hated giving interviews, being put on the spot. Her nerves got all frazzled, and she never knew what to say. Cam usually handled any type of interview that came their way, but she couldn't shove this one off on her friend.

Nope. Because I had to jump in and be the 'hero of the day.'

"Are we going to be on TV?" Charlotte asked, gazing up with big, bright eyes.

Okay, totally worth enduring the agony of an awkward interview for that sweet smile.

"Looks like it, sweetie."

"Yay!"

At least someone was excited.

"Cam, Ellie."

The radio on Cam's hip crackled. Cam grabbed it, bringing it to her mouth to respond as the EMTs continued to check Charlotte and Ellie.

"Go for Bird Force One."

She chuckled at her friend's code name for them. Across

the way, Tammy shook her head. The director didn't always care for Cam's humor. Ellie thought her bestie was hilarious.

"The teacher called the child's father. He should arrive soon."

"Daddy's coming?" The young girl bounced in her lap at the prospect of seeing her father.

"I need Ellie to give the news crews an interview. Be ready in ten, Ellie. And try not to…just, be professional."

"Crews? As in plural?"

Her question answered itself as she saw more people with cameras and microphones arriving, setting up gear.

"Craaaaap!"

"Daddy says that's a bad word."

Shit! At least she hadn't said that out loud. Glancing down at the child in her arms, she smiled. "Your daddy is right. It is a bad word and I'm sorry I said it."

Charlotte grinned, revealing one missing lower canine. "That's okay. Daddy said the S word once when he stepped on my blocks. I forgot to put them away, but he said he wasn't mad. I just had ta remember next time."

It was clear this little girl was the apple of her father's eye. Poor guy must be a mess right about now.

CHAPTER 3

*S*ullivan Green was a mess. From the moment his daughter's teacher called and told him there'd been an accident involving Charlotte on their field trip to the zoo, he hadn't been able to breathe, think, do anything except drive with a furious purpose to get to the one person in his life that meant more than anyone else.

His daughter.

He'd rushed out of his office, grateful that his practice employed multiple doctors and nurse practitioners. Emergencies happened to people in all walks of life, even doctors. There'd be people to cover his patients for the day.

His foot pressed hard on the accelerator. The zoo was only fifteen minutes away from his office. Sunlight wasn't a big town, but it resided on the outskirts of Denver, Colorado, and drew in the city's overflow, so sometimes traffic could be a bitch. Thankfully, this Friday afternoon did not seem to be one of those times. Hoping he wouldn't run into any speed traps along the way, he drove with hurried caution. He needed to get to his daughter, but he needed to get there in one piece.

"Mrs. James said she was okay," he spoke the words out loud to remind himself his daughter, his heart, his entire fucking world, was fine. "Charlotte is fine."

He repeated the mantra in his head as he pulled into the zoo parking lot. Not bothering with searching for a parking spot in the crowded lot, he pulled right up to the front-loading area. Throwing the car into park, he jumped out, turning at the shout of a large white man in a security uniform standing there with a perturbed look on his face.

"Sir, you can't park your—"

"Charlotte Green! I'm her father. I was told she fell into an animal enclosure." And how in the fucking hell had that happened? Someone better have some damn answers for him. After he had his baby girl safely in his arms.

The guard's expression morphed into one of guilt and fear. *That's right buddy, you better be worried.* Until he saw his daughter, Sullivan didn't give a shit about rules and parking.

"Mr. Green, sir. I've been instructed to take you to your daughter right away."

He nodded to the guard, fear and anger stoking the fire of urgency within.

"The EMTs are with her now, but I believe she's fine."

He'd be the judge of that. Then he'd decide what the hell he was going to do about this whole mess. If the zoo had faulty safety standards putting people—namely his kid—in danger, he'd pull all the power he had to see it rectified.

The guard motioned to a small golf cart emblazoned with *Sunlight Zoo Security* on its hood. He hopped into the passenger side while the man in uniform slid behind the wheel. The guard started the dinky cart. Sullivan jerked as they took off, surprisingly faster than he was assuming the vehicle could handle. Sullivan's leg bounced up and down, twitching nervously as his heart pounded a furious beat, blood heating his entire body as it pumped viciously through his veins. Never had he felt fear like this.

As a doctor, he'd seen the worst of the worst. Car crashes with mangled limbs, construction accidents with missing appendages, violent crimes that made him question his faith in humanity. He practiced Internal Medicine now, but he'd done his rotation in the ER during residency. He knew how to stay calm in an emergency when you were fighting with death, the stubborn bastard. A cool head was needed to make split-second decisions. You couldn't think with emotions when saving someone's life.

But this wasn't just someone. This was his daughter. The person who came screaming into the world after fifteen hours of labor and stole his heart away forever. A tiny bundle of joy who spit up on him after every meal for the first six months of her life. The girl with his green eyes. This was Charlotte.

How could he stay detached from her?

He couldn't.

The golf cart slowed as they approached the penguin enclosure. Before the guard even turned off the vehicle, Sullivan jumped out, sprinting toward a sight that made his heart race with fear and joy all at once. There across the metal railing and clear blue pool of water was his angel, his life, his Charlotte. She was sitting in the lap of a woman with dark brown hair plastered about her head. They both appeared to be soaking wet, but thankfully unharmed. Two EMTs crouched by their side.

"Charlotte!" he yelled, chest aching with the need to hop over the rail and swim to her. *Not a good idea, dumbass. Get ahold of yourself. Find your calm. You don't want to scare her any more than she already is.*

He knew that, but it was damn hard to control his emotions when all he wanted to do was hold his baby in his arms and promise to protect her from every bad thing in the world for the rest of her life. Couldn't be done, he knew, but try telling a stressed parent that.

Her little blonde head turned, that beautiful, life-giving smile lighting up her sweet, round face. "Daddy!"

At that one uttered word in her precious voice, his heart rate slowed to a normal rhythm. She grinned up at the woman holding her, cheerfully saying, "That's my daddy."

The woman smiled at Charlotte. "I bet he's happy to see you."

She had no idea. He was so relieved he could soar across all the putrid smelling water just to get to his daughter.

"Mr. Green?"

Turning his head, he saw a tall, Black woman wearing a charcoal pantsuit and a badge hanging from a lanyard around her neck proclaiming her to be Tammy Hughes, director of Sunlight Zoo.

"Yes, I'm Dr. Green."

"I'm Tammy Hughes, director of the Sunlight Zoo." He'd ascertained that already but didn't interrupt. "I'm sure you have a lot of questions and I'd be happy to answer them all, but why don't I take you to see your daughter first?"

"Thank you."

Points for the zoo on knowing his priorities. Yes, he wanted a full explanation of how something like this could happen. Before he left the premises with his daughter, he'd damn sure know who was responsible and see them take responsibility. But right now, all he cared about was getting Charlotte into his arms. The rest could wait.

He followed Ms. Hughes into the aviary, brushing off Charlotte's panicked teacher with a wave of his hand. He liked Mrs. James. She was a good educator, but he didn't have time for her apologies or explanations right now. He needed to get to his daughter.

The zoo director led him through a blue door labeled employees only. Beyond the door, he found himself in a large gray room with a huge silver industrial fridge against one wall and a line of sinks against the other.

"Right through here to get to the outside exhibit." Ms. Hughes motioned with her hand to another blue door. This one led him out into the sunshine, this time inside the penguin enclosure. The sour smell of animal feces filled his nostrils, but he didn't care. All he cared about was—

"Daddy!"

Charlotte jumped up from the woman's lap and ran toward him. He jogged a few feet forward before bending down on one knee and scooping her up into his arms. He clutched her to him until she wiggled with complaint.

"Too tight, Daddy."

"Sorry, Angel." He couldn't hold her tight enough, couldn't smell her deep enough. She smelled like stinky penguin water, but underneath that was play-dough and strawberry shampoo. The familiar scent of his daughter. A balm to his frazzled nerves. His hands ran over her, checking for injuries. He finally let out his last breath of worry when he discovered none.

"I fell in the water, but Ellie saved me." Her little hands slapped against his cheeks as she whispered in utter seriousness. "She says you were right about the elephants, but I could come here, and she'd show me their secret playground."

"She sounds like a very smart woman, and I think she's due a huge thank you from the both of us." He glanced up from his daughter's precious face to see the woman in question stand and walk over to them.

"Sullivan Green, this is Eleanor Clark, one of our head aviary keepers," Ms. Hughes said, motioning toward the soaked woman standing before him.

"Ms. Clark, I...I can't thank you enough for saving my daughter." The words were tense and filled with emotion as they left his throat, his arms tightening around his daughter once again.

The woman blushed, appearing uncomfortable with his gratitude. "Call me Ellie, please, and I just did what anyone would do."

Really? He didn't see anyone else soaking wet from rescuing a seven-year-old girl from drowning. Charlotte knew how to swim. He made sure of that the day she was old enough for baby swim lessons, but he also knew falling into the water with all your clothes and shoes on could be a death sentence.

"You're a hero, Ellie. Our hero," he insisted.

Ellie shrugged, tugging on her right ear lobe. "You have a very special little girl there, Mr. Green. Such a brave one."

She bopped Charlotte on the nose and his daughter giggled with glee. It seemed the two had formed a bond. Life and death situations did that, he supposed.

"I one hundred percent agree, and please call me Sullivan."

"Of course, Sullivan."

Something shot up his spine at the soft utterance of his name from her lips. A spark of something he hadn't felt in far too long. Strange. Probably just leftover zing from his haywire emotions. His gaze glanced over her. She was a tiny thing, couldn't be more than five feet and a hundred and ten pounds soaking wet. Which she was. His doctor's eye assessed her physically, scanning for any wounds, satisfied when he found none.

His male gaze, however, roamed over her with a different intent entirely. Though the woman had just come out of smelly animal water, he noticed her eyes were a deep brown. Like dark chocolate, delicious and easy to indulge in. Her dark hair looked as if it had once been contained in a braid, but now pieces were plastered to her forehead and neck, bits sticking up here and there. Her lips, like everything about her, were small and slightly blue—no doubt because of the icy plunge she took saving his daughter—but they curved with the most delightful smile as she laughed at something Charlotte said.

Fascinating.

He couldn't remember the last time he'd felt this instant draw to a woman. Probably just a bit of idol worship for her gallant heroics today. That was all.

The EMTs, having packed up their gear, came to join the small group. It did not surprise Sullivan to discover he knew them both. Though he worked in private practice now, he still did the occasional shift in the county ER when needed.

"Hey, Jay, Jayla."

"Hi, Dr. Green."

The taller man reached out to shake the hand not currently wrapped around Charlotte. Jayla simply gave him a nod and a smile. He thought he heard Ellie mutter the word *doctor* under her breath. Most people had two reactions to discovering he was a doctor, delighted interest—usually from single women looking for a rich husband—or curiosity, namely they'd ask if he could look at some ailment or diagnose their cousin's strange symptoms. He always told the latter he'd be happy to see them during office hours and the former...well, he tried to be polite in his refusal to "get to know them more." His hands were full enough already—literally at the moment—he didn't have time for a woman in his life.

But Ellie's tone inflected neither of those things. In fact, if he wasn't mistaken, the moment she found out he was a doctor, her bright smile dimmed. Had she had an unpleasant experience with a doctor before? It happened. Doctors, like all professions, were humans. They made mistakes. Sometimes life-ending ones. And not always by accident. He'd always prided himself on his attention to detail, his commitment to his patients, but he knew some former colleges who cut corners, dismissed patients' complaints because they thought they knew better.

Didn't matter what Ms. Clark thought of him. All that mattered was she saved his daughter, and he was eternally grateful to her for that. If she had some issue with doctors, it had nothing to do with him and it shouldn't bother him.

So why did the slight ache in his chest say it did?

"Charlotte's vitals are good. Her lungs sound clear. We can take her in for a scan if you want, but—"

"It's fine, Jay." He trusted team JJ, as they were called around the hospital. Plus, he was one of the top specialists in internal medicine in Sunlight. He knew what symptoms to look for. He knew how to care for his daughter better than anyone. "I'll keep a close eye on her tonight."

The EMTs nodded, passing off a clipboard to Ms. Hughes to sign before heading out. With a heavy sigh, Ms. Hughes turned to speak to him and Ellie.

"The news crews are going to want to do some interviews. Dr. Green, I understand if you would rather not. I'm sure you want to get your daughter home and changed—"

"I get to be on TV?" Charlotte squealed with glee.

As much as he agreed with Ms. Hughes, there'd be no avoiding the cameras now. Charlotte's big green eyes were staring at the cameras across the way with avid interest. Though he'd prefer avoiding the whole circus, he knew his daughter wanted the thrill of "being famous" even if it was only the local channels. And he could deny her nothing. Not today. Little stinker knew it too. He'd bet his medical degree she'd be asking for ice cream for dinner. He made a mental note to stop at the store on the way home for some mint chocolate chip.

"Do you want to talk to the camera people, Charlotte?"

"Yes, yes, yes!"

She bounced up and down in his arms, soaking his dress shirt and slacks, but he didn't care. He'd ruin every item of clothing he had just to make sure she never knew fear like today ever again.

Wishful thinking, man. You know how life goes. You can't protect the ones you love from pain.

No, but he could do his best.

"Ellie, they want to interview you, too."

Ellie's face paled at her boss's words. So, she didn't like doctors or reporters. Interesting.

"Um, can't Cam do it? She usually does all the news interviews."

The director nodded. "True, but this isn't a promotion for the zoo. They want to talk to the hero of the hour."

Now the woman shifted uncomfortably on her feet, gaze falling to the ground. "I'm not a hero."

He begged to differ. "You're our hero, Ellie. Mine and Charlotte's."

Her eyes snapped up at his words, gaze colliding with his. Did she not see what an amazing thing she did? Could she not realize she'd just saved his entire world with her actions?

"You're like a real-life superhero," Charlotte exclaimed. "Like Wonder Woman!"

"Wow," Ellie smiled at his daughter. Damn, the woman had a beautiful smile. "I think that's the best compliment I've ever received."

"If you're all in agreement, I can take everyone over to the staging area." Ms. Hughes motioned to where the news crews were setting up outside the enclosure. "Best to get started right away so you can all go home and, um, wash the delightful smell of the day from you."

Charlotte wrinkled her nose. "I smell like yucky poop."

He laughed along with the two women. "I think you smell perfect, Angel."

His daughter glanced at him like he was out of his mind, and he was. Out of his mind with happiness that she was okay.

They followed the zoo director back through the aviary building and into the sunshine of the outside once again. As they walked, the director explained what had happened and how his daughter fell into the penguin pool. His anger rose at the mention of the boys teasing Charlotte. He knew his daughter had been having some trouble with a few bullies at school, but he had no idea it had gotten this bad. The principal would get a visit from him very soon. He knew kids could be mean, but this was taking things too far. Something had to be done. He'd see to it.

Ms. Hughes set them up behind a podium that someone had placed in a shady area underneath a large tree. The penguin enclosure framed perfectly behind them. Ms. Hughes introduced herself, Ellie, Charlotte, and him, and the questions began.

"Ms. Hughes, Dan Stevens, channel four. Can you tell us what happened?"

The director explained in sparse detail how the incident occurred, framing it as visitor error and not a lax in zoo security. Sullivan was fine with that since that's exactly how the situation played out. After hearing all the details, he knew the zoo was not at fault. Though he hadn't spoken to the director about it yet, he had no intention of holding the zoo responsible. The fault lay with the bullies' and chaperone's supervision.

The interviews continued. They asked him about his take on the events.

"I'm very grateful to the zoo and Ms. Clark for her quick thinking and selfless act of jumping in after my daughter. She's our hero and we're very thankful for her."

He glanced at Ellie, who was blushing furiously, her pale skin almost red. She tugged on her right ear as the reporters started firing question at her. The woman stumbled over her words, shrugging off everyone's praise as she stated she was simply doing her job.

"I think Charlotte is the true brave one," she said, shifting the focus off of her. "She was swimming like a champ to get to me."

Charlotte beamed as all eyes and cameras turned toward her, soaking up the attention. "I tried as hard as I could, but my shoes were heavy and the water smells like poop!"

Everyone laughed, enamored with his daughter. He couldn't blame them. She was something special. So was the woman who saved her, he was coming to realize. This odd woman who thought nothing of risking her life to jump in after a child she didn't know. A woman who seemed to have hidden depths that tugged at him for some odd reason to get to know better. A woman whom he owed more than he could ever repay.

Because she'd saved his very life, the moment she saved his daughter.

CHAPTER 4

*E*llie stumbled into her apartment, cold, smelly, and slightly wet. Her socks squished with each step because no matter how long one wore wet socks, they never seemed to dry. Her hair, once pulled back into a neat, tight French-braid, now hung stiff, the ends sticking out all over the place in a haphazard mess. The slight amount of eyeshadow and blush that she wore had smudged off long ago. Thank the makeup companies for waterproof mascara so she didn't have raccoon eyes. Her clothes crackled as she moved into the tiny living room, dropping her keys in the bowl by the door.

She closed and locked her front door, checking three times, as was her routine. A ritual that always annoyed her mother, but since she lived on her own now, she didn't cover it up. Her therapist said if her rituals didn't harm her or interfere too severely with her daily activity, it was fine to continue them. The important thing was not letting the dark thoughts control her. If she needed to perform a repetitive motion to keep that at bay, so be it. Other people might not understand, but what they thought didn't matter to her.

Yes, it does.

Okay, so it bothered her when people made comments or gave her *those* looks. The ones that said she was a few cans short of a six-pack. But in the long run, all that mattered was what she thought of herself and her ability to function. And she could. Function. She was doing great. Okay. Fine. She was doing fine. She might be a little lonely now and then, but who wasn't? Cam was only a phone call away. Her bestie was great like that. And she had the animals at the zoo. Bingo and the other birds. So what if she didn't have someone to greet her the moment she got home? A warm presence in her bed at night? She didn't need a man to keep her company. That's what dogs were for.

"Yeah, like I can afford a dog."

Zookeeper was not a career one got into to hit it rich. After her internship, they had offered her barely more than minimum wage. When she was appointed head aviary keeper, she'd received a slight raise, but with her debts from school, rent, and basic amenities, she was barely breaking even these days. No. She hadn't gotten into this field for the money. Ellie did it for the love of the animals. Those amazing creatures who needed someone to care for them, protect them, educate the public on their behalf. It was a job she loved, and it filled her with happiness. That was enough for now.

"Besides, who needs a dog when I have a whole zoo full of the greatest creatures on earth?" It was like having every pet you could ever want, and her apartment didn't smell like poo.

A pungent, sour smell wafted up into her face. She curled her lips as the scent turned her stomach. Her apartment might not smell, but she sure did. "Ew."

She sniffed her shirt, gagging at the stale smell of penguin feces. Normally, it wouldn't bother her. She was used to the pungent smell being around her, but she wasn't used to it being *on* her. A shower was needed, pronto. After the interviews—which thankfully hadn't been too awful—Ellie spent over an hour filling out paperwork for security and emergency personal. Tammy was a good boss and let her leave her shift early, but in that time her clothing had dried. Stinky, stiff, and uncomfortable. She couldn't wait to get out of it.

She was exhausted, smelly, and oddly hungry. A glance at the clock over her microwave revealed the reason for her grumbly tummy. It was two hours past lunch. Now for the real question, food first or shower?

The air conditioning in her apartment kicked on, the cool breeze wafting the aroma of sour animal waste up her nostrils. Shower. Definitely shower first. If she tried to eat now, she might get another whiff of herself and puke all over her food.

As she made her way to the bathroom, her cell's ringtone chimed from her purse. Thankful she hadn't been carrying the phone in her pocket during her shift that day—she really couldn't have afforded a new phone if the poor thing had taken the icy plunge with her in the penguin pool—she reached into her bag, answering without glancing at the caller ID.

"Hello?"

"Eleanor, darling, I saw the news. Are you alright?"

Her mother. Of course, she'd be calling the moment Ellie needed some alone time to decompress. Guilt twisted inside her at the harsh thought. That wasn't fair. Her mother loved her and if she saw the news report, she had to be worried.

"Hi, Mom."

"Don't you 'hi mom' me, young lady. I've been sitting here with your father watching the news, worried sick. Why didn't you call us?"

Because it literally just happened, and she'd been

swamped with paperwork, followed by the need to get home and shower. She figured a call to her parents could wait a few hours. Silly her.

"I'm sorry, mom," she apologized, taking the easier route with the woman who birthed her and could get frantic at the slightest breeze of wind heading her only daughter's way. "I was wrapped up with filling stuff out for work and then I drove home to shower and change. You know I don't use my cell in the car."

"Yes, dear, and I'm very proud of your maturity."

Not so much maturity as the innate fear of glancing at her phone and causing a seven-car pile-up, resulting in mass casualties. Sometimes her paranoid brain was good for things like keeping herself and others safe.

"Are you home now or back at the zoo?"

"Home."

She crossed to the kitchen. Resigning herself to a delayed shower. If she couldn't clean herself right away, at least she could put some sustenance in her belly. Nothing too stimulating or the combined smells might make her hurl. Opening a cabinet, she pushed around the boxes of instant noodle soup until she found a package of crackers. Perfect! Mild, salty, filling, and best of all, odorless.

Opening the package, she leaned against the counter, phone tucked between her ear and shoulder. "Tammy gave me the rest of the day off."

"Good," her mother said as Ellie shoved a cracker in her mouth. The salty, buttery flavor exploded on her tongue, reminding her she hadn't eaten anything since that apple she grabbed on her way out the door this morning. She really had to get better at eating breakfast. "They should give you an entire week off for your heroics."

"Mom, I'm not a hero."

"Yes, you are, dear. All those reporters said so."

Right, and if it was on the news, her mother took it as law.

"You saved that poor girl from certain death."

That was a bit dramatic. Sure, Charlotte might have drowned if no one had gotten to her in time, but there were plenty of people there. If Ellie hadn't dived in, she was sure Cam or one of the other adults present would have. She just happened to be the closest and first person to do so. This wasn't a big deal.

"You're discounting your worth again."

Dr. Mitchell's words rang in her ear. Reminding her she was quick to judge herself for all the things that went wrong in her life, but slow to accept praise from others about her accomplishments. Something she'd been working on but having trouble accepting.

"I just wanted to help," she replied, trying her best to acknowledge her part in saving Charlotte.

"And you did, dear. That poor child's father looked very grateful for your actions. Very grateful and very handsome. Did I hear right that he's a doctor?"

Yes, the reporters had directed questions to him as Dr. Green, though how they knew he was a doctor on such short notice was beyond her. She didn't know how journalists got their scoops. The EMTs were interviewed first, so perhaps they disclosed the doctor's profession? Didn't matter. She knew where her mother was going with this line of questioning, and she was going to shut it down right now. Before it went any further.

"Yes, Dr. Green expressed his gratitude, as did Charlotte."

"Charlotte? Is that the child's name?"

"Yes."

"She seems like such a sweet thing."

She had been so sweet. *Odd*. Ellie had a hard time relating to most people, but there was something about the tiny girl that reached out and grabbed her heart, making a unique connection she couldn't seem to deny.

"She is and very smart too."

"I can imagine. Having a doctor for a father, she must be very intelligent."

Her mom just would not let that go.

"Did he examine you to make sure you weren't injured in the rescue?"

While she phrased it as a question, Ellie heard the intonation behind the seemingly innocent remark. Deciding not to rise to the bait, she answered honestly. "No, mother. He was there to get his child, who'd just suffered a traumatic experience. I'm sure work was the last thing on his mind."

"Yes, but you experienced the event, too. Shouldn't someone have checked on you?"

She sighed, reaching the end of her cracker package, and tossing the empty wrapper into the small trashcan under the kitchen sink. "The EMTs looked me over and declared me fit as a fiddle. I didn't need another exam from Sullivan."

"Sullivan? You're on a first name basis with the man?" her mother preened over the phone, glee practically dripping from the line.

"No, we…I mean, yes, I suppose so. I saved his daughter, after all."

"You did indeed. And as a mother, I'm grateful you weren't harmed in your daring heroics."

She really wished people would stop calling it that.

"I'm sure the child and her father are very grateful, along with his wife?"

Boom. There it was. Done beating around the bush, her mother tried horribly to slide in the question of the good doctor's relationship status into the conversation. Honestly, she had no idea if Sullivan—Dr. Green—had a wife. Charlotte had mentioned not having a mommy with sad little eyes that broke Ellie's heart, but that didn't mean the girl's father wasn't involved with anyone. How could he not be? Not only was the guy a doctor and genuinely sweet—if his treatment of his daughter was anything to go by—but he was also one of the most handsome men Ellie had ever seen. And Ellie knew hot guys. She worked at the zoo. She could create a whole Instagram page on the DILFs of Sunlight Zoo. But she didn't need to...because Cam had.

"I don't know if he has a wife, mom. They just called him, and he left with Charlotte. No one else came."

"Oh really? That's interesting."

No, it wasn't. Not unless you were a retired music teacher who watched way too many romantic comedies and was constantly trying to push your only daughter down the aisle despite her abysmal track record on dating. She loved her mother, but the woman saw romance everywhere. Their local grocery manager smiled at her. Start shopping for save the date cards. The cop who pulled her over gave her a warning instead of a ticket. Reserve the church now. A man on the train gave her his seat in a crowded car. Buy the white dress because wedding bells can't be far behind!

It got exhausting trying to talk her mother down from her starry-eyed fantasies.

She just wants me to be happy.

Ellie sighed, rubbing at her chest, where guilt ached. The small meal of crackers soured in her stomach, like the smelly water still clinging to her clothes and skin. She felt so ungrateful for thoughts like that, but what her mother didn't realize was that Ellie was happy. Mostly. She was working on it, but her and her mother's visions of what happiness looked like were very different. Ellie didn't need a man. Sure, it'd be nice, but it wasn't necessary.

Maybe it was a generational thing.

Whatever the case, she knew her mother loved her and

that was all that mattered. But it would be nice if the woman could at least pretend like her daughter was a whole person without the help of a man. The prodding for a husband and the pitter-patter of little feet had only gotten worse since her older brother recently separated from his wife of five years. At least when Oliver had been married, her mom had laid off her love life for a while. Now that his wife left him, and there was little chance of grandkids from that failed marriage, her mother had again set her sights on Ellie.

Yay.

"He's a rather handsome man," her mother mused at her continued silence, Beverly Clark always comfortable filling in empty spaces in conversations. "And the way he dotes on that child, well, the sign of a good man is through the love he shows his children."

Couldn't argue with her mother there.

"He seems like a wonderful father." There, a nice generic statement. Her mother couldn't read too much into that. Could she?

"Just how well did you two get to know each other after you saved his daughter's life?"

Guess she could.

Ellie wouldn't be surprised if her mother was planning her wedding to Dr. Green in her head as they spoke. The woman let her fantasies take her away far too often. Better to nip this thing in the bud before her mother ordered mono-grammed his-and-her towels.

"We barely spoke more than a dozen words to each other, mom. But he was concerned and kind. He didn't yell at Tammy or blame the zoo."

"Well, of course not! It wasn't the zoo's fault. From what the lovely reporter lady told us, it was some hooligan bullies. Shame how cruel kids are to each other these days."

True, but it wasn't anything new. Kids had been mean to

each other since the dawn of time. She knew that firsthand. Having an anxiety disorder for most of her life hadn't led to being the most popular girl in school. Quite the opposite, in fact. Friends had been few and far between in Ellie's life. Bullies? Sadly, those had been plentiful and painful.

"Their teacher said they'd receive proper punishment." And she knew Sullivan would follow through to make sure of it. It'd been in the determined set of his hard jaw, the cool gaze of his emerald eyes. He would make sure the parties responsible for hurting his little girl would face the consequences. While she knew next to nothing about the man, she could see he was fair and loved his daughter. He'd fight for her.

A pang of longing pinched her chest. How she wished she had someone like that in her life. But no, she got stuck with a mother who was more concerned with marrying her off than facing her daughter's mental health struggles.

She needed to decompress and that would involve getting off the phone with her mother and into a hot shower to wash the smell and...weirdness of the day from her.

"Thanks for checking in on me, Mom, but I need to hop in the shower and get the smell of penguin off of me."

"Oh yes, dear. Of course. I imagine you aren't smelling too fresh after a dip in that bird water. It must be dreadfully uncomfortable. You were fidgety on the television." Her mother's voice lowered as if confessing some great secret. "I noticed you...tugging again, dear."

Ah yes, the ear compulsion. When she felt nervous or overwhelmed—like during live TV interviews—she coped by tugging on her right earlobe. A small ritual that helped keep the anxiety from crushing her. Something her mother found extremely distasteful.

Ellie knew her mother hated that she wasn't "normal."

Whatever the hell that meant. If only it was as simple as stopping those *unseemly* habits, as her mom liked to call them. She'd give anything to stop the rituals, the dark thoughts, the anxiety. But that wasn't how it worked. There was no magic cure. Only hard work and acceptance. She was doing the best she could. It took her years with Dr. Mitchell to figure that out. Now if her mother could only see it, things would be aces.

"I gotta go, Mom. Love you."

"Love you too, dear. And be sure to let me know if *Sullivan* stops by."

Rolling her eyes—because she knew her mother couldn't see over the phone and scold her for bad manners—she sighed. "Why on earth would *Dr. Green* come by my apartment?"

"Why to thank you for saving his daughter's life. Perhaps he'll take you out for a nice dinner and a movie."

Her mother, ever the romantic. "Goodbye, Mom."

"Bye, Ellie."

Making her way to her bedroom, she plugged her phone in on her nightstand before stripping off all her stinky clothing. Most of the cloth had dried now into stiff fabric that was a bitch to get off, but she managed. She shoved the smelly garments directly into her tiny washer before slipping into the bathroom. She turned on the ancient taps in the tub and pulled the device to get the showerhead flowing, but she didn't step in. This apartment building had fifty residents and one very tiny water heater. Those drops would be icy cold for about two minutes, and she had enough of freezing cold water today, thank you very much.

Once the water reached an acceptable scalding temperature, she pulled back the cherry print curtain left by the last tenant and stepped in.

"Ohhhhhh, yes," she sighed in bliss as the hot water

pounded her back, washing away all the stink and stress of the day.

Grabbing her favorite occasional splurge—lilac-scented body wash—Ellie squeezed a generous amount onto her loofa and reveled in the luxurious feel of the sweetly scented soap cascading over her body. Oh man, did this feel good after the day she had. Her eyes closed in ecstasy, mind floating away as the events of the day played out. Getting to work, discussing speed dating with Cam, the school group, Charlotte's fall, and diving in after her. Stress mounted again, remembering, but then a vision filled her mind.

A man rushing to his daughter's side, holding her so tightly, like he would never let her go again. Love for the tiny child he held in his arms plain on his face. His very handsome face. The suit and tie he'd been sporting worked for her, too. She'd never given much thought to the clothes people wore, men especially, but Sullivan Green in a suit was what Cam would call "spank bank material."

With her eyes closed, she could see clearly in her memories the dark green of his eyes, the slight blonde scruff on his jawline. His nose had a slight kink to it, as if it had been broken and repaired long ago. It gave him a devilish sort of appeal to his almost perfect appearance. A slight flaw, so his beauty didn't overwhelm. And when he'd smiled at Charlotte, Ellie had lost her breath. The man had a killer smile. Made a woman wonder how powerful it would be aimed at her. How delicious those lips would taste as they captured her own in a—

Hold up!

Eyes snapping open, Ellie realized, rather embarrassedly, she had been stroking the loofa over her breasts as she daydreamed about kissing Sullivan. Oh crap! She really needed to get laid if this was how she got her jollies now. Making a dirty movie in her head about a man she barely knew? Cam was right. She needed a date, or at least a tumble between the sheets.

She rushed through the rest of her shower as efficiently as possible. No more lingering soap fun.

Deciding to forgo actual clothes since she didn't plan to leave her apartment for the rest of the evening, she threw on some sweats and grabbed her fully charged cell, texting Cam.

Ellie: I'm in for speed dating.

She waited a moment for the reply. Her friend never took long.

Cam: Yay! I knew you'd cave. Sucker.

"Yeah, yeah. Well, I realized I needed human contact when I almost made love to my glorified cleaning rag five minutes ago," she said to the phone, but texted,

Ellie: Yes, yes, you're always right.

Cam: Duh! I'll come over in the afternoon with some outfits.

Ellie: I have clothes.

Cam: Not for speed dating, you don't. See you tomorrow! XOXO.

Fantastic. Speed dating. A forced hour of social interaction with a bunch of strangers trying to get in each other's pants. Only she wouldn't be wearing her pants because they weren't *appropriate* or whatever. She'd be wearing some uncomfortable, slinky outfit her best friend could pull off, but she'd look like a toddler trying on her mother's clothes.

Falling back onto her bed, she clutched her cell phone to her chest, allowing herself one small pity party of the events of her day.

"I should have stayed in the penguin pool."

CHAPTER 5

"*Y*ou are not wearing that."

Ellie looked down at her shirt. Sure, it might be a little casual for speed dating, but it was cute and funny. Plus, it had a sweetheart neckline, which gave her some semblance of boobs. Her poor A-cups needed all the help they could get.

"What? Why?"

Cam shook her head, fiery, curly hair bouncing with the motion. "It says *Nice Ass*."

"Yeah, because there's a donkey on it, see?" She pointed to the comically adorable jackass, tushy on full display, head turned to show a long pink tongue hanging out of the side of its mouth. "It's a pun. It's funny."

Ellie couldn't resist a funny animal shirt. She didn't think she owned any plain T-shirts. Who could resist a soft, cuddly kitten with the words "I'm purrrrrfect" written on it? Adorable and hilarious…to her, at least. Not everyone appreciated puns. And those people had no sense of humor.

"Ellie," Cam sighed. "You're going speed dating. An event where some guys will be looking for a quick and easy lay.

Now think about how they're going to interpret that shirt. Do you really want to deal with hours of lewd jokes and disgusting come-ons?"

It wasn't fair. Why were women responsible for what men thought or did? Why couldn't she wear a punny shirt that—okay, yes—maybe had a slight sexual connotation to it? Was it too much to ask for people to enjoy her weird sense of humor without using it as an all-access pass to bone town?

As unfair as society and gender constructs were, her friend was right. The people close to her rarely got her punny T-shirt humor. It'd be a lot to ask a bunch of strange dudes looking to hook up to see it as the joke it was meant to be and not an invitation for sex. Dang it! This was why she hated dating. She wasn't any good at it.

"Fine. I'll change, but I am not wearing that red scrap of floss you brought for me."

Cam threw up her hands in exasperation. "It's not a scrap. It's a five-hundred-dollar dress, but you're right." Her friend picked up the miniscule garment, masquerading as clothes with a wince. "I forgot you kind of need…a bit more up top to fill out the bodice on this thing."

"Did you bring any dresses from the pre-teen department?"

"Stop that!" Cam scowled. "You are beautiful and perfect just the way you are. Every woman is. Tall, short, big, small, double Ds or amazing As, we are women, hear us roar! Variety is the spice of life, and we keep it delicious!"

She loved her friend. The woman had this unique ability to see the good in everyone and everything. She had the confidence of a toddler who'd just gotten ahold of their parents' phone and thought they could outrun them. Ellie didn't hate her body, sure she lamented the fact that she didn't always feel *womanly* enough, but she liked herself just fine. Cam *loved* herself, but not egotistically. The woman just saw the benefit of every angle and curve. She never judged and Ellie found that to be an asset and a goal to aspire to.

"Here, try this."

Cam tossed a wad of black cloth at her. Ellie grabbed it out of the air—okay, so she grabbed it when it hit her in the face. Sports were never her things.

"What's this?"

"Something I bought on sale but neglected to check the washing instructions. Damn thing shrunk like a man's junk in ice water. I hate it when things can't be tossed in the wash. Who has time or money for dry cleaning?"

She agreed. If she couldn't wash it in a machine, she left it on the rack.

Unballing the material, Ellie quickly shucked her clothing and slipped the dress over her head.

"Wow! It's a good thing I accidentally washed that. You look amazing, Ellie!"

At her friend's words, she turned to face the mirror attached to the back of her bedroom door and sucked in a gasp. The little black dress was gorgeous. Ellie didn't own many dresses. She found them uncomfortable and never had occasion to wear them. But this. This dress she would wear on the walk to the mailbox downstairs.

The fit and flare style of the skirt gave the appearance of actual curves, and the knee-length hemline made her look flirty and fun without causing her short stature to give the appearance of a child, as some dresses did. The neckline of see-through mesh paneling gave the dress a peek-a-boo kind of sultriness without being so daring that she felt uncomfortable. And when she slipped her hands down the side, she discovered the best thing of all.

"Does this dress have pockets?"

"Yup. One of the reasons I bought it."

A cute dress with pockets. If only it was machine washable, it would be the trifecta. The Unicorn of dresses. Oh well, two out of three wasn't bad.

"How much did it cost? I'll reimburse you for it."

"Forget it. You keep it. It looks amazing on you. Not like I can squeeze into that thing anymore."

She turned from the mirror to frown at her friend. "Seriously, Cam. I'll pay you for the dress." She knew her friend was in a similar money conscious situation as she was, though Cam had family money, she hated using it. Cam highly valued her independence. Zookeepers were rarely high rollers.

"And I'm serious too, Ellie. I don't want your money. Consider it a birthday present."

Rolling her eyes, she smiled at her friend. "My birthday was three months ago, and you already got me a present."

"Happy Arbor Day then. That's next week, right?"

"Yeah, but I'm pretty sure people don't give Arbor Day presents. I think you're supposed to plant trees and stuff."

Cam shrugged, leaning against the dresser. "I'm starting a new present tradition. Besides, we are hoping some guy plants his big, thick—"

Ellie reached over to smash her hand over her friend's mouth, fighting to hold in her laughter. "Stop! Don't utter another filthy word or I'm not going to be able to look any of these guys in the eye tonight without thinking of that .. mental image you put in my head."

"What mental image?" Cam muffled around Ellie's palm.

"Going to bed with a man and having him pull down his pants to reveal a pine tree between his legs where a penis should be."

Cam doubled over with laughter, her forehead smacking Ellie's hand as she bent. Ellie pulled her slightly stinging hand to her chest. "You know how weird my mind is."

"Yes, and I love you for it."

That made one person.

Two if she counted herself, because as much as she got frustrated and angry at the thoughts in her mind, she really did like herself. Everything in her strange brain made her who she was, the good and the bad, and it all rolled into a neat little Ellie ball. At least she enjoyed her own company and Cam did, too. Who knew, maybe there'd be a guy at this thing tonight who was just looking for a game of Ellie ball. Wait, that sounded weird. That metaphor needed work, but she'd have to think about that later.

Cam straightened from her slouched position against the dresser. "We're looking fabulous. We get two free drinks. And if there aren't any good matches, at least we'll have some hilarious stories."

Ellie slipped her feet into a pair of heels, black Mary Janes with three-inch heels. She had a feeling she'd need all the heights she could get tonight. "Hilarious stories?"

Her friend laughed as they left the bedroom and headed to the front door.

"Oh, sweetie. You have been out of the dating game too long."

She'd never really been in it. A few disastrous first dates and one nice, but quickly fizzled steady boyfriend in college did not a game player make.

"This event is going to be crawling with skeevy guys trying to get into every available woman's pants."

"Then why the hell are we going?" She asked in horror. She wasn't good with guys in everyday situations, let alone ones where they were trying to take her out back for a little game of hide the eggplant emoji.

Cam opened the apartment door, turning to grace her with an optimistic smile. "Because there's always that diamond in the rough. The guy who's looking for the real thing, and Ellie, my friend, tonight he's going to find you."

CHAPTER 6

*W*here the hell is this diamond in the rough guy? All I'm seeing is rough.

Ellie sucked down her second soda, wishing she had taken up the event organizer on the addition of rum to the drink, but she wanted to keep her head clear. Alcohol made her mouth open, and her brain shut off. She didn't have a problem with that around Cam, but she was trying to make a good impression here. Too bad none of the men she'd met seemed to be concerned with the same thing.

DING!

"Okay, everyone, that's ten. Switch tables," the perky coordinator's voice rang out in the large front bar area of the busy restaurant.

Ten minutes. How could anyone make a genuine connection in ten minutes? She'd barely gotten her name out before the guy in front of her yammered on about his new startup and how many investors he was bagging. As if that would impress her. She hadn't understood more than a dozen words the dude said. Not that she could have told him that with his verbal diarrhea.

"Damn, has it been ten minutes already?" Mr. Self-involved said as he stood. "Nice talking with you, Abby."

"It's Ellie," she said, but he'd already moved on to the next table and the next woman.

Crap, how much longer was this thing? She was going to kill Cam. The new season of Nailed It just came out. She could be at home in her PJs eating donuts and watching other people epically fail at something. Instead, she was here. At speed dating. Epically failing, herself.

"Hi there."

She glanced up to see an attractive Asian man with slightly graying hair at his temples and warm brown eyes standing before her. He seemed older than most of the people here, but she wasn't one to let a little age gap get in her way if the man was nice enough and they clicked.

"Hello."

"I'm Louis." He took the chair opposite her, extending his hand.

"Ellie." She offered her own, happy when he shook it instead of kissing it like the guy twenty minutes ago had done. *Ew!*

"So, Ellie, what do you do?"

Standard first question. She smiled, taking a sip from her drink and unconsciously tapping the straw three times before answering. "I'm a zookeeper at the Sunlight Zoo. And you?"

Louis's eyes darting to her straw, her fingers, then back to her. A knowing look filled his gaze as he replied. "I'm a psychiatrist."

Hell no!

She had no problem with psychiatrists. Saw one herself, as a matter of fact, but in a professional manner, not a sexual one. There were two types of guys she could never be in a relationship with; abusive assholes and shrinks. The former because obvious reasons. The latter because she'd never know if they were being a supportive partner or trying to fix her.

"Oh, that's nice." She placed her hands in her lap, trying hard not to let the panic inside her show.

Louis laughed. "No, it's not. I enjoy my job, but most people here either think I'm fodder for stories about *crazies*. I hate that word, by the way. Or they want me to cure them of their neuroses."

She didn't want him curing her of anything. No, thank you. She already had a doctor for that, and she was doing just fine. Shame, because Louis seemed like a nice guy. At least the nicest she'd run across tonight.

"Can I confess something to you?" He leaned in as if to impart some big secret.

"Um, sure." Ellie tilted her head his way.

His lips parted in a smile. He was a nice-looking man. Some might even call him a silver fox, but sadly, he did nothing for her. Even if his occupation hadn't been a deal breaker.

"I really didn't want to come to this thing tonight. My daughters signed me up. They told me it's time I got back out in the dating world."

Hmmmm, strangely similar phrasing to what Cam had said. Was anyone here of their own willingness, or had everyone been pushed into it?

"My wife passed five years ago, and they think I need to stop mourning and move on."

Her heart clenched, breath leaving her in a whoosh. "Oh, I'm so sorry."

"Thank you." A sad smile tilted his lips. "We had twenty-five wonderful years together before the cancer took her and while I miss her every day, I'm not mourning her like my children seem to think. I'll always love and miss her, but me not dating has nothing to do with her loss. I just haven't found my boom. You know."

She shook her head, leaning forward, willing to lap up all the advice this man who seemed to love his late wife so profusely had to say. He placed his hands on the table, and she caught a whiff of the same aftershave her father used. Comforting, but would have been another deal breaker. Being reminded of her dad every time she kissed her lover? Not a flying chance in hell.

"That someone who makes your heart race and the blood rush in your veins. The person who steps into a room and you can't help but smile because just their presence makes the entire room brighter. Someone you love to talk to about everything under the sun, from the weather to dreams of the future. The person who is not only your other half, but your best friend, too. When you wake up one day and realize *boom*, they make everything in your life better. I had that once and I'm okay if I never have it again, but I won't settle for anything less."

She sniffed, a hot tear leaking from the corner of her eye and rolling down her cheek. She brushed it away, only slightly embarrassed by the show of emotion. Honestly, how could anyone hear that and not shed a tear or two? They'd have to be some kind of heartless monster.

"Your wife was a lucky woman."

Louis shook his head. "I was the lucky one. We both were."

"Ellie?"

Her head turned at the familiar voice calling her name. Shock infused her, followed quickly by a rapid heartbeat and rushing blood as she stared up at the last person she expected to see tonight. "Sullivan?"

"Are you okay?"

His green eyes narrowed as he glanced at Louis and back

at her. His gaze caught on her cheek. Oh crap, had there been more than one tear? She brushed at her wet cheeks. Yup. A few other sneaks had followed the first.

"I'm fine."

"You sure?"

His suspicious gaze went back to Louis, but the menacing look in Sullivan's eyes didn't seem to bother the older gentleman. Louis stood, stepping away from the table and motioning to Sullivan.

"I was actually just leaving." Her gaze came back to her. "Thank you for your time, Ellie. Why don't I leave you with your friend here?"

"Oh, you don't have to—"

He cut her off with a wave of his hand. "I'm not going to find my boom here." Brown eyes shifted to Sullivan and back. "Maybe you'll find yours, though."

Louis walked away and Sullivan kept his gaze on him the entire time. What was the deal with that? She'd disliked people after a few minutes of talking to them—prime example, every single guy before Louis who'd sat down tonight— but Sullivan hadn't even talked to the guy before he gave the older man the stink eye.

"Five more minutes."

At the chipper call of the hostess of tonight's event, Sullivan turned back to her with a smile.

"Five more minutes of what?" He took Louis's recently vacated seat across from her. "What is this?"

She groaned, dropping her head to the table. "Speed dating."

He laughed. "What?"

Reigning in her embarrassment, she huffed and lifted her head. "Speed dating. My friend Cam, you remember her from the zoo?" He nodded, so she continued. "It was her idea, and she dragged me along and here I am."

"Here you are."

"And here you are, too. You're not..." she trailed off, not sure if the prospect of Sullivan looking for his boom made her excited or nervous.

"Ah, no. Not really my style."

Of course not. He had a daughter at home. He probably logged on to some single parents dating service. *If* he was single. She still didn't know his relationship status. Charlotte said she didn't have a mommy, but that didn't mean her daddy didn't have a "special friend." And why the hell did Ellie care again? She didn't. Right. Not at all.

"I'm here to pick up dinner because this place makes Charlotte's favorite spaghetti and meatballs. She suckered me into promising it for dinner after she gets back from the movies with my brother, who she also suckered into taking her to the new superhero kid movie."

Ellie laughed. "She's milking the zoo thing for all it's worth, then?"

"And how." He shook his head. "Honestly, it's not like I say no to her that much, anyway."

"She's a good kid. She deserves to be a little spoiled."

Green eyes flared with pride and something else...heat? No, couldn't be. That was just her imagination running away with her. Call it the ridiculous speed dating in the air. Whatever it had been, it disappeared in an instant. Sullivan smiled wide, revealing a small dent—not quite a dimple, but almost —in his right cheek.

"Yeah. She's pretty great."

"And you're a great dad, too."

Aw, crap. Why had she said that? It was true, but now he was staring at her like she was a weirdo. No, not a weirdo, but...something. She couldn't decipher any of this man's looks. Heat crawling up her cheeks, she took a sip of her drink, tapping the straw three times and then three times again until her nerves were back under control. Sullivan glanced at her drink but said nothing. Most people didn't even notice her compulsions, but those who did almost always commented on them. Asked why she did that "weird tapping" thing. She tried to explain most times, but how did you tell someone you had to perform repetitive motions to get your mind to leave you alone? It sounded crazy.

Crazy is a word people use when they fear something that they don't understand. You're not crazy. Your brain is just wired differently.

Her therapist's words rang in her head, reassuring her.

"Thanks. I try to do my best, but sometimes being a single parent is tough."

She had no idea, but she imagined it was.

"Sullivan Green? Order for Sullivan Green!"

His gaze turned to the host stand where a man dressed in black pants and a shirt with the restaurant's logo on it held a large brown paper-bag that looked very full.

"That's me. I better…" He rose from the chair, mouth open, but whatever he was about to say got interrupted by the ding of the bell.

"Your ten minutes is up. Gentlemen, move on to the next lady."

"Oh boy," she muttered, wondering if she could fake sick and grab a cab home.

Sullivan chuckled. "Need me to call you in five minutes with a fake emergency?"

What she wouldn't give for that. But no, Cam would have her ass if she ducked out on this. In fact, her friend was staring at her from across the room now. Mouth widely forming the question *is that Sullivan Green?* She shook her head, trying to inform her friend with a look that they'd talk later. Cam just smiled and gave her two thumbs up.

"No. Thank you, Sullivan, but there's only half an hour left. I think I can suffer through it."

"All right." He started to leave, but then turned back.

"Hey, dude." Her next "date" approached the table, grimacing when he saw Sullivan still there. "It's time to move on. The lady said."

"Give me one more second, *dude*."

She rolled her lips in to stop the laughter threatening to escape. Damn, she really wished she could talk to Sullivan for the rest of the night instead of moving on to the guy standing two feet away currently pouting and sipping on a—gross, a margarita? She hated tequila. Ever since a fateful night in college she couldn't quite remember. What she did recollect was puking up everything she'd eaten the entire week before. Even the smell of the alcohol made her queasy. Her next ten minutes should be a blast. Too bad she could only hold her breath for two.

"So, um, Charlotte would really like to see you again."

"I'd like to see her too." The adorable seven-year-old had burrowed under her awkward exterior and right into her heart.

"Great, then how about coming over for dinner sometime this week?"

"Dinner? At your place?" That's what he said, so why couldn't she wrap her mind around it?

"Yeah. I swear I can cook." He laughed as he gestured to the host stand where the host had his to-go order waiting. "I know a meal can in no way make up for what you did for Charlotte, what you did for me, but I'd like to thank you."

He didn't have to thank her, but she would like to see Charlotte again, and if she were being truly honest, she'd like to spend more time with Sullivan too.

"Dinner sounds lovely, thank you."

His lips pulled wide in that cheek-dent revealing smile

again. Her body flushed with heat as her heart raced. Good grief, she really needed to get ahold of herself. All the man did was smile at her.

Yeah, but what a smile. He could make a mint doing toothpaste commercials.

She chuckled at her own joke as Sullivan reached into his jacket pocket and pulled out a white piece of paper.

"Here's my card. Text the cell number and let me know what evening works for you."

She reached out, taking the card from him. As she did, their fingers brushed, and she felt a zing, like a bolt of lightning, shoot from the contact point straight to all the erogenous zones in her body. There were quite a few more than she realized.

"Okay."

He gave her one more smile before motioning to the chair. "All yours, *dude*." Then he turned and left, grabbing his order on his way out.

Her new date sat down, but Ellie didn't hear a word he said. She didn't hear a word any of the next three men said. Her mind was consumed. For once, her frustrating brain was filled with nothing but good thoughts. Thoughts of Sullivan Green and his dented cheeked smile.

CHAPTER 7

*S*ullivan glanced quickly at the clock on his car's dashboard, grateful his last appointment of the day had cancelled so he could duck out of work early today and miss traffic. The bold, red numbers informed him he had five minutes until Charlotte's after-school program let out. Perfect. Just enough time to find a spot in the tiny elementary school lot. Normally he joined the line of cars in the drop off/pickup zone, but today was special. Today, they were having Ellie over for dinner.

Charlotte practically bounced off the walls two days ago when he mentioned Ellie's text asking if tonight would be good. His daughter had taken a liking to the sweet, but slightly awkward, zookeeper. Truth be told, he had too. The woman saved the life of the one person he valued most in this world. How could he not be a little enamored by her?

Be honest, that's not the only reason.

Okay, so he felt...something around her. The first time he'd met her, he noticed his pulse speeding. The hairs on his arms stood up like the sensation he got right before a lightning storm, but he chalked that up to his haywire emotions over Charlotte's accident. Then, when he saw her the other night at the restaurant in that amazing black dress looking for all the world like she'd rather be drenched in penguin water again, he felt his body react the same way.

There was something about Ellie, something special. She made his daughter happy and for that alone, he wanted her in their lives as much as possible. Charlotte hadn't had enough positive female attention in her life. Since his ex-wife ran out on them six months after Charlotte was born, Sullivan concentrated all his attention on his daughter. He did his best to raise her right, give her everything she needed, love her with everything in him.

He couldn't see himself getting married again. Risking his heart like that. It was too painful, and he wouldn't do that to Charlotte. Thankfully, she'd been a baby. Too young to feel the soul-crushing pain of her mother's abandonment. But he saw the confusion in her eyes whenever the school had a Mother's Day project and Charlotte had no one to make paper flowers for. Sometimes he wondered if not remarrying, not providing another stable adult in the house for her, had harmed her development.

"We all screw up our kids unintentionally. That's half the fun."

His late father's words rang out in his mind. The man had an unusual sense of humor, to be sure, but he'd been a wonderful dad. Both his parents had been. His childhood hadn't been perfect. No one's was. But he'd been loved, had a roof over his head, food in his belly. He had nothing to complain about. His only qualm was that his parents both died in a car accident before Charlotte had been born. They would have been amazing grandparents had life given them the chance.

Luck was on his side today as Sullivan found a parking

spot right next to the school's front doors. He parked, hopping out of the car right as the teachers led the students out in a single file line.

"Daddy!"

Charlotte screamed his name, jumping up and down and waving her arms wildly in the air. He chuckled, knowing she wanted to run to him, but would never disobey the school rules of no running at pick up time.

"Hi, Angel." He hustled over to the line, which was quickly becoming a blob of children. "Did you have a good day today at school?"

"Yeah, we had a spelling test, and I only missed one word. And in art we made paper matches flowers!"

"I think you mean papier mâché."

"Oh, right."

Charlotte launched into a whirlwind explanation of her day as he smiled at the after-care teacher and signed her out on the clipboard. Her boisterous chatter lasted all the way to the car and the twelve-minute drive home.

"Okay, Angel, I want you to put your backpack away and wash up for dinner," he said as he pulled the car into the garage and shut off the engine.

"Daddy, Ellie is coming over tonight, right?"

"That's right."

Charlotte squealed with glee as she unbuckled herself and slid out of her booster seat. He got out and walked around the car. But as always, she'd already opened her door and had hopped out.

"Uh, uh." He nodded to the interior of the car as she went to shut to door. "Aren't you forgetting something?"

Her pale brows furrowed, green eyes staring in confusion until recognition dawned. "Oh, right."

As she did every day, Charlotte reached back in the car to grab her backpack from the floor. If he didn't remind her, that thing would live in his SUV. Homework would never get done and leftover lunch would rot. His daughter was always so excited about life she sometimes forgot things. Typical seven-year-old. He didn't mind reminding her. That was his job, after all.

He used his keys to unlock the garage door, and they headed inside to discover a man sitting at the kitchen counter sipping on a soda. Sullivan wasn't surprised. He'd seen his brother's car parked outside the house. He knew Gavin would have let himself in using the spare key Sullivan had given him.

"Uncle Gavin!" Charlotte squealed again, running into the kitchen, arms wide open.

Gavin slid off the barstool and crouched down, allowing the tiny girl to plow into him as he faked falling over with a laugh.

"Wow, Cheeky Monkey. When did you become so strong? I think you broke my shoulder."

Charlotte laughed as he scooped her up in a bear hug "You're silly."

Sullivan hung his keys on the wall hook. "Nice to see you've made yourself at home. And that better not be the last of the root beer you're drinking."

"Well, hello to you too, brother. Hard day at the office?"

No. Most days were fairly smooth in private practice. He'd left the chaos of the ER behind him after Charlotte was born. His annoyance at seeing his brother in his living space had nothing to do with his day and everything to do with his plans for the evening.

"What are you doing here?" he asked, ignoring his younger brother's baiting.

Gavin shifted Charlotte onto his back. "Came to see if you and Charlotte wanted to grab dinner."

It wasn't unusual for his brother to stop by for dinner. He

lived in a duplex a few minutes away and came by often. Since their parents died a decade ago, the brothers kept a tight bond.

"Can't tonight."

"Why? You have a hot date?" His brother's chuckles turned to shock when Sullivan said nothing. Hazel eyes, inherited from their father, widened. "Holy shit, you do have a hot date."

"I do not, and don't swear in front of Charlotte."

"It's okay, Daddy," the sweet girl said, peeking out from behind her uncle's back. "You said the S word in the car. Remember?"

"Road rage, big brother?"

He silently counted to ten in his head. It had been the day he picked up Charlotte from the zoo. *That* day. The one where his nerves were already riding high and his patience thin. Some jackass had cut him off, nearly swiping his fender. He might have uttered a curse or two. Leave it to a kid to remember a naughty word from days ago but forget to hang up her coat every single day, even with a reminder.

"I was stressed." He scowled at his brother, but then softened his face into a smile for his daughter. "But you're right, Charlotte. Even when we're upset, it's not nice to swear. Can you go wash up now, please?"

"Yes, Daddy."

She wiggled until Gavin put her down, then ran to the hall, her tiny feet pounding up the stairs making more noise than should be possible for a forty-five-pound seven-year-old to make.

"So," his brother started when they heard the slam of the upstairs bathroom door. "Who's your date with and why didn't you ask me to babysit? Is Nancy coming over?"

Gavin was his go-to babysitter. Sullivan didn't go out much, but he had the occasional conference or office party he had to attend. Now and then, when he needed some adult time, he'd make plans with Gavin and a few of the guys to go out for beers or a game, and he'd pay his weekly housekeeper Nancy to stay and watch Charlotte. But not tonight.

"No, Nancy isn't coming over and I don't have a date." He made his way over to the fridge, pulling out the ingredients for tonight's dinner. "I'm having a friend over for dinner."

"What friend?" Gavin nudged his way into the open fridge, pointing at the remaining three root beers with a knowing smirk. "You don't have any friends."

He shoved his brother out of the way. Grumbling in annoyance when the guy moved off with a chuckle. Little brothers could be a real pain in the ass sometimes.

"I have friends."

Or he did, before Carla left and he became consumed with putting Charlotte first. There was always that kernel of guilt wedged in the back of his mind that somehow his ex-wife's addiction problem was his fault. Her inability to be a wife and mother was because of something he'd done, or not done. That she'd left because of him, and he needed to do everything in his power to make up for that fact. Make sure Charlotte didn't suffer because of his failings. Whether it was true, it shaped his life, his parenting, his social activities.

"So, who's coming over?" Gavin hopped on the counter, grabbing an apple from the fruit bowl, and biting into it. Juice dripped off his chin as he crunched loudly. At Sullivan's perturbed glare, Gavin grinned and wiped his face with the back of his hand. "Oh, come on, you can tell me. We're family."

Yeah, just the reason he didn't want to tell. His baby brother loved to rile him about anything and everything. There must be something in the younger brother handbook about annoying your older siblings into an early grave.

"It's not a big deal. I'm just making dinner for Ellie Clark."

Gavin frowned. "Ellie Clark...why do I know that name?"

"She's the one who saved Charlotte at the zoo. I invited her over for dinner tonight to thank her." And because Charlotte had been begging him to take her back to the zoo so she could see Ellie again.

"Oh, yeah." Gavin's expression lit up. "Damn, I'd like to thank her too. Amazing what she did for Charlotte."

His brother's lips curled into a smile. If anyone on this earth loved Charlotte even close to what Sullivan did, it was his brother. When Carla left, Gavin had pitched in as much as he could to help Sullivan out. The man was almost a second father to Charlotte. He would be forever grateful to his brother for all the love and support he offered them.

"Yeah, well, she's going to be here in half an hour, so go home."

"What? I can't stay and meet her?"

"No." He set the oven to preheat, while gathering the rest of the ingredients for dinner.

"Why not?" Gavin tossed his apple core in the trash, sliding down off the counter and moving to, yet again, get in Sullivan's way. "She hot or something? You wanna keep her all to yourself?"

"Geez, Gavin." His brother was a nice guy, but a well-known ladies' man. None of them ever complained, but neither did they stay long. Something Sullivan never minded before, but the thought of his little brother working his charms on Ellie didn't sit right with Sullivan. "I invited her over to dinner, at my house, with my *daughter*. It's not like I'm planning to jump her on the dinner table."

Or anywhere else. Sullivan had a busy life. It didn't lend itself to relationships. And Ellie, well, Ellie was a relationship kind of woman. Why else had she been at that speed dating thing the other night? She was clearly looking for something.

Something more than a single overworked father could give her.

Gavin just stared at him with a big stupid grin on his face. "What?"

"Oh man, you are so far gone already, my brother. This is going to be fun to watch."

"What's going to be fun? The hell are you talking about?"

"Daddy, you said the H word!"

He groaned as Charlotte came back into the room. Of course, his daughter would pick the absolute worst timing to return. No, worse would have been if she came in during his rant about taking Ellie on the kitchen table. He didn't want to have *that* talk for another, oh, *never* years. Sadly, he knew he'd have to have it eventually. Sooner rather than later. Unfortunately, she'd already heard some talk on the playground. He didn't even want to think about what misinformation she'd be hearing over the years. That's why, as uncomfortable as he knew it was going to be, he'd already started gathering age-appropriate information for their talks.

"I did, Angel, and I'm sorry. Uncle Gavin was just leaving."

"You're leaving?" Her tiny bottom lip came out in an adorable pout. "Don't you want to stay for dinner? Ellie is coming!"

At the last part, her mouth turned up in a wide smile. He shook his head, unable to contain his smile too. Tearing the plastic covering off the chicken and setting it in the glass dish, he drizzled olive oil and lemon pepper over the skinless breasts.

"I'd love to—"

"But Uncle Gavin can't stay."

His brother raised one eyebrow but didn't contradict him. Gavin knew better than to question his parenting decisions in front of Charlotte.

"He's right. I have some work to do tonight. Big order to work on."

Gavin made custom furniture. Amazingly beautiful pieces designed specifically to the client's request. Over the years, he'd built up a reputation and made quite a name for himself.

"Can we go to the park on Saturday? You promised to take me on the carousal."

Gavin bent down to get eye level with Charlotte. "I did?"

"Uh huh." She gave him a toothy grin. Everyone in the room knew he'd promised no such thing, but Sullivan's daughter was a charmer like her uncle. Hard to say no to. The reason she had three ridiculously expensive collector dolls in her room. "You did."

"Then I guess I better take you to the park for a carousel ride on Saturday."

"Yay!"

She threw her arms around Gavin's neck. The big man rose to his feet, taking the small girl with him. His gaze met Sullivan's, arms tightening around the tiny child they both loved so much. He knew his brother was thinking about what happened at the zoo. How close they'd come to losing another family member. But they didn't. He didn't. Thanks to Ellie.

The oven beeped, letting him know it had reached the temperature for cooking. He slid the baking dish with the seasoned chicken into the hot range, setting a timer after he closed the door.

"I'll see you Saturday."

Charlotte nodded as Gavin set her down. "Bye, Uncle Gavin."

"Bye, Cheeky Monkey." His brother headed toward the front door. "I'll be by around ten?"

"Works for me."

"You be sure to give Ellie my thanks, too." A mischievous gleam entered his brother's eye. "Have fun tonight, brother."

"We'll have a nice dinner together. *All* of us." He nodded his head to Charlotte, but his annoying brother just laughed, waving his hand as he left.

"Can I help with dinner, Daddy?"

"Sure, angel. Want to help me butter the garlic bread?"

"Let me get my stool!"

He chuckled as Charlotte ran to the pantry to grab the three-foot step stool she used to help him in the kitchen. As he set her up at the counter with slices of bread, a plastic kiddie knife, and the soft butter. While she buttered, he set about getting a salad prepped. He was no Bobby Flay, but he could cook a decent dinner.

"I can't wait for Ellie to get here. Do you think she'll like the cupcakes?"

Last night, he and Charlotte had made cupcakes after dinner. They'd both sampled a few to make sure they were good enough to serve their hero.

"I'm sure she'll love them, angel."

Even if she didn't, he suspected Ellie wasn't the kind of person to disappoint a child who'd worked hard on a gift. He didn't know her well, but from the brief interactions they'd shared, he knew she had a kind heart. The night she'd been speed-dating, it had been clear she was suffering through the event for the sake of her friend.

He noticed something else that night, too. Something he'd observed the first time he met her. Ellie had compulsions. Nervous habits exhibited in times of stress like the TV inter-view and the speed dating event. He noticed her pull her ear and tap her straw. Another person might think nothing of it, but Sullivan was a doctor. Trained to observe. He suspected Ellie struggled with some type of anxiety disorder. Since he wasn't *her* doctor, he wouldn't bring it up unless she did.

People kept matters like that private from random acquaintances in their life. Maybe if they grew closer, she'd share with him—

Whoa, hold on! What the hell was he thinking? Grow close to Ellie? That wasn't what this night was about. He was simply thanking her for saving his daughter's life. Contrary to what his brother thought, this wasn't about starting a relationship or getting in Ellie's pants. He didn't have time or desire for any of that. And he was certain she was too young for him, anyway. She had to be in her twenties and although he was only thirty-five, sometimes, he felt much older. It was a symptom of single parenthood. Not that he would give up Charlotte for anything in the world, but raising a kid on your own could wear on a person.

"I'm done!"

He shook himself out of his thoughts and glanced at the bread. "Great job."

"Really?"

Chubby cheeks rounded with her wide smile.

"Yup." Her less than gentle butter spreading had destroyed only two pieces of bread. Less than usual. "You want to sprinkle the garlic? Not too much, remember?"

"I remember, Daddy."

He watched as she carefully tipped the spice shaker over the first few slices of bread, growing impatient and dumping heaps of garlic powder on the last two. Thankfully, those were the ripped pieces and would likely go straight into the trash.

"Great job, angel. Now I'll pop them in the toaster oven. Can you set out the silverware, please?"

"Yes, Daddy."

Charlotte jumped down off her stool, running to the cutlery drawer, excited to be helping. His heart swelled watching his daughter, the light in his life, and thought again how if not for one amazing woman, he could have lost her. A woman who would be here soon, in his house, eating the meal he prepared for her. When was the last time he'd made a woman a meal? He couldn't remember. He also couldn't remember the last time he'd felt this strange fluttering of anticipation in his gut.

And he had no damn clue what to do about it.

CHAPTER 8

*E*llie stood outside the address Sullivan had texted her. Spit lodged in her throat as she tried to swallow. This place was enormous! There was a three-car garage and the home itself towered above the midsized pines perfectly manicured out front. She knew by the address he lived in the nicer part of Sunlight, but she did not expect...all this.

Duh, he's a doctor. Of course, he had a big house. Probably has a big bank account too.

Suddenly, she felt out of her element. Dinner to her usually meant noodles from a box or a frozen pizza. Sullivan probably had all his meals made by a personal chef or something.

"Crap."

The nice, but cost-efficient, bottle of twelve-dollar wine in her hand would be used to water the houseplants in a place this nice. How could she have forgotten Sullivan was a doctor and therefore brackets above her in the income department?

"Doesn't matter," she muttered to herself. "I'm not here to

date him. I'm here to enjoy a thank you dinner and see Charlotte."

At the reminder of the spirited little girl, her nerves calmed. That's right, she was here to see Charlotte, not the girl's father, or at least, not only him. This was a simple, friendly thank you dinner. Nothing more. Panic averted. For the moment. She ran a hand over her hair. The wind today had picked up the second she got out of her car and, of course, she'd chosen to leave her hair down for once. What she wouldn't give for a brush right now. The fine strands always became a tangled mess at the slightest breeze. Oh well, nothing she could do about it now.

She also couldn't do a thing about her outfit. Sullivan had indicated the dinner was casual, so she'd dressed as she normally did. Jeans and a T-shirt. Cam would kill her for wearing the graphic tee with an adorable tabby and the words "you've gotta be kitten me" printed on it. But Ellie wasn't on a date—no matter how much her friend insisted it was when Ellie accidentally spilled the beans about her dinner at the Greens' house tonight—so she didn't need to impress anyone. She just needed to be herself. She liked animals and puns. Put them together and bonus points.

She raised her fist to knock on the beautiful dark wood double door. Insecurities rising again. Seriously, who had double doors? This place wasn't even a house. Weren't homes this big called mansions or manors or something? What if he had a butler? What would she do? She'd never met a butler in real life. Only seen them on TV shows. Okay, there had been the one at the Haunted Mansion at Disney, but that guy had been an actor playing a role.

Visions of the horrible ways she was going to screw up tonight's dinner, and how angry Sullivan would be, filled her mind. He'd toss her out for being uncouth. Gossip about her with his society friends. Word would get back to her boss and she'd somehow lose her job, fall behind on her bills, be forced out on the street!

"Stop it!" she chided herself, hand going up to tug on her earlobe. "None of that stuff is going to happen. Stop doing this."

She closed her eyes and took a deep breath. Acknowledging the radical path her brain had taken her on was not logical and in no way probable. The negativity and dark thoughts were trying to force her down again, but she wouldn't let them. Sure, tonight might not go swimmingly, but she'd been invited, and Sullivan knew full well where she worked. He had to know how vastly their lifestyles differed. All she had to do was be herself and everything would be fine.

She'd just finished calming herself down when the door swung open, and she found herself face to face with the most handsome man she'd ever laid eyes on.

Sullivan Green.

"Hi."

"Hello." She thanked her lucky stars there was no stodgy old butler to contend with. "I, um, thanks for inviting me." Then again, if she'd been dealing with an old wrinkly dude, instead of Sunlight's hottest doctor, maybe she could settle for a coherent sentence.

"Thanks for coming."

"This is for you." She thrust the bottle his way, suddenly unsure about everything. Her hands trembled as he took the wine from her grasp.

"Shiraz." He smiled as he read the label of the bottom-shelf alcohol. "My favorite."

"Really?"

"Yup. I know most people prefer cabernet or merlot, but I can't palate the stuff."

Neither could she. She wasn't a big drinker as it was, but when she had wine, it was usually a Shiraz.

"Come on in." He stepped back and motioned her inside.

"Thank you. You have a lovely home."

He grinned, the cheek dent making its panty-melting appearance. "You haven't even seen it yet."

"Oh, well, the, um, outside is nice. I just figured the inside would be—"

Her words were cut off as a squeal of delight ripped through the air.

"Ellie!"

Suddenly she was hit with forty-five pounds of pure excited seven-year-old.

"Oof! Hey there, Charlotte."

"You came, you came, you came!"

The little girl jumped up and down while still locked on Ellie's legs, causing her to wobble slightly. A firm hand closed around her upper arm, holding her steady throughout Charlotte's wiggling.

"Charlotte, give Ellie some personal space, okay?" Sullivan chuckled as he stepped even closer, bracing her with his shoulder against her back. "Sorry," he whispered in her ear as Charlotte dutifully released her tight grip and took a step back. "She's been really excited to see you."

A shiver that had nothing to do with the cool breeze blasting from the AC vents washed over her.

"It's fine," she squeaked out, not sure what to say. It was fine. She didn't mind Charlotte's excitement. Few people were all that excited to see her in her life. Animals, sure, she fed them. But people? Not so much.

"Did you bring sparkling juice?" Green eyes peeked up at the bottle Sullivan held in his hand.

"No, Angel, this isn't for you. This is grown up juice."

73

Her tiny face fell. Ellie's heart would have been crushed, but she had another gift yet to give.

"I'm sorry about the juice, Charlotte, but I do have something for you."

Her little frown turned upside down, eyes going wide. "You do?"

Reaching into her purse, she pulled out the small stuffed animal she'd purchased at the Zoo gift shop this morning.

"An elephant! Daddy, it's an elephant!" Charlotte grabbed the soft toy, squeezing it to her chest in a smothering hug. As she did, the animal let out a recorded trumpet blast of sound. "And it talks! Oh, thank you, thank you, thank you, Ellie! She's the bestest elephant ever! I'm going to call her El."

"El?"

The seven-year-old glanced at her with the brightest smile in the world. "Yeah, for Ellie the Elephant. Because you gave her to me. Come on, dinner's ready!"

Charlotte raced off through the house. Moisture blurred Ellie's vision as tears formed in her eyes. Ellie the Elephant. No one had ever named anything after her before. This kid was seriously carving out a large portion of Ellie's heart and settling right in.

"Hey."

She turned at the softly spoken word to see Sullivan had come around to her side and was now staring at her with concern. Blushing from embarrassment, she blinked until the tears disappeared.

"You have a special kid there, Sullivan."

His expression softened into an understanding smile. "Don't I know it. Shall we?"

"Lead the way."

He took her out of the entryway, showing her the living room complete with gas fireplace, a window seat she'd love to spend an afternoon reading on, and dark leather furniture that looked like it came straight from those expensive home redecorating shows her mother loved to watch. Next, he pointed out the guest bathroom, which, despite not having a shower or tub, was bigger than the *one* bathroom in her apartment. In fact, her entire apartment could probably fit in the living room and entryway alone.

They passed the stairs to the second floor, where he mentioned the bedrooms and his home office location. Finally, they made it to the dining room where Ellie was currently sitting at the table, El sitting in the seat next to her with a banana on the plate in front of her.

"Is El joining us for dinner?" Sullivan asked his daughter, winking at Ellie as he showed her where to sit and headed into the kitchen that was visible through the large open doorway.

"Yes, but she only eats bananas because she's an elephant." Charlotte nodded, then quickly backtracked. "And peanuts. Bananas and peanuts."

Ellie took a seat at the dining table, noticing the cheerfully colored yellow tablecloth with white daisies and the three place settings. Two in a beautiful bone ivory color and one plastic clown face child's plate. Choosing to take the seat on the other side of Charlotte—the one not occupied by a stuffed animal—Ellie once again noticed how different she and the Greens lived. She didn't even think she owned a tablecloth. Her plates were dollar-bin plastic. Dishwasher, and microwave safe out of necessity.

"Actually, Charlotte. Elephants can eat up to three hundred and seventy-five pounds of vegetation every day."

The little girl's jaw dropped open and her brow furrowed. "What's vegetation?"

"Things like plants, grass, fruit, twigs, tree bark, even some roots."

"Wow. They must fart a lot. Joey Freemont says vegetables make you fart, and that's why he doesn't eat them." She leaned in close and whispered. "But I think he eats them anyway because I've heard him fart in class and it's smelly."

"Charlotte." Sullivan called from the kitchen.

"Oops, I'm not supposed to talk about farting at the table."

Huh, she wondered how many times the girl had brought up the topic before that it had to become a rule. Seemed like an odd thing to want to discuss, but then again, she was seven. Bodily functions were all the rage at that age if Ellie remembered correctly.

"Sorry, Daddy!"

"It's okay." Sullivan entered the room again, arms full of serving dishes.

"Oh, let me help you." She started to rise but sat back down when Sullivan shook his head.

"You're the guest, besides I can handle this. I used to be a waiter in college."

"You were?" Somehow, she couldn't imagine Dr. Green taking orders at the local burger joint.

"Yup. Med school isn't cheap."

So she'd heard. She'd also heard doctors made out like kings after a few years of practice. Looking around the place, she guessed it must be true. Still, it made her feel a little better knowing Sullivan had endured his share of roughing it. Maybe they had more in common than she thought.

"Dinner is served."

She glanced down at the serving dishes Sullivan had placed on the table. Delicious aromas wafted from the food. Garlic and butter flew up her nostrils, making her mouth water as she spied some golden slices of garlic bread. A large wooden bowl held crisp-looking leafy greens, red cherry tomatoes, thin slices of bright orange carrot, and chunks of white, which she assumed to be feta. The last platter held three yellow and black speckled chicken breasts, steam still rising off the meat.

"Charlotte?"

Sullivan grabbed a serving fork, holding his free hand out. Charlotte passed her plate along, thanking her father as he piled it high with food. When he held his hand out to her, Ellie did the same. Extending her plate for him to serve. So far, this night had gone nothing like she feared, thank goodness. Once everyone had their dinner served, Sullivan took a seat opposite her and Charlotte.

"Dig in, everyone."

No one argued.

Ellie cut into her chicken, the tender meat slicing with the barest of pressure. The second it hit her tongue; the flavor exploded. Sharp, spicy pepper combined with the tangy, tart lemon and moist juices of the chicken to create the most wonderful zest.

"Wow! Sullivan, this is amazing."

"Surprised I can cook?"

Honestly, a little. She expected him to have a chef or something. Didn't all doctors have that? Her father had never cooked a day in her life. The only thing she'd ever seen the old man heat was coffee. Her mother cooked all the meals when she was a child. Tried to teach her, but after one fateful night when Ellie almost blew up the oven, her mother had declared her a lost cause in the kitchen. Thank goodness for takeout and cereal, or she'd starve to death.

"I just…wasn't expecting it."

He chuckled. "I've always enjoyed food, and I discovered in med school cooking was a great way to take my mind off studies. Whenever I got stressed or my brain wanted to explode, I took a break and baked cookies or cupcakes."

"Huh, bet you were popular among your classmates."

"There was a time or two I suspected our professor gave

us extra homework just so I'd bring in my double chocolate brownies."

Double chocolate brownies? Oh yes, please! She really hoped he made those for dessert tonight. She was a brownie addict.

"I made the garlic bread," Charlotte stated proudly, taking a huge bite of her own bread. "Daddy, let me do the sprinkle."

Ellie picked up the slice on her plate, the smell of garlic hitting her like a punch to the face. Lifting the food to her lips, she took a small bite. Immediately, her eyes watered as garlic overpowered every taste bud she possessed. Charlotte must have been very generous with her sprinkling. Not wanting to hurt the child's feelings, she forced herself to chew and swallow, wondering how on earth Charlotte could sit there and eat her slice without gagging.

"It's delicious." She pasted on a big smile she hoped was convincing. Thankfully, it worked as Charlotte beamed and focused on her dinner.

"Sorry," Sullivan whispered, covertly taking her slice, and slipping it under his napkin while grabbing her another piece. "You must have gotten one of the heavy shakes. I apologize. I thought I took all those out."

She took a small nibble of her new piece of bread, sighing in relief. This time, a garlic bomb didn't explode on her tongue. She could actually taste the butter on this slice.

"The last few slices are always a little...enthusiastic with the flavoring." He chuckled. "But Charlotte loves to help in the kitchen."

"You like to cook, Charlotte?" She smiled as the little girl shoved a large forkful of salad into her mouth.

"Mmmmm, hmmmm."

Sullivan pointed his fork in his daughter's direction. "Charlotte, no talking with your mouth full."

Ellie tried to hold back laughter as Charlotte rolled her eyes, making big dramatic chews before swallowing.

"I love cooking, but sometimes I get the 'gredients wrong. But Daddy's teaching me. Jayne's mommy taught her how to make chocolate chip cookies, but I don't have a mommy."

The child said it so matter-of-factly, but Ellie felt the temperature in the room drop ten degrees at those words. Her eyes slid to Sullivan. He was looking at his food, cutting his chicken with a single determined focus, but she noticed the tightness in his jaw. When he raised his gaze, it clashed with hers. Green pools of pain and anger filled his eyes, but in a blink, all the emotion was gone, and he'd once again plastered a smile on his face.

See what you did with your questions? You ruined dinner!

Ellie focused on her food, resisting the urge to tug at her ear. She told the dark voice in her head to shove it all while wishing she had a magic wand to wave the awkwardness of this moment away.

CHAPTER 9

urns out she didn't need a magic wand. After the small blip of discomfort, the rest of the dinner passed uneventfully. Charlotte asked her dozens of questions about the zoo and the animals there. Ellie happily answered all the girl's questions. Talking about animals was something she loved to do and didn't have in common with many people, so it was nice to find someone else who loved listening to her blabber on. Even Sullivan seemed interested, asking a few questions himself. She discovered while elephants were Charlotte's favorite, the elder Green preferred the lions. Of course he did. With their sleek beauty, relaxed demeanor, and tightly leashed power, Sullivan reminded her of the beautiful creatures.

Once dinner was over, they enjoyed some homemade cupcakes that weren't brownies, but they were scrumptious. She might have to change her stance on favorite desserts. Charlotte talked them into playing a game of Candy Land, which she won. Ellie suspected Sullivan had let the girl win. She sure had.

At eight-thirty, Charlotte let out a jaw-cracking yawn.

Sullivan scooped her into his arms. "Okay, Angel. Time for bed."

"Can Ellie tuck me in?"

He lifted his brows in question. Was he asking if she wanted to? She'd never tucked in a kid before. Couldn't even remember the last time someone had tucked her in. She was sure her parents had at one point in her childhood.

"Um, sure. I can do that."

"Yay."

The excited cry was softer than normal as the girl's eyes started to droop.

"We better get a move on." Sullivan turned and headed toward the stairs. "Once she's out, she's out. I'd like her to at least make a pass at her teeth before that happens."

Ellie followed them up the stairs and down the hall. She stood by awkwardly as Sullivan helped Charlotte brush her teeth and hair, staying in the hall as Charlotte changed into her pajamas and used the bathroom. She followed Sullivan and the drowsy little girl into a room decorated with pictures of elephants and princesses. A small bookshelf held several children's books, some of which Ellie fondly remembered from her own childhood. A scattering of toys spilled out of a chest in the corner, dolls, animals, some blocks. Ellie even spotted a truck or two. It seemed the little girl had everything her heart desired. The thought made her smile right before she remembered the little girl didn't have a mother.

Maybe not everything her heart desired. Ellie knew no one's life was perfect, no matter how it looked from the outside.

"Ellie?" Charlotte asked sleepily as she brought the covers up in the white princess bed and tucked them around the child.

"Yes?"

"Do you want to come to my birthday party next week?"

She glanced at Sullivan, who simply smiled, nodding his head.

"Sure, sweetie. I'd love to."

"Yay..."

The word trailed off into soft little snores. Ellie knelt there next to the bed, gazing at the sweet sleeping girl who truly looked like the angel her father so often called her. Sullivan leaned over to place a kiss on his daughter's head. He rose and held out a hand to her. She placed her palm against his and was stunned by the shock that ran down her arm. Not an electric shock, like from static electricity, but a shock of awareness. One that went straight to all her core, awakening something inside her she'd never felt before.

The moment they were out of the room, Ellie dropped her hand. Sullivan glanced down but said nothing. Instead, he put a finger over his lips then indicated with a nod of his head they should head back downstairs.

"Would you like a cup of coffee or tea?"

More caffeine was definitely not what her nerves needed right now, but for some strange reason, she was hesitant to leave. "Tea sounds lovely."

"Come on. I have a whole stash. You can take your pick."

They headed back down to the kitchen, where Ellie realized he wasn't kidding. Sullivan had every type of tea under the sun. With all the weirdness going on in her body right now, she settled on a nice, calming cup of chamomile. While waiting for the water to boil, she tried to fill the silence with something. She didn't do silence well.

"So, what happened to Charlotte's mother?" Crap! She didn't do talking well either. Why the hell had that come out of her mouth?

Because you're starting to care about these two and you want to know more about them.

Sullivan paused in his reach for a mug.

"I'm sorry. That was rude of me. You don't have to answer."

He let out a weary sigh, grabbing two mugs and turning to face her. "No. It's fine. My ex-wife…she had some problems. We met in college, and I think she liked the idea of me being a doctor, but when I started my residency and my shifts at the hospital, she realized the life of a doctor's wife wasn't all prestige and yachts."

Wait, he had a yacht? She'd never even been on a rowboat.

"I was away a lot in the beginning of our marriage. Long shifts, late nights, emergency calls. We drifted apart. I thought having Charlotte would bring us back together, but after her birth…"

Sullivan's grip on the mugs tightened. Pain radiated off him, so potent she couldn't help herself. Ellie hurried over to his side, placing a supportive hand on his shoulder. He didn't look at her, but she felt some of the tension leave his body.

"She didn't seem to enjoy being a mother. I thought perhaps it was postpartum depression, but she never talked about it. I was so busy, so wrapped up in my own things, I didn't push. At that point, our marriage…well, she didn't seem to enjoy being a wife either. I thought if I was patient, she'd come around."

"But she didn't?" Ellie asked when he didn't continue.

"No. She left. Packed up one day while I was on shift, dropped Charlotte off with my brother, and left town. I got the divorce papers in the mail two months later, complete with the paperwork to sever her parental rights to Charlotte."

Whoa. She knew people got divorced for various reasons, but it was rare for a parent to give up rights to their own children. She wondered what the woman could have been going through to abandon her baby like that. Her heart ached for all of them. There was no winner here, no happy ending. Everyone had suffered.

"I'm so sorry, Sullivan."

The water in the electric kettle clicked. Sullivan moved to pour the boiling liquid in the mugs, dumping the tea bags in the steaming water.

"She made her choice."

He sighed. A heavy sound Elli could practically feel weigh down the air in the room.

"Thankfully, my brother stepped up helping with Charlotte until I could figure things out."

"Have you ever thought of getting remarried?" she asked before she could stop herself. Ellie didn't mean to poke a sore subject, but Sullivan seemed so great, and Charlotte was a doll. She couldn't imagine why he hadn't found someone else.

Sullivan frowned, his jaw hardening as the rough words escaped tight lips. "No. Charlotte was a baby when her mom left. She didn't feel the...I couldn't risk trying again with someone new and having it not work out. I won't do that to my daughter."

Stupid Ellie! Look what you did. You upset him with your invasive questioning. No wonder no one stays around after date number one. Why would anyone want someone as annoying as you?

She squeezed her eyes shut as the insidious voice whispered the dark thoughts into her head. She wasn't being rude. They were just talking. If Sullivan hadn't wanted to talk about his ex-wife, he would have said so. Besides, this wasn't a date. There were no worries about him dumping her because they weren't together. And probably never would be, according to his distaste for relationships. She got it. Hard to bounce back from heartbreak. Even harder when you had a kid whose well-being depended on you.

"For what it's worth," she said, giving him a soft smile. "You're doing a great job on your own. Charlotte is wonderful."

He glanced up at her words, a hesitant smile on his face. "Yeah?"

She nodded. "She really is."

His lips curled into a full-fledged grin. "Yeah," he said, handing her a mug. "She really is something. Thank you, Ellie. Thank you for saving my daughter and thank you for agreeing to come to her party."

She blew across her mug to cool the tea. "My pleasure. I like hanging out with Charlotte. She's very sweet. Such a special girl."

Sharp green eyes focused on her, the intensity in them causing every nerve in her body to spark to life.

"You know what, Ellie?"

She shook her head, tongue too thick to form a single word as the intensity of his gaze captured her, refusing to let her look anywhere but deep into his eyes.

"I believe you're something special, too."

CHAPTER 10

"So, how was the date?"

Ellie glanced up from checking the bucket of fish for the penguin's morning meal. Cam sat on the metal countertop, legs swinging in the air, a mischievous smile on her face. *When had she come in?*

"It wasn't a date." She went back to checking the food, the fishy smell of, well, fish, so common to her she barely noticed it anymore. "It was a thank you dinner with his *daughter* present."

"How is Charlotte?"

"Great. She's such a sweet kid. She really liked the stuffed elephant. Thanks for suggesting it."

Cam snorted. "Of course she liked it. She's a kid. Kids like stuff. I have seven nieces and nephews to prove it."

Cam came from a large family. Being the baby of the bunch, she was the only one without kids, but unlike Ellie's mother, Cam's didn't pressure her daughter to find a man and start popping out babies before her biological clocked ticked off. Whatever the hell that meant. She'd never heard a tick from any part of her body, especially the baby-making parts. Screams of agony once a month, sure, but no clock ticks.

"So, the date—excuse me, *thank you dinner*—was good then?"

Cam corrected herself at Ellie's sharp look. Her friend smiled, sliding off the counter and walking over to the cabinet to grab the headset for the feeding hour show.

"Yeah, it was nice. Sullivan can cook, like, actually cook."

"Most people can, Ellie. You're the only person I know who can live off fast food and box pasta and still be that tiny."

All the people in her family were tiny. They had small genes. Even her dad was barely over five foot eight. Plus, she ran. A lot. Early on in her therapy, Dr. Mitchell had suggested exercise in addition to her meds and therapy to help manage her OCD. Not a big fan of gyms, she'd tried out morning jogging and fell in love. Rising with the sun to hit the streets. Only her and the chirping sounds of the early birds.

There was a park by her apartment with a great running trail that weaved through a small, wooded area. No cars, busses, or morning commuters to harsh her vibe. Only the crunchy sounds of her feet hitting the dirt path. The cool crisp morning air filling her lungs as she pushed herself until her legs burned. She ran out her anxiety, and while it wasn't a cure-all, it helped calm her mind.

"You could always come running with me."

Cam's mouth dropped in horror. "Bite your tongue. There's not a sports bra in this world strong enough to keep me from getting a black eye the moment I even attempt a jog. The girls would knock me out for sure." Her friend glanced down at her generous chest and shook her head. "No, thank you. I'll stick to my spin class."

She understood. Actually, she didn't since she was a member of the itty-bitty titty committee and her girls wouldn't even bounce on a trampoline, but she realized everyone had their own body issues no matter what the shape or size. She liked to jog. Cam liked to cycle. Friends didn't have to do everything together. She was just grateful she had a friend to do stuff with sometimes.

"Hey," Cam spoke to her as she hooked the hands-free mic headset around her ear. "I noticed we're running low on Bingo's vitamins. I told Stephan to order more."

"Thanks, I made a note on yesterday's end of day sheet as well."

She placed the bucket of fish on the metal counter, checking through the birds' food once more to make sure everything was in order, wishing she could be satisfied with one check. But she couldn't. She knew how illogical her rituals seemed. They freaked people out. Her parents, her exes, former friends. They even annoyed her most days. Didn't mean she could suddenly stop them. There was no stopping the dark voice in her head, insidiously whispering that if she didn't check one more time, didn't tap that or flip this, everyone she loved would die and it'd be her fault.

A warm palm landed on her shoulder. Turning her head, she glanced up to see Cam smiling at her.

"You good?"

"Yeah, I'm good."

"Damn right you are."

Her friend pulled her in for a brief side hug. Emotions threatened to spill over, but she tucked them back. What had she done to deserve such an amazing friend? Someone who might not fully understand what went on in her head but accepted her no matter what. No judgment, no fear or scorn. Just support, friendship, and love. That's what Cam gave, and Ellie did everything in her power to give it back.

"Now let's get out there." Cam headed toward the inner door to the outside penguin enclosure, tossing over her shoulder, "I hope we don't have another kid go overboard this week."

"Why would you say that? Are you trying to jinx us?"

Her friend headed outside with a laugh. She shook her head but let a tiny giggle escape. No one would fall into the water today. Tammy had made sure of it by placing a three-foot barrier in front of the enclosure until the zoo decided if they needed extra safety measures for the penguin enclosure. The committee would evaluate and vote on it next week. Until then, they had pushed the visitors back. Good thing too, since their feeding time crowd had doubled in size since the incident with Charlotte.

People loved an exciting story.

Thankfully nothing exciting happened at today's feeding time. Unless seeing Bingo shoot a stream of poo into the pool filled people with excitement. Judging by the laughter of the three middle school boys in attendance, it did.

Ellie finished feeding the tiny tuxedoed birds, making sure each got the right vitamins, according to Stephan and Rob. Cam finished her talk and invited the crowds to ask questions. A dozen hands went up.

"Yes, you sir. In the back with the red shirt." Cam pointed over the huddled mass to a large man standing in the back.

"Yeah, so I was wondering about that kid that fell in last week?"

Ugh, this again. People had been asking about Charlotte and what had happened for the past week. Didn't anyone follow the news? They'd already reported the entire story. Cam's smile tightened.

"I'm afraid we're not at liberty to discuss the events that took place last week. Any other questions?"

"It was bound to happen," the guy continued to shout. "Animals shouldn't be locked up in cages. It goes against their natural instincts."

Oh great, another one of those people who thought they knew everything about how zoos operated, but in reality, had zero clue. Ellie took a deep breath. She didn't get mad often, but it really burned her butt when people accused zoos of being animal prisons. There were laws, codes, all kinds of checks and balances in place to assure the animals were treated with the best of care. It wasn't like they were plucking creatures out of the wild. Most zoo animals were bred in captivity according to the SSP; species survival plans. And Sunlight Zoo was a member of AZA, the Association of Zoos and Aquariums. If they violated any safety requirements, they'd have their funding pulled faster than a cheetah could run.

She loved animals. Everyone who worked here did. They would never let these precious creatures suffer, and shame on anyone who thought otherwise.

"Little boy in the front, yes, you have a question?"

Cam plowed right over the guy's yelling.

"How far can they shoot their poop?"

The crowd chuckled, forgetting about the loud guy in the back as Cam launched into a very fun but educational lesson about penguin feces. Eventually, the questions ran out, and the people wandered away. Ellie noticed Cam pulled out her walkie, speaking into it as she stared at the guy in the red shirt who still stood a dozen feet away, an angry scowl on his face.

"You notify security?" she asked, following her friend back inside.

"Yup. Man, I am getting really sick of all the people asking about what happened last week. And I really hate all these so-called animal activists trying to stir up trouble. If they really cared about animals, they'd donate to the zoo or to the wildlife rescue and rehabilitation program."

She agreed. People liked to talk a lot, but they rarely put their money where their mouth was.

Walking over to the large sink, she turned on the taps and rinsed out the bucket. Placing it in the rack to dry. After feeding time, they let the penguins bask and swim while they tended to the other birds in the aviary. Ellie and Cam gathered the food she'd prepped earlier that morning, Cam waiting while she checked it over again. Once they were ready, they took the interior hallways, the ones the public didn't have access to, to each bird enclosure. Squawks and chirps greeted them at every door. The birds were always happy with feeding time.

After they'd visited the individual enclosures, they headed to the tropical walk-through zone. A wonderful enclosure where zoo guests could walk a designated path in the building and see the birds flying and nesting all around them. There were plants specific to the bird's native habitat and even a small waterfall that fed into a little pool of three-inch deep water. The guests loved it and the birds loved to pose for snapshots.

Especially Bill the parrot.

"You're fabulous, Doll-face!" The beautiful blue and gold macaw bobbed his head in greeting when she stepped up to his feed bowl.

"Hey there, Bill. Ya hungry today, buddy?"

"Ellie's got a boyfriend. Ellie's got a boyfriend," Bill replied.

She stumbled in shock, almost dropping the scoop of nuts, seeds, and fruit she'd been about to place in his dish. Heat burning her cheeks, she turned to face her friend, who held a hand over her chuckling, meddling mouth.

"Where did he learn that?"

Cam held her hands up in exaggerated surprise. "I have no idea."

"Yeah, right. He's not my boyfriend. We just had dinner."

"Strictly platonic." Cam nodded.

"Totally platonic."

"No sparks at all over the course of the night."

She hesitated, not wanting to lie to her best friend, but also not entirely sure what had gone on the other night. Something had been going on under the surface of the evening. But maybe that had just been her? Who's to say Sullivan felt anything for her? He certainly didn't say anything or make a move...

"Ellie's got a boyfriend. Ellie's got a boyfriend."

She turned a grumpy scowl on the parrot. "Can it unless you want nothing but pellets for the next week."

Bill tilted his head. "You're fabulous, Doll-face."

"That's better."

She filled his bowl, not blaming the parrot. Wasn't his fault her bestie taught him that ridiculous phrase. *Boyfriend.* What a silly word. Did adults even use the term? Wasn't lover the preferred nomenclature?

How would I know? I haven't had sex in ages.

Okay, not *ages*, but it had been a while. After her last breakup, she'd had a disastrous one-night stand and decided men just weren't worth it. Not when she had her trusty BOB in her bedside drawer.

"I'm going to get you for this," she muttered to Cam. The woman just laughed and moved on to fill the other bowls.

Once all the animals were fed, they moved back to the kitchen area to clean up. Ellie's phone chirped in her pocket.

"You really need to change your notification." Cam placed a hand on her chest. "Every time someone texts you, I think there's a bird loose."

She chuckled because besides Cam and her mother—who rarely texted because she *preferred to speak to real people*—not many people texted her. So, unless her friend was sending

her a funny meme or an article on the latest breeding prac-
tices for penguins, her phone didn't chirp much.

Curious about who could be messaging her, she pulled
the device from her pocket. Her lips pulled into a wide grin
when she saw the sender.

Sullivan: Does the zoo sell elephant-themed party supplies?

An odd question for a doctor to ask. Unless said doctor
had a seven-year-old daughter in love with elephants.

Ellie: I think we might have something to fit the bill.

*Sullivan: Yes! Charlotte decided she wants an elephant-themed
birthday party and every store I've been to has zero options.*

Ellie: Let me see what I can scrounge up.

Sullivan: You are a lifesaver.

She laughed. No one had ever called her a lifesaver
before. Weirdo. Crazy. Odd. Quirky. All those, sure. Lifesaver was new.

She liked it.

"What?" Cam finished washing the last of the feed
supplies, drying her hand on a towel and gazing at Ellie with
narrowed eyes. "What's with that giggle?"

"I didn't giggle."

"You most certainly did. And you've got a big goofy grin
on your face."

"I do not."

"You do…ohmigod it's him! Isn't it? You're texting Dr.
Sexy."

Dr. Sexy?

"His name is Sullivan and yes, I'm texting him—"

"Holy crap, you're sexting him!" Cam slapped her play-
fully on the shoulder. "At work, you bad girl, you."

How in the heck had her friend made that leap? "I'm not
sexting him!"

"Yes, you are. Your face is bright red."

She placed a hand on her cheeks, which were indeed hot.

"Only because you brought up sexting. Which we're *not* doing. He's asking me about decorations for Charlotte's birthday party."

"Oh," Cam slumped against the sink. "It's not sexting, but it's still something, I guess."

Honestly, she had no idea what went on in her friend's mind most days. Sexting at work? Yeah, right. She'd never even sexted someone at home, or ever for that matter. The very idea made her...actually it made her kind of hot. The thought of sending naughty texts to Sullivan in the middle of the day. Getting him all worked up until they could get off work and come together to—

Whoa! Okay, back it up there. Her mind was running away from her again. She wasn't dating the guy. They were just...friends, she supposed? Yeah, friends. No getting together, no sexting. Just two people who had dinner and were now discussing party decorations. Nothing dirty or naughty.

"He has a kid, and he's not looking to get married because..."

She hesitated, not wanting to share what Sullivan had told her about his ex-wife. It was personal and heartbreaking. Something she suspected he didn't want spread about the Sunlight zoo.

"He has his reasons, but he very clearly stated he was not looking for a wife."

Cam snorted. "Doll-face, I'm not looking to get you wifed. I'm just trying to help you get some action."

"I like the way my life is just fine."

"I know you do. And I wasn't suggesting you change it. I'm just pointing out if a person, any person, makes you smile like that with just the thought of them. Well then, maybe you should try to spend a lot more time with that person. Not with the intention of putting a ring on it. Just for fun."

More time with Sullivan? She liked the sound of that. He was smart and funny. A good dad, kind, and fair without being a pushover. After what he told her the other night about Charlotte's mother, she knew he'd faced some pretty hard times, but he didn't let them drag him down. He did his best for his daughter. How could anyone not like spending time with a person like that?

"Just take it one day at a time and allow yourself to be happy, okay?"

She glanced up at her friend. "I think I can do that."

Cam winked. "I know you can. Now let's get a move on. You're on poop duty while I give everyone their baths."

"How come I have poop duty?"

Cam grabbed the rubber gloves they used when cleaning the animals' pens and tossed them. Ellie caught them mid-air, sliding them on as her friend pointed a finger with a smile.

"Because one of us is going home tonight to frozen pizza and a Schitt's Creek marathon and the other is heading over to Dr. Sexy's house to save his kid's birthday. I think the good doctor will be very grateful, once again, and those with the possibility of sex in their future get poop duty. Now let's go."

She highly doubted there'd be any sex for her tonight or in the near future, but she couldn't argue with the fact that her night sounded like a lot more fun than her friend's. Unable to keep the goofy grin off her face—she didn't even want to try anymore—Ellie set about to poop duty and after that...who knew what could happen?

CHAPTER 11

Sullivan gently closed the door to his daughter's room. He swore the child could hear the squeak of a shoe on the way out of her bedroom but wouldn't budge a muscle if the entire kitchen exploded downstairs. Normally she went to sleep on her own just fine, but today had been tough on her. Him too. They'd had a meeting with the boys responsible for pushing Charlotte into the penguin pool. The school had reached a decision on proper punishment. Three days of suspension and a ban from all field trips for the rest of the year. In addition, the boys had to write Charlotte letters of apology and read them to her in the principal's office.

A fair punishment in his mind. He hoped reflecting on their behavior helped the children to see what they did wrong, but who knew if it would have any lasting impression. What he knew was he was damn proud of his daughter. Charlotte sat in that office with her head held high, listening to the letters, and at the end she'd told each boy she had forgiven them. He knew she was still frightened, but she put on a brave face and showed poise and maturity far beyond what most people—let alone a seven-year-old—would have.

After the meeting, he'd taken her out for her favorite dinner. They'd gotten extra dessert because she deserved it. Putting her to bed, he discussed with her a little more about her feelings on the day. Most of the time, he had no idea what he was doing. He was just winging this parenting thing. All the books he'd read when Claire had been pregnant had conflicting advice. He'd ended up just trashing them all and going with his gut. Seemed to be working out okay seeing how today turned out.

He headed down the stairs, pulling out his phone to text Ellie that Charlotte was in bed, and it was safe to bring the decorations over. A smile curled his lips as he typed out the message. He enjoyed texting Ellie. Texting her, talking to her. Hell, even thinking about her gave him a thrill he hadn't felt in a long time. The woman fascinated and awed him. He might have a bit of hero worship, considering she saved his daughter, but that was just another aspect of her he found himself enthralled by. She had jumped in without a thought to her own safety to save a perfect stranger. Few people would do that.

The more he got to know her, the more he liked her. She had a unique sense of humor and a kind heart. The way she listened to him the other night, no judgment for him or his ex, just an open ear and a sympathetic heart. Who did that? Ellie did, apparently. He had no damn clue what was going on between them, but he knew whatever it was, he didn't want it to end. He wanted to see where their budding friendship led. If nothing more than for Charlotte's sake. She adored Ellie.

He still held true to what he told her the other night. Sullivan wasn't looking to get remarried. A fact that a few of the staff at the office had refused to acknowledge. The nurses kept trying to set him up with their friends and daughters. He finally had to put his foot down and make it clear he wasn't on the market. Ellie knew he wasn't looking for a wife. Would she be amenable to something...more than friendship, but less than permanent?

He shook his head. He was getting ahead of himself here.

Walking into the kitchen, he debated making tea or opening a bottle of wine. Normally he enjoyed a glass after Charlotte went to bed, but he didn't want Ellie to assume... what? That he'd invited her over to seduce her? His body heated at the thought of sharing a glass of wine with Ellie by the fire. The dim glow of the flames illuminating her soft round face. Talking in hushed tones, edging closer as their bodies naturally gravitated toward each other. He could see it all in his mind, almost taste the sweetness of her lips as he sampled the vintage bouquet from the depths of her mouth.

Sullivan groaned, his body tightening with need. What the hell just happened? He'd been debating what drink to offer his impending guest and somehow it became a cheesy porno in his mind. *Not cheesy, hot.* Yeah, it had been hot. He'd be lying if he said he hadn't imagined himself and Ellie in an intimate scenario more than once since meeting the woman. But he didn't want to do anything to make her feel uncomfortable.

Grabbing the teakettle, he filled it with water. Tea it was, then. He liked Ellie, in more ways than one. More importantly, Charlotte liked Ellie. He didn't want to do anything to jeopardize the budding relationship between his daughter and a woman he knew would be an excellent influence. Sullivan wouldn't let his sudden raging hormones get in the way of his daughter finding someone she could relate to.

The water started to boil. Sullivan grabbed the box of chamomile from the cabinet, remembering it being Ellie's choice the other night. He took two mugs down from another cabinet and dropped the bags in just as his phone pinged with an incoming text message. Pulling it from his pocket, he smiled as he read.

Ellie: At the front door. Didn't want to knock in case it would wake up Charlotte.

He hurried to the doors, pulling one side open to reveal the person currently taking up a large portion of his thoughts these days. Ellie Clark.

"Hi."

"Hi." She smiled, holding up two large paper bags. "I got some party goodies for you."

His eyes took her in, grin widening as he read her light blue shirt with a picture of a toad and the phrase *Toadly Awesome* on it.

"You are *toadly awesome* and I owe you for this."

She blushed. "Happy to help."

A shrill whistle sounded from the kitchen. He opened the door, stepping back to motion her in. "I'm making tea. Want to come in for a cup and show me what you got?"

"Okay."

She stepped in with a smile that made his heart skip a beat. He was in so much trouble. Damn good thing he hadn't opened that bottle of wine. The woman messed with his head as it was. No need to muddle the night with alcohol, too.

Ellie headed to the kitchen. After closing and locking the door, Sullivan followed. He lifted the kettle from the base, pouring the steaming water into the prepped mugs as Ellie set the bags on the counter and pulled out the contents.

"There was a lot of fun things left over from the celebration we had last year when we opened the new elephant enclosure."

He remembered that. They'd spent two years building an expansive new paddock for the large animals. Charlotte had been so excited to see it when it finally opened last year. She'd begged him to take her out of school for the opening and he'd almost caved, but education came first. He'd taken her the following weekend, and she'd spent hours exploring every inch of it. He chuckled, remembering how he wondered if the gleeful grin would ever leave her face that day.

"I've got biodegradable plates, cups, and napkins. All with happy elephants' faces on them, of course."

"Of course." He smiled as she pulled the items from the bag, her enthusiasm reminding him very much of Charlotte's glee whenever the subject of elephants were brought up.

"There are also some balloons. You'll have to rent a helium tank. We don't have one on hand at the zoo, but I can give you the number of the place we rent from. I promise they'll give you a good deal."

"Thank you."

"Oh!" She reached into the bag, pulling out a large elephant statue. No wait, it wasn't a statue, it was a—

"Is that a piñata?"

"Yes. We ordered it, but then decided against using it because the crowd was so big, we didn't want any of the kids hurting themselves or anyone else swinging a bat around blindfolded. But I figure it will be perfect for a birthday party. Can't have a birthday without a piñata, right?"

"Indeed." He placed the hot mug of tea on the counter in front of her. "Ellie, thank you for all this. I really appreciate it."

She smiled with a small shrug. "Anything to make Charlotte's big day special."

"You're amazing."

Her gaze locked on his, and the surrounding air crackled with energy. He felt himself being pulled toward her as if by an invisible wire. A live wire, shocking him with bolts of lust.

Her lips parted, and it drew his gaze to their soft, plump pinkness. He wanted nothing more in this moment then to lean forward and capture them, see if they tasted as good as they looked. He found himself stepping forward, hand raising to reach out.

"It's nothing, really."

Her softly spoken words broke whatever spell he found himself under. Sensing her need for space, he leaned back against the counter, lifting his mug and blowing across the top before taking a small sip.

"How much do I owe you for all this?"

She snorted. "Are you kidding? When I asked Tammy, she practically shoved the stuff in my arms."

"Tammy? The zoo director?"

"Mmmm, hmmm." She grabbed her mug, blowing the hot beverage as he did. "I think she's worried you'll sue because of what happened with Charlotte. You could probably ask for free lifetime membership and she'd give it to you."

He chuckled. "No need for that. I know what happened wasn't the zoo's fault and the boys responsible have been properly reprimanded. No suing from me. Tammy can rest at ease."

She smiled. "That's good to hear."

Ellie took a sip of her tea, wiping the edge of the mug with her thumb and tapping the side three times. It was a move he'd seen her do a few times at dinner the other night. He assumed it was a compulsion tied to whatever anxiety disorder she had, so he said nothing. It wasn't his place. However, when he glanced up, the worried expression on her face told him she'd observed him noticing.

Dammit.

Her smile vanished, along with the cheerful mood in the room. Shit, he didn't want Ellie to feel uncomfortable. The last thing he wanted to do was upset her. Especially when she'd done so much to help his daughter.

"I'm sorry," she said, setting down her mug.

"You don't have to apologize, Ellie. Ever."

She closed her eyes, taking a deep breath before opening them again. The beautiful, deep brown gaze staring him directly in the eye. "I…I have obsessive-compulsive disorder."

"OCD."

She nodded. As a doctor, he was familiar enough with the condition. He didn't treat it, as he wasn't a psychologist, but he had referred a few patients he suspected suffered from the disorder. It wasn't what most people thought. Movies and other entertainment forms got it completely wrong—as they did with most mental health issues.

"You don't have to explain anything if you don't want to."

She smiled then, a small one, but enough of a curl to her lips to make his heart race again.

"It's okay. My therapist said I shouldn't feel shame about discussing it with people."

Very good advice. Society held ridiculous stigmas over neurodiversity and mental health conditions. He always believed talking about things, educating people, helped reduce the fear and stigma surrounding things. It was one of the reasons he became a doctor in the first place.

"My specific type is harm based," she said with a small sigh. "It used to be really bad."

"How bad?"

She glanced down, her right hand coming up to tug on her earlobe. Another compulsion he'd noticed in the time they'd spent together.

"I had to drop out of school after I got diagnosed. I home-schooled for a little over a year. Saw a few different therapists. Got put on some meds."

"And now?"

The tugging stopped. She dropped her hand, raising her chin to stare him directly in the eye again. "I'm better. I don't need my meds as often. I see my therapists once a month. I'm not claiming every day is a cakewalk, but I'm managing now."

He'd say she was more than managing. OCD was a condition with a varying severity. Ellie appeared to be handling it fantastically as far as he could see. Every new thing he learned about this woman amazed him.

"Okay."

She raised a skeptical brow. "Really?"

"What?"

She crossed her arms over her middle, clearly something on her mind, though her mouth stayed shut.

"Whatever it is, Ellie. You can say it." He was a hard man to offend, mostly because he rarely cared what people thought of him. If they didn't like him, so what? No one could like everyone. But oddly, he cared what Ellie thought. He wanted *her* to like him. Because he sure as hell liked her.

"It's just, I figured with you being a doctor and all you'd have…an opinion about all this."

She gestured vaguely to her head.

"I try to leave the white coat at work."

A euphemism, since he didn't actually wear a white coat, but he tried to leave doctoring at the door when he came home. Some days were harder than others, especially whenever Charlotte got sick. As a physician, he had seen the worst of the worst and it was hard not to turn every cough and sniffle into the nightmares that had come across his exam table. But over the years he'd learned to trust his fatherly and doctor instincts when his child became ill and not jump to the worst-case scenario. So yes, he could turn off the doctor in him. Or at least mute it for a while.

"Most people, when they find out, either think I'm crazy

or think they can fix me. When they discover they can't, they usually bail."

"There's nothing to fix, Ellie. You're not broken or crazy. You're a kind, funny, smart, beautiful woman and anyone who can't see that is an idiot."

Her eyes widened, arms dropping to her side. "Wow. I don't think anyone's ever said so many nice things about me at once."

He pushed off the counter, taking a small step toward her, encouraged when she didn't shy away. "Then you know some pretty thick-headed people."

She tilted her head. "You're a very strange man, Sullivan Green."

He grinned. "I'll take that as a compliment."

She smiled then, a full-fledged, light-up-the-room smile. His heart skipped a beat. Never had he seen a more beautiful woman than the one standing inches in front of him. She'd shared a very intimate part of herself with him tonight. Something he wouldn't take lightly. It humbled him and he didn't want to do anything to shatter the trust building between them. Which was why, as much as he wanted to lean forward those few inches it would take to capture her lip, he didn't. Instead, he grabbed his tea, taking another sip.

"So. Anything else in those bags? You wouldn't happen to have a real elephant in there, would you?"

Ellie laughed. "Um, no. I don't think Tammy would go that far to ensure you don't sue. Besides." She glanced around. "As big as this place is, it still couldn't house an elephant."

"It's not that big."

One dark eyebrow arched. "Sullivan, my entire apartment could fit in this house four times over."

She had to be exaggerating. Sure, his place was big, but it wasn't a mansion or anything. Counting the partially finished basement where he kept his treadmill and free-weights, there were just over three thousand square feet. Made him wonder how big Ellie's apartment was. And that made him think of Ellie in her apartment, eating, getting ready for work, washing her endearing animal pun shirts, sleeping. He wondered...did she sleep naked?

His slacks tightened as his body hardened with the image of a naked Ellie covered only by silk sheets, the fabric caressing her soft skin. Since dress pants were notoriously bad at hiding erections, he shut those thoughts down. Tonight was not the time to make a move. Not after what she'd shared. It felt like a big step for her, for them. He didn't want to move too quickly, push too hard and lose...whatever it was they had going on.

He could be patient. Somehow, he knew Ellie was worth it.

"Okay, so no live elephant. I guess the piñata will have to do."

"Trust me, when the candy comes pouring out of that thing, it'll be the hit of the party."

"True enough."

Thankfully Charlotte was at the age where candy was still exciting and fun. He had no idea what he was going to do in a few years when she left behind the dolls and sweets for makeup and boys. Or girls. Or whoever she wanted to crush on. As long as she was happy, he was happy. He just didn't want to think about any of that yet. At times he wished he could keep her his little girl forever, but he supposed all parents wished that. Those who cared and didn't abandon their kids, that was.

At the thought of his ex, his mood soured a little. Something must have shown on his face because he felt Ellie's hand softly grip his. He glanced up into concerned eyes.

"Hey, you okay?"

"Yeah." He did his best to smile. "I just sometimes wonder if I'm doing enough for her. If *I'm* enough for her."

"You're a wonderful father, Sullivan. You love that girl with all your heart. That's all she needs. Well, that and a roof over her head. And I gotta tell ya, this is a really nice roof."

He chuckled along with her. Amazed yet again at the wonders of Ellie Clark. The woman was truly something special.

"It's getting late," she said, glancing at the clock on the microwave. "I should probably go."

"Let me walk you to your car."

"Oh, that's not necessary—"

"Please."

"I'm parked in your driveway."

"Good, then it won't be a far walk. I shouldn't leave the property while my daughter is sleeping."

She shook her head but laughed softly. "Very true."

He laced his fingers through hers, walking to the front door and leaving it open as they walked hand in hand to her small coupe parked in his driveway. She hit the fob, unlocking the car and pulled her hand from his to open the door. He immediately missed the soft warmth of her palm.

"Goodnight, Sullivan."

A slight breeze picked up, blowing a few strands of her hair into her face. He reached out, brushing the dark tresses across her smooth cheek and tucking them behind her ear. He could feel the rapid beat of her pulse as his fingers trailed down her neck. Her sudden sharp inhale sounding piercingly loud in the stillness of the dark night. Her eyelids dropped, a needy haze entering her dark brown eyes.

"Goodnight, Ellie."

He stood still as a statue, wondering if she would make a move, lean in, ask for a kiss. But she didn't. Instead, she gave him another soft smile and got into her car, starting the engine, and giving a little wave as she backed out and pulled away into the night. Sullivan let out the breath he was holding, disappointment and exhilaration filling him all at once. He wanted Ellie, and he was pretty sure she wanted him. But there was no need to rush. They'd figure this out. Whatever the hell *this* was. Because he knew one thing for sure, good things were worth waiting for and Ellie was one of the best damn things he'd run across in a long time.

CHAPTER 12

"*W*ake up! Wake up! Wake up!"

Sullivan groaned when a ridiculously sharp, pointy elbow stabbed him in the back as Charlotte flung herself on him in excitement.

"Wake up, Daddy. It's time for my party!"

Cracking one eye open, he glanced at the bedside clock. "It's six in the morning, kiddo. Your party isn't for another eight hours."

He never understood how Charlotte could wake up at the butt crack of dawn on the weekends, but on school days, he could barely drag her out of bed before seven. Made no damn sense.

"Daaaaaaaddyyyyyy!"

Tiny hands tugged at his T-shirt. Knowing there was no way he would get any more sleep this morning, he reached behind him, securing an arm around his daughter as he jumped out of bed.

"Yay! Pony ride!"

Charlotte squealed with glee as he hopped around the room, her little arms clinging tightly to his neck, almost to the point of suffocation. He didn't care. He'd gladly forego oxygen if it got his little girl to laugh.

After ten minutes, he needed a break. At thirty-five, he was beginning to feel all the aches and pains of his creeping age. He kept in shape—wouldn't be much of a doctor if he told his patients to do something he wasn't willing to do himself—but sometimes he swore having a kid aged him ten years. Charlotte seemed to drain him, gaining more energy with every ounce he spent.

"Okay, cowgirl. It's breakfast time."

"Yay, pancakes!"

"Yup, birthday pancakes." And coffee. Lots and lots of coffee.

Twenty minutes later, Charlotte was happily stuffing her face with fluffy pancakes dripping with far too much syrup while he was on the way to feeling semi-normal enjoying his second cup of coffee. After breakfast, Sullivan got them both dressed and started party preparations while Charlotte watched her favorite Saturday morning cartoons in the living room. At exactly ten o'clock, the door opened, and someone called out.

"Knock, knock. Is there a birthday girl in here?"

"Uncle Gavin!"

Sullivan continued pouring candy into the elephant piñata, ears attuned to his brother's heavy footsteps heading his way.

"Happy birthday, Cheeky Monkey. So how old are you now? Sixteen, twenty-one?"

"Uncle Gavin," Charlotte giggled, held aloft in his brother's arms as they both entered the kitchen. "I'm eight."

"Eight? Wow, you're old. Time to move out and get a job. Am I right, Sully?"

He glanced up from stuffing fun size sour gummy bags into the minuscule hole in the elephant's back.

"Don't call me Sully and Charlotte won't move out until she's thirty."

"That's gonna make it awkward when she starts dating."

"She's not dating until she's thirty."

"Right, keep telling yourself that, big brother."

"Daddy, what's dating?"

He speared his brother with a death glare. Gavin, the jackass, just smiled.

"Dating, Angel, is when two people who really like each other go out to movies or the park and spend time together."

"We went to the movies. We saw the pig cartoon."

A smile curved his lips at the memory of their special daddy daughter day to Charlotte's first movie. She'd been so excited to see a movie in the real theater and he'd gone all out for it. Large popcorn, soda, all the candy she wanted. A move he regretted later that night when all that sugar gave her a stomachache. But the outing had been a special moment for Sullivan as a father and it warmed his heart to know it had become a cherished memory for his daughter. In a few years, she'd probably ask him to drop her off at the movies with her friends a block away so she wouldn't be seen with her uncool dad.

He wished she could stay a kid forever.

"Yes, we did, but that's not like grown up dating. Grown up dating is, um…" Shit, how did he explain this to an eight-year-old?

"Is it when you kiss and stuff?"

His heart stopped. Pausing mid-beat in his chest.

"What do you know about kissing?"

"Janey said she had a babysitter last week because her mommy and daddy went to a show and when they came home, they were kissing, but they didn't see her because she was supposed to be in bed, but she wasn't because she wanted a glass of water and she saw them kissing. Is that dating, Daddy?"

There was something to be said for being a single parent. At least his kid couldn't inadvertently stumble upon him and his wife making out, or worse. It had been so long since he'd gotten any, he'd almost forgotten how to do it.

"Yes, Angel, it's something like that and it's only for grow-ups."

"Uncle Gavin is a grownup." Her little head turned to his brother, still holding her in his arms. "I saw him kissing the lady at the mall last week. Are you dating her, Uncle Gavin?"

His brother had the decency to look abashed. "No, Cheeky Monkey. She's, um, just a friend."

"A kissing friend?"

"Hey, Angel, how would you like to test out the bounce house?" Her eyes lit up, and he knew his distraction had worked. Charlotte wiggled out of his brother's arms and ran to the backyard where the rental company had set up a deluxe bouncy castle just half an hour earlier.

"Sorry," Gavin winced once Charlotte was safely out of hearing range.

"The mall lady?"

His brother shrugged. "It was when I took Charlotte to buy her party dress. Lucy works at the pretzel shop there."

"Who the hell is Lucy?" He loved his brother, but the guy ran through women. He didn't think he'd ever seen his baby brother with the same woman for more than a month.

"Just some woman I dated a few times. She's nice, working on getting a law degree. She's not looking for anything serious."

And neither was Gavin, so he bet the two worked perfectly.

"Can you please keep the PDA with your non-serious *friends* away from the keen eyes of my daughter?"

"Sure."

Gavin walked over to the fridge, opening it, and helping himself to a soda. He offered one to Sullivan, but he waved his brother off. Raising his cup of coffee for a sip before returning to the piñata. Gavin shrugged and popped the top of the soda.

"But the kid's gonna see things like that, eventually. Not from you, of course, but movies and stuff."

"The hell do you mean, not from me?"

His brother laughed. "Come on, Sully. You haven't dated a woman since the divorce."

"I don't want to get married again. You know that." His brother had seen him at his worst after Claire left. If anyone could understand the reasoning behind his desire to remain unattached, it was Gavin.

"I'm not saying run to the altar, dude. You can enjoy time with other people without promising them forever. When was the last time you got laid?"

"None of your damn business." He finished stuffing the rest of the candy into the elephant and plugged the hole again. "Besides, not all of us can have a parade of women gracing our bed. Some of us have responsibilities. And don't call me Sully."

Gavin snorted. "I'm not as big a man-whore as everyone seems to think. And I know you have Charlotte, but just because you're a dad doesn't mean you can't date. DILFs are a thing you know."

"I don't even want to know what that acronym is supposed to spell out."

"Dad I'd like to fu—"

He shoved a leftover pancake into his brother's mouth. The bastard grinned, chewing the fluffy, cold breakfast food and swallowing.

"Yum."

Gavin helped him with the rest of the party set up. They filled the balloons Ellie brought over with a helium tank he'd rented from the party rental place. He also had half a dozen chairs and a few small tables he'd rented. His brother helped him get everything squared away in the backyard. He was grateful his daughter had been born in the late spring when the finicky Colorado weather usually held to the state's boastful three hundred days of sunshine. His birthday was in late January. He never had an outside party as a kid. There was always at least a foot of snow on the ground around his birthday.

The caterer came over just after one to set up the buffet. Since the party was scheduled for after lunchtime, he'd gone with small plates. Appetizers and finger food with cake and ice cream, of course. Everything was set up and ready to go by the time the doorbell rang with the first party guest. Within fifteen minutes of the first guest's arrival, his backyard had become a screaming mass of gleeful children and gossiping parents. And all Sullivan wanted was the one person who had yet to arrive.

CHAPTER 13

*E*llie rushed down the sidewalk, the sounds of laughing children audible from blocks away. Dang it, she hated being late. It was rude. Her mother had drilled that into her as a child. *If you're not ten minutes early, you're ten minutes late.* Extreme, some might say, but a hard habit to break. She wouldn't have been late today if not for the accident she'd gotten stuck behind. It wasn't even a bad one. Just some fender bender everyone had to rubberneck and clog up the roadway.

"Dammit!"

She stumbled on the sidewalk, wishing she could blame it on her shoe. However, since she was wearing sneakers and not heels, all she could do was claim klutzy. Great, she was late and about to break an ankle. Perfect party guest material.

She hurried up the walkway to the Greens' house. Noting the large number of cars parked along the street. She'd had to park a few houses back herself. Charlotte was a popular girl. The thought made her smile. And why shouldn't she be? The child was a sweetheart. She should have multitudes of friends.

Where were those friends the day those boys were picking on her at the zoo?

Ellie had no idea. Maybe Charlotte's friends weren't in her class, or maybe all the people here today were family or something. Did Sullivan have a large family? He hadn't mentioned anything. They were just getting to know each other. She really didn't know the man all that well. But she wanted to. More and more she was discovering she *really* wanted to know Sullivan Green a lot better.

Making it to the front door—without falling and breaking a limb, yay—she reached out to knock, but one of the large doors swung open. A tall man with light blond hair and hazel eyes stood there, a wide grin on his face. His gaze took her in, pausing on her shirt. Today's was an elephant with the phrase *Your Opinion is Irrelephant* in honor of Charlotte. His lips split into a wide grin.

"You must be Ellie."

"Um, yes, and you are?"

The man thrust out a large hand. "Gavin Green. I'm Sullivan's little brother."

Little was an operative word. Gavin had to be at least three inches taller than Sullivan and had double the muscle mass. Sullivan was no slouch, from what Ellie could observe, but he had a much leaner body type than the muscle-bound man in front of her.

"Nice to meet you," she said, accepting his handshake.

"Oh, believe me, the pleasure is all mine." He motioned for her to come inside. "I've heard so much about you."

She stepped into the house, the loud party noises quieting to a din as Gavin shut the door. "Really?"

"Okay, not a lot, but I know you're the woman who saved Charlotte's life." The cheerful man's smile slipped. His face took on a serious cast as emotion welled in his eyes. "Thank you. That little girl means the world to a lot of people."

Ellie choked back the feelings that welled suddenly at Gavin's heartfelt words, happy to know how loved Charlotte was. "She's a very special girl."

Gavin tilted his head, almost identical to the motion she'd seen Sullivan do when he was trying to figure her out. Eerie, but she supposed brothers were similar like that.

"Yeah, she is."

"Gavin, where's the tape? I asked you…"

Sullivan's words died out as he came around the corner and saw them. His gaze focused on her, eyes lighting up, lips tilting in a smile that revealed the dent in his cheek. That was all it took. One smile, that silly dent, and she was a goner. Her heart raced, palm sweating as they gripped the present in her hands.

"Ellie, you came."

"Yeah, um, sorry I'm late. There was an accident."

Suddenly he was by her side, hand grasping her arm as he glanced over her with a furrowed brow.

"Are you okay?"

"Yes, oh no, not me. I got stuck behind a fender bender. Everyone was okay, from what I could see. It just clogged up the road a bit."

His smile returned and his hand stayed on her arm. "Good. The party is going full swing in the back. You want to come wish the birthday girl a happy birthday?"

"I'll just run out to my car and grab that tape you asked for, right Sully?"

She turned her head to see Gavin staring at them, an amused expression on his face.

"Yeah sure, whatever."

Sullivan didn't even glance at his brother, his focus solely on her as he placed his hand on her lower back, guiding her to the backyard. A thrill of excitement shot up her spine. She prayed he couldn't feel her body quiver from his touch. One touch. Just a casual hand on her lower back. Nothing intimate at all. But here she was, a quaking mess of hormones. Cam was right. She needed to get laid if a man's touch through layers of clothes did this to her.

But it wasn't just any man's touch. It was Sullivan's.

The moment they stepped outside, the noise returned, louder and higher pitched. She'd seen Sullivan's backyard the few times she'd been over, but she hadn't spent any time outside. It was lovely. Huge. The lawn was covered in lush, green blades of grass that looked soft enough to tickle your feet if one were to take off their shoes. Large pines were scattered along the back fence, giving the illusion of privacy from the neighbors. Lilac bushes lined one side of the yard. Their sweet, floral smell wafting in the air, mixing with the savory smells coming from the long table set up with what looked like a buffet of finger foods.

Children ran about, laughing, screaming, throwing foam darts and balls at each other. There was a large bouncy castle set up on one side of the yard where half a dozen kids were jumping and falling all over each other. There was also several adults. Parents of the children in attendance, she assumed. The men had on jeans and polos while the women wore sundresses or fancy leggings with silk tunics. Suddenly Ellie felt very out of place. Looking at all these people, it reminded her of the gaping economic status between her and Sullivan.

"I had to invite everyone in Charlotte's class," he whispered in her ear. "She didn't want anyone to feel left out."

Of course, she didn't. Because his daughter had one of the biggest hearts Ellie had ever seen.

"Most of the parents stuck around. I barely know half of these people, so don't leave my side, okay? I need a buffer of protection."

She turned to face him, finding her smile. "You want *me*

to protect you from the suburbanite hordes? You're the one who lives here."

"And you're the hero who works with animals. Now come on, spout some of those fun animal facts so I don't have to talk about PTOs or bake sales or whatever the hell the HOA is up in arms about this week."

"You have an HOA?"

"Sadly, yes."

She chuckled at his despondent look, knowing full well he probably bought this home because it had an HOA to keep home values up. This whole schtick was just to make her feel better about being so out of place. Somehow, he'd sensed her discomfort. It touched her that he was trying to ease it.

"Ellie!"

Charlotte's squeal of glee was the only warning she got before the tiny girl plowed into her. She grunted, falling against Sullivan as his daughter threw her arms around Ellie's legs. She really had to remember how strong the small child could be when excited.

"Hi, Charlotte."

"You came, you came, you really came!"

"Yup. Happy birthday, sweetie."

Kneeling, she held out the bag in her hands. Charlotte glanced up at her father with big puppy dog eyes.

"Can I open it?"

Sullivan nodded. "Go ahead."

Charlotte tore into the tissue paper, pulling out the small cardboard box.

"What is it?"

Ellie nodded to the package. "Open it and see."

Nimble hands opened the flaps of cardboard, reaching into the box to pull out the small elephant necklace and packet of paper inside. On the front of the packet was a picture of an elephant.

"Her name is Dolly. She lives in Africa, but you adopted her."

Charlotte glanced up from the picture, a puzzled expression on her face. "Adopted?"

"Yup. It means she's your elephant. You're going to get pictures of her and stories about how she's doing. She can't come and live with you, but you're helping take care of her in her home, so she's your elephant."

Green eyes grew so big Ellie was afraid they just might pop out. Charlotte's mouth dropped open as she exclaimed, "I have a real-live elephant of my very own?"

"Sure do."

Squealing, the girl jumped up and down, hugging the picture to her chest. "I have a real-live elephant! Thank you, thank you, thank you, Ellie. It's the bestest present ever!"

She laughed as Charlotte almost toppled her once again with an exuberant hug before running off, shouting to her friends about her new elephant.

"Well, thanks for that," Sullivan chuckled in her ear, his body pressed up close against hers from his daughter's forceful excitement pushing them together. "Now anything I give her will pale in comparison."

A sense of dread dropped in her stomach. Crap! Had she overstepped her bounds? She turned to face him. "Oh, Sullivan. I'm sorry. I didn't think. I just know how much she loves elephants, and we have this program at the zoo where you can sponsor an animal and so I—"

"Shhhh." He placed a finger over her mouth. Stopping her apology. "I didn't mean it to sound like that, Ellie. It's a wonderful present. Anything that makes my daughter smile like that is…well, thank you. You really are amazing."

She couldn't quite make out what he was saying because of all the blood pounding in her ears. Her heart raced from the feel of his hands on her lips. She had the insane urge to open her mouth and suck his finger inside, swirl her tongue around the digit just to taste the salty heaven of his skin.

But she didn't. Because she was frozen. A frozen mass of quivering need and lust in the middle of a child's birthday party.

Totally inappropriate, Eleanor.

Someone called Sullivan's name, and the spell broke. He pulled away to attend to something. She headed to the food table, praying there was something cold to drink because she felt as if she was on fire.

The party continued into the evening. Gifts were opened, cake was had. She actually enjoyed herself. The kids were rambunctious, but mostly sweet, and the adults weren't as bad as she feared. A few of the women introduced them-selves, commenting on her bravery when they discovered she'd been the one to save Charlotte from the penguin pool. They seemed nice enough, but she wasn't used to socializing in such large crowds or with so many people she didn't know. Anxiety caused her muscles to jitter. Her nerves rose with every second of conversation. The need to run to soli-tude overwhelmed her, but she knew it would be rude to disappear in the middle of a party, so she pushed the feelings down.

"Is there something wrong with your ear, Ellie?"

One of the mom's—Jennifer, she thought the woman's name was—tilted her head, staring at the hand Ellie hadn't realized was tugging on her lobe. Dropping her hand, she took a deep breath that did nothing to calm her anxiety and pasted on a bright smile.

"Oh, um, no. It's fine. I just…" Feeling the walls closing in on her—which was impossible since they were outside and there were no walls—Ellie blurted out the first excuse to come to her mind. "Excuse me, I need to use the restroom."

Ignoring the confused expression on Jennifer's face, Ellie

tucked her head down and made a beeline for the back door. Thankfully, no one stopped her to chat as she hurried inside the back door. Making her way through the kitchen, she quickly slipped into the empty bathroom. Her heart pounded in her chest as her brain screamed at her.

What is wrong with me? Why can't I just be normal?

With shaking hands, she turned the tap on the sink. The cool water pooled in her cupped hands, calming the frantic nerves. She splashed the water onto her face. The chilly liquid just the slap in the face she needed to ease her racing heart.

After a moment or two, she shut off the water, glancing up to gaze at her dripping wet, harried reflection.

"Get a grip, Ellie," she admonished herself. "It's just a party. A *kid's* party. Everyone is here having a good time. Don't freak out and ruin everything."

But the dark voice whispered that she already had. Taking another deep, calming breath, she pushed the voice away. So one person had caught her ear compulsion. No big deal. The woman probably thought she was adjusting her earring or something.

Dammit! That was a good excuse. Why couldn't she have thought of that in the moment?

Didn't matter. Her abrupt escape may have startled Jennifer, but no one else noticed her leave the party. Everything was fine—

"Ellie?"

The soft knock on the bathroom door caused her to gasp, whirling away from the sink to stare at the dark wood, recognizing the person belonging to that deep, familiar voice standing behind it.

"Are you okay?"

Great. Just perfect. Someone had noticed her frantic rush inside. And not just anyone. Sullivan.

See? You're ruining his daughter's party. Way to go.

She squeezed her eyes shut. Counting to three. Willing the dark voice back into the little box in her mind, she preferred to keep it locked up. If only she could lock that box and throw away the key.

The voice would just get out anyway. It always did.

Determined to rise above this, she opened the door.

"Hi, Sullivan. I'm fine." She tried for a cheery smile. "Just needed to use the bathroom."

His brow furrowed, green eyes taking in every inch of her expression. Her fake smile must need improvement because Sullivan's lips turned down.

"You don't have to pretend." His gaze swung to the right where sounds of the boisterous party filtered down the hallway. When he glanced back to her there was a fiercely protective glint in his emerald eyes. "If someone said or did something to upset you, I will—"

"No."

She reached out to place a hand on his arm. The moment she touched his bare skin, her fingers burned like they were on fire. Not painful, but hot and heady. She immediately released her grip, curling her hand into a fist at her side to resist touching him again. Sullivan said nothing, simply raised one eyebrow and waited.

"No one did anything to upset me. I just…" Oh damn, this is why she didn't have many friends. Why dates always dumped her after a few weeks. Social situations were a nightmare for her, especially large gatherings with perfect strangers. But she'd wanted so badly to be here for Charlotte's special day. "I get a little…anxious in large groups of people I don't know. I'm sorry. I didn't mean to ruin Charlotte's birthday party."

Sullivan smiled, taking a step toward her. His hand came up to cup her cheek. Ellie sucked in a sharp breath at the contact. All the tense anxiety she'd been experiencing a few minutes before shifting into something that felt just as tense, but much flutterier and more enjoyable.

"Ellie, never apologize for being who you are. And you didn't ruin Charlotte's party. No one even noticed you left."

She swallowed past the dryness in her throat. "You did."

He stared at her, something she couldn't read in those beautiful green eyes, leaving her breathless.

"The party is almost over, but if you need to leave—"

She shook her head. "No. I'm better now." And she wouldn't disappoint Charlotte by leaving early. She was not her OCD. She would rise about this tiny setback.

"Are you sure?"

She nodded, a genuine smile curving her lips. "I just needed a little breather."

"Okay, then."

Sullivan dropped his hand from her face, and she had to hold back a whimper. She wasn't a cat. She didn't need his touch to soothe her. But man, oh man did it.

CHAPTER 14

*W*ith Sullivan at her side, Ellie returned to the party that was indeed winding down. A few of the guests had already left while she'd been in the bathroom, and more were gathering their things to say goodbye to the birthday girl.

After the last guest left, Ellie felt completely relaxed again. Charlotte asked her to stay for pizza and she didn't have the heart to say no. Plus, she had no other plans. So, she stuck around with Sullivan's brother Gavin, who also stayed behind to help clean up. By the time nine o'clock rolled around, Charlotte was fast asleep on the sofa, clutching the picture of Dolly and the ballet shoes her father had gotten her.

"Well, the kid's asleep." Gavin stood from his spot on the floor, stretching his large frame. "That's my cue to go." He leaned down to place a soft kiss on his niece's forehead. "Night, Cheeky Monkey."

Gavin came over to where she sat in the large armchair. "Ellie, it was a pleasure to meet you. I hope to see you again sometime."

"Ditto."

He grinned, waving to his brother before he headed out the front door.

"Let me put her to bed, then I'll be back down," Sullivan said as he scooped his daughter into his arms.

"I want Ellie to tuck me in," the sleepy soft voice complained.

Sullivan lifted his brow. She nodded with a smile. Who was she to deny the birthday girl? She followed Sullivan up the stairs and helped tuck Charlotte in. The sweet girl didn't even stir as Ellie tucked the blanket around her. The whole situation felt...oddly comfortable. She shook off the weird sensation, heading back downstairs with Sullivan to the kitchen.

They had cleaned most of the party up, but there was still some leftover cake. They'd all had second pieces after cleaning. Well, the brothers had. She and Charlotte barely finished half of their second piece.

"Ellie, you don't have to help clean."

Sullivan put a hand over hers as she grabbed the plates full of half-eaten cake from the table.

"It's fine. I don't mind." After the way he'd helped her bathroom freak out, she owed the man something. And cleaning always calmed her down.

He tried to grab the plate from her, and she lost her grip. Cake went flying through the air, landing smack dab on Sullivan's nice white polo. She didn't know whether to laugh or gasp, so she settled on an indelicate snort, covering her open mouth with her hand.

"Oh, Sullivan. I'm sorry. I didn't mean..."

He glanced up at her, a mischievous gleam in his eyes. Scraping off a chunk of frosting from his shirt, he started forward. She held out her hands, backing away, but unable to keep the laughter out of her voice as she pleaded.

"No, no, don't even think about it. This is my favorite shirt and I—Sullivan!"

She squealed as he grabbed her around the waist, smearing the frosting across her face. He backed them up until she was flush against the kitchen wall, caught between the hard plaster and his hard body. Laughing, she glanced up into his eyes. Seeing something that made her breath catch. Desire. The same driving need she felt pulsing through her body every time this man got close to her.

"Ellie." Her name was a low growl deep in his throat. "You know I'm not looking for anything long term, but I'd be lying if I didn't admit I'm attracted to you."

Her mouth dried. All the moisture gone as his words sunk in. She felt parched, dying for something to cool the fire that had taken over her body. A fire that could only be quelled by the man in front of her.

"And I think," he continued. "That you're attracted to me, too."

"Yes." Somehow, the word left her lips even as her brain stopped functioning. Sullivan wanted her. Her!

He pressed closer, impossibly close, and still not near enough to satisfy her. There were too many barriers between them, too much fabric for what she wanted to do with this man.

"I feel like a jerk even asking you, but—"

"I don't need forever," she spouted, knowing forever wasn't in her future anyway. People always gave up on her, eventually. Besides, she'd never ask him for more than he was willing to give. "Why don't we just enjoy each other's company and see what happens?"

He grinned, that cheek dent making her breath catch in her throat.

"I can get on board with that."

Lifting her hands, she gripped the front of his cake-stained shirt, pulling him to her, lifting on her toes so she could crash her lips against his. And it was a crash. A total and complete wreck. Nothing like the minor accident she'd been delayed by this afternoon. No. This was a full contact, body-destroying kiss like she'd never experienced before.

Sullivan dug his fingers into her hair, angling her head to fit his mouth over hers perfectly. Ellie moaned as she parted her lips to taste the sweetness of his mouth. Or maybe it was her lips that tasted sweet. After all, she was the one with chocolate frosting all over her face. But no, it wasn't chocolate she was tasting. It was Sullivan. Pure, delicious, sexy, Sullivan.

"Ellie."

He moaned her name, pressing against her so she could feel the effect she was having on his body. Something in her roared in triumph. Like a lion knowing he'd won the battle to mate with the pride. Her entire body burned, every nerve ending connected to her lips. To the place Sullivan was currently worshiping. She never wanted it to end.

"Daddy!"

Sullivan paused, his lips frozen on hers.

"I need a glass of water!"

He pulled away, panting. Or maybe that was her. She couldn't tell anymore.

He placed his forehead against hers, a soft chuckle escaping those perfect lips she'd been enjoying just a few second earlier.

"I better go to her."

"Of course." The words came out hoarse, so she cleared her throat and tried again. "Yes, of course. I should get going anyway."

He stepped back to let her pass. "Your car's in the driveway?"

She nodded. She'd moved it after all the guests left at his request.

"Good."

"Good."

She needed to leave. He needed to attend to his daughter, but neither of them moved. They stood there, staring at each other. She didn't know who moved first, but suddenly they were kissing again, his hands tangled in her hair, her own clutching his shoulders.

"Daaaaddddy!"

With a chuckle, Sullivan pulled away. "I have to go."

"I know."

"I'll call you tomorrow."

"Okay."

He called up to Charlotte, letting her know he'd be right up before walking Ellie out to her car. She drove away, watching in her rearview mirror as he went back in the house to attend to his daughter. A smile affixed to her face the entire way home. Her lips still tingled. Even after she'd brushed her teeth, she still had the taste of chocolate cake and Sullivan on her tongue. As she drifted off to sleep, one thought kept bouncing around in her brain.

Best. Party. Ever!

CHAPTER 15

*E*llie walked into work the next day, surprised to find Cam already there. Normally she arrived at work much earlier than her friend, who loved to say that anything before the sun rose shouldn't be legally considered morning.

"You're here early."

Cam hopped off the metal counter, two paper cups of coffee from her favorite local coffee shop in her hands. She passed one to Ellie. The aroma of coffee beans and vanilla wafted from the open spout on the lid, tickling her nostrils and waking up her sluggish brain. Typically, she was a morning person, but today she hadn't even made time for her run. She'd been too busy lying in bed, enjoying the remnants of a very naughty dream involving her and a certain sexy doctor.

He'd checked her temperature and then some.

She'd woken late, her breathing heavy as if she'd run five miles.

"Not so much as you're late," her friend replied, taking a sip of her coffee.

Ellie glanced at the clock. "I'm not late. I'm right on time."

"Exactly. You're always here before me. Right on time in Ellie world is late." A sly grin turned up the corners of her friend's lips. "Soooooo?"

Opening the lid of her coffee, she blew across the hot beverage. The first sip ran over her tongue like liquid magic. She might be a morning person, but Ellie loved her coffee as much as the next person. The legal stimulant coursed through her veins, waking up all the muddy parts of her brain that were still rusty and distracted from her late-night fantasies.

"So what?"

Cam rolled her eyes. "So how was yesterday?"

She shrugged, taking another sip to stall before answering. "Fine. It was a kids' party. They ran around, screamed, ate cake. Charlotte liked her gift, though. I thought she might cut off my circulation with the bear hug she gave me when she opened it."

"I told you the elephant adoption plan would be an excellent gift."

She had, because her friend was fantastic at picking out presents, especially for kids. She had to be with the number of nieces and nephews she had to buy for. Cam always said she loved being an aunt. All the fun, none of the responsibility. Ellie knew that was true for her friend. But for her, watching Sullivan with Charlotte, seeing how much joy the little girl brought into his life, she thought the responsibility might make it all the better.

"Thanks for the idea. She loved it. You were right."

"Duh, of course I was, but enough about the party."

"You're the one who asked."

"No, I asked how yesterday was."

Had Cam put whiskey in her coffee this morning? Maybe she'd enjoyed a few of her mother's "special brownies." That was the only reason her friend wasn't making any sense this morning.

"Yeah, and yesterday was the party."

Cam shook her head as if Ellie was being the exasperating one. "I know, but I wasn't asking about that sweet girl's birthday bash. I was asking how your night went with her sexy, single father."

Ellie had chosen that unfortunate moment to take a sip of her coffee. She choked, snorting hot, sugary liquid up her nose. Her eyes watered as the sting burned her nostrils. Cam grabbed a few paper towels from the dispenser on the wall. The tall woman held them out with an apology.

"Oh sweetie, I'm sorry. Are you okay?"

She nodded, unable to talk as the back of her throat was currently on fire.

"So, can I take that as the night went well?"

The twinkle in her friend's eye was back. Cam was like a dog with a bone when she wanted to know something. She never gave up.

"How do you know I didn't go home right after the party?" For some reason, she didn't want to spill the beans about her and Sullivan just yet. Right now, it was simply a wonderful moment between the two of them. Something she could hold close and take out whenever she needed a little pick me up. To reveal what happened against the wall in his kitchen last night to someone else would make it…real. And real things could end.

"I went by your place last night around eight to see if you wanted to go to Toppers with me, but you weren't there. Figured you were still at Dr. Sexy's house."

"His name is Sullivan, and you could have texted me."

"No, because then you would have made some excuse not to come out."

True. She didn't like bars all that much and while Toppers

wasn't that bad, she still preferred a quiet night at home to a crowded, loud, bar full of strangers where the drinks cost three times as much as what she could make them for at home. Plus, at home she could drink in her comfy jammies.

"Soooooo?"

"So what?"

Cam sighed as they repeated their earlier back and forth. "So, did you and the doc do it?"

"Cam! He has a kid!"

"What? Single parents can't get it on? I'm pretty sure that's how they got into their situation in the first place."

"We didn't…do *it*."

One dark eyebrow rose. "But you did do something?"

Her right hand came up to tug on her ear. Holding it in was killing her. She wanted to shout from the rooftops and seal her lips shut forever. How could her feelings be so contrary?

"It's okay, Ellie." Cam's expression softened. "You don't have to tell m—"

"He kissed me! Or I kissed him. We kissed. I can't really remember who started what."

For one stunned moment, Cam stood perfectly still. Then her best friend let out a loud whoop, throwing her hands in the air and shaking her hips in a celebratory dance.

"I knew it! That's awesome! It was awesome, right?"

So much more than awesome. It had been overwhelming, intense, breathtaking, the most astounding experience she'd ever had with another human being.

"Yeah. It was pretty awesome. But…"

Cam frowned. "But?"

Dipping her head, she admitted. "It might have gone further, but Charlotte woke up and needed him, so he walked me to my car."

"So, you two kissed in his…?"

"Kitchen."

"Nice." Cam winked. "Okay, you make out in the kitchen, then when his daughter needs him, he gallantly walks you to the safety of your car and tends to his child. Plus, he's handsome and a doctor. I swear if I didn't love you so much, I'd steal him right out from under you."

No, she wouldn't. Cam would never break up a happy relationship. Or a miserable one. Her friend had been on the receiving end of a few jerks who thought they could have their cake and eat it, too. She would never hurt someone like that. But she got the message. Sullivan was a very special person. She agreed.

"You two would never work out," she teased. "He's an inch shorter than you and in heels you'd tower over him."

Cam waved a hand in the air, moving off to grab her equipment for the morning. "Like I care if a guy's shorter than me. That's their hang-up. Not mine. What's wrong with short kings? It just means they're closer to where they ought to be."

She pointed down toward her crotch and Ellie nearly choked on her coffee again. She had to remember how outlandish her bestie could be and how dangerous it was to consume hot beverages around her.

"Well, don't get your hopes up," she said to herself as much as her bestie. "We're not serious. He has a lot of responsibilities and a kid. We agreed to keep this thing casual."

An arrangement that sounded a lot better last night when it meant she got to kiss Sullivan. In the light of the day, she wondered if this plan was smart. She'd never been good with casual. Then again, she'd never been good with long term either.

Cam shrugged. "You never know where casual can lead."

Casual or long term, didn't matter. For Ellie, it usually ended in disaster.

They started prepping for their morning. Today Stephan was coming by to give the penguins their monthly checkups. Ellie had to prep the exam room in the back, and they'd have to bring the birds there one at a time. It was a long and arduous process, as some of the birds didn't like to be separated from their partners, but it was necessary. The health of the animals was the number one priority of the zoos and hers as well. Last year, they had a sweep of avian flu. She'd gone home most nights crying, watching her beloved birds fall ill, their mournful chirps and squawks haunting her late into the night.

Everyone made a full recovery thanks to the efforts of Stephan and Rob, but it had been touch-and-go there for a while. Ellie might have spent a night or two in the aviary sleeping next to the cages of her sick friends. The animals were her friends. All of them. She loved them and they loved her. She'd always preferred the company of animals to humans.

Well…

She usually did, but lately things felt different. Recently, she was finding she very much enjoyed spending time with one human in particular. Sullivan Green.

At the mere thought of his name, butterflies took flight in her stomach. She'd never felt this way about anyone before. She'd had crushes. Liked guys. Dated. She'd even had sex. It had been a while and not anything to brag over honestly. But with Sullivan, everything was different. The things he made her feel were different from anything she'd ever experienced before.

It was exciting.

And scary.

"Hey." Cam popped her head in the room Ellie was

preparing. "Stephan says he'll be by in five. I'm going to bring Bingo in first."

"Perfect."

Less than a minute later, Cam came back in carrying the sweet old bird. The moment he saw Ellie, his flippers began to flap.

"Easy, old timer." Cam laughed. "Don't jump or you'll break a knee."

She grabbed the squirming bird out of her friend's hands, cuddling him close to her chest. "I don't think that's possible."

"I know. It's a saying."

"Hello, ladies," Stephan said as he entered the small exam room.

Cam moved out of the way to make room for him. As he put his bag on the table, pulling out the instruments he would need for the exams, Ellie placed Bingo on the table, keeping her hands on the penguin so he wouldn't waddle off the edge.

"Hola Bingo. Cómo estáis hoy?"

Stephan addressed the bird as he did all the animals.

"How do you know they speak Spanish?" Cam asked from her position in the doorway.

Stephan turned his head to glance at her. "How do you know they speak English?"

"Fair point." Her friend winked at the doc. "I'll go get Bubbles."

Bubbles was their second oldest penguin and the self-appointed matriarch of the colony. Ellie thought Bingo might have a thing for her. She'd seen the old guy pecking about the rocks lately, looking for shiny ones. Some penguin species gave rocks to future mates, called pebble proposals. Not unlike the rocks humans gave each other, she supposed.

Halfway through Bingo's exam, Ellie's phone pinged.

Normally she would leave it on vibrate at work, but she'd been so frazzled this morning she'd forgotten.

"Go ahead, Ellie," Stephan said with a smile, never taking his eyes off the flipper he was checking. "I won't tell Tammy."

They weren't supposed to check their phones during work hours, but she really, *really* wanted to see who the message was from. Or maybe she didn't. If it wasn't from who she thought…

Her phone pinged again.

"First you're late and now your phone isn't on silent?" Cam entered the room with Bubbles held calmly in her arms. "I think after all these years of friendship, I'm finally having a bad influence on you."

Stephan shook his head, but the smile never left his face. "Cam, you have a bad influence on everyone. It's why we love you."

"I love you too, Stephan. And I'm not a bad influence. Your husband just can't hold his rum."

He chuckled. "Now there's an accurate statement. Bingo's all set."

The two exchanged birds and Cam headed back out to the penguin enclosure to return Bingo and grab the next bird up for their exam, Libby. Bubbles sat like a queen on the exam table. No hint of movement as Stephan examined her. This left Ellie's hands free. Free to check her phone. She really shouldn't but….oh screw it. After two minutes, she couldn't stop her curiosity. Pulling her phone from her pocket, she held her breath and swiped to unlock it. A smile split her face as she read the text.

Sullivan: Thanks for coming yesterday. Charlotte loved her gift, and I really enjoyed having you.

He texted! And it wasn't even three days! She quickly typed out a response.

Ellie: Thank you for inviting me. I had a lot of fun and that cake was delicious.

She waited, anxiously staring at her phone as those three little dots appeared. Then suddenly words replaced them, stealing her breath away.

Sullivan: It was sweet, but you tasted sweeter.

"Calm down, Libby." Cam's footsteps echoed on the hard floor as she came back into the room with a wriggling squawking bird in her arms. "It's just Dr. S. You like him, remember? He just wants to make sure you're in tip-top shape, silly bird."

Her friend's voice barely registered in her brain as she reread those last three words.

"Hey, Ellie, can you…why is she grinning like a fool?"

"I'd say she got a very important message from an admirer," Stephan continued the conversation without ever glancing up from his examinations.

"Ohmigod! It's him! He texted you. What did he say?"

Cam eased up to Ellie's side, head tilting over her shoulder to glance at her phone. With her friend's tall stature, it wasn't hard for Cam to see the messages, but Ellie was feeling shy sharing the details of last night. She pulled the cell close to her chest. Pressing the breathtaking words to her heart.

Libby—still tucked securely in Cam's arms—pecked at Ellie's shoulder, the bird making her agitation known. Ellie understood. She didn't particularly like going to the doctor either, but it was necessary to give each animal a full health exam to ensure they were in optimal health. She reached out, stroking the upset bird on her neck, trying her best to soothe the sweet animal.

"He's just thanking me for yesterday."

"Which part of yesterday?" Dark eyebrows wagged.

"Cam!" She liked Stephan, but she didn't want her

personal life aired out for the whole zoo to see. This thing with Sullivan was new. She didn't want to jinx it.

"Trust me, Ellie," Stephan said as he handed off Bubbles to Cam, taking the next penguin from her arms. "I may be an old married fart, but I wasn't always in love with Rob. I've had my wild days. Nothing you can say will shock me."

"It's nothing." She reached over to place her hands on Libby. She was a squirmer. Hated to have her vitals checked. "There's just this guy and...it's new. Ya know?"

He smiled, squeezing her shoulder reassuringly. "New is always fun and a little scary."

He had that right. She felt like a hundred peacocks were doing their mating dance in her stomach. Feathers unfurled and tickling her from all ends. The thought of Sullivan made her heart race and her palms sweat. When she was with him, all she wanted to do was touch him and when she wasn't with him, it seemed like he was always on her mind. Maybe not right up front, but always there, somewhere. It was consuming, and that terrified her.

But no matter how scared she was, the pull outweighed the fear. For once in her life, she found herself so drawn to something, to someone, that the nasty voice in her head telling her everything would go wrong, and it would all be her fault, was softer, quieter. Make no mistake, it was still there, but she found it easier to ignore.

"I love new," Cam sighed.

Ellie's phone pinged again, and she glanced down.

Sullivan: Sorry if this is too cheesy but...

And then he texted a gif of a toad in the mud with the words *I toadally dig you* flashing above it.

"Holy shit, he's into your animal puns." Cam leaned over her shoulder, glancing at her phone. "You two are perfect for each other."

She scoffed, but a piece of her heart couldn't help but

agree. For once, she shoved the negative thoughts in her mind into a tiny box and closed them tight. For now, for one moment, she would allow herself to enjoy this. To be happy.

She sent back a gif of a seal with the words *That's the sealiest thing I've ever heard.*

He quickly responded.

Sullivan: Can I call you tonight?

Ellie: You better.

Then she flipped her phone to silent and slipped it back into her pocket. Tonight! He was calling her tonight. For the first time since she'd started this job, she was looking forward to the end of the day.

CHAPTER 16

*S*ullivan sat at the desk in his office on Monday morning with a big grin on his face. He wasn't particularly fond of Mondays, but he had a lot to be grateful for. A job that he loved, a kid he loved even more. A slightly annoying younger brother who he loved despite wanting to strangle at times. A roof over his head, money in the bank. But none of those were the reason for the curl of his lips on this sunny Monday morning.

No, the current cause of his sunshiny mood had nothing to do with any of those things and everything to do with the woman he was currently texting.

Ellie: I forgot to tell you last night that Cam wanted you to tell Charlotte she says hello.

He chuckled as he read the message. Ellie most likely forgot because after two seconds on the phone late last night, he'd brought up their kiss again and the conversation had turned a bit...naughty. Who knew the sweet woman could have such a filthy mouth? She'd been shy at first, but once he'd mentioned how sorry he was their kiss got interrupted, she'd opened up. Telling him in explicit detail what she'd wanted to do to him and have him do to her the other night. Sullivan had now made it his goal to fulfill every single one of her wishes. Soon.

After their call, he'd taken care of himself in the shower. It had taken the worst of the edge off, but not by much. Knowing Ellie wanted him as much as he wanted her ramped up the need inside him to epic proportions. He couldn't ever remember wanting a woman this badly before. Not only that, he enjoyed spending time with Ellie. She was funny and smart, and she made him feel comfortable. Like he could be himself. Not just a doctor, or a dad, but Sullivan. All the bits and pieces that went together to make him who he was.

Sullivan: I'll tell her.

He texted back, pausing a moment before adding.

Sullivan: Is she the "giant lady" Charlotte keeps talking about?

Ellie sent a laughing cry emoji.

Ellie: Yup. Cam is almost six foot, so I'm sure to a child she would be a giant. I feel that way around her too, but don't you dare tell her.

He chuckled. Ellie had told him a little about her best friend, Cam. He vaguely remembered meeting her that day at the zoo, but he'd been so worried about Charlotte everything else was a blur. Anyone Ellie considered a friend had to be a good person.

Sullivan: My lips are...

Then he texted her a gif of a seal.

Ellie: I've created a monster.

Sullivan: What? I like your love of animal puns. They...

He grabbed the meme of a duck with the words *Quack me up* written on it he'd saved from an earlier internet search and sent it.

He took a sip of his coffee as he waited for her reply. It

didn't take long for a picture of a bear to pop up along with a kissy winky face emoji.

Ellie: You're unBEARably cute.

Laughter burst from him. Gavin would call him the corniest cornball ever—if Charlotte was present, if she wasn't—he'd say Sullivan had lost his damn mind. That wouldn't be far from the truth. He didn't recognize this strange, playful side of himself. Ever since his parents died, he'd felt this immense pressure on his shoulders. Gavin had only been seventeen at the time, so Sullivan had taken a semester off school and filed the paperwork to become his brother's legal guardian. He'd helped his brother finish school and apply to college, going back himself to finish undergrad and head right into medical school.

When he met Claire, it just felt natural to propose after a year and a half. Like the right thing to do. What he was supposed to do. Finish school, get a job, get married, have kids. Be an adult. That was the life his parents wanted for him, and he didn't want to disappoint them. Didn't want their death to derail the grand plan they imagined for him. They had been wonderful parents. They deserved him following through on their plan.

It wasn't that he didn't like his life. He loved being a doctor, helping people. He also loved being a dad to Charlotte. The happily ever after marriage thing had failed, but it wasn't entirely his fault. It took two to destroy a union. He couldn't fix his marriage when his wife walked away, sending divorce papers and no forwarding address.

So, he'd failed a bit, but he was trying like hell to stay on track with the rest. He'd been so obsessed with toeing the line all these years, he'd forgotten what silly fun felt like. This bubbly excitement low in his gut every time he got a text from Ellie. The terrible animal puns they sent back and forth. The late night, naughty talk. This was something for him. *Just* him. Ellie made him feel good, happy. He liked it. He liked her.

Sullivan: Do you have any plans for Friday night?

Ellie: Well, I was planning on watching Planet Earth for the seventh time again, but...

His lips curled, imagining Ellie sitting on her couch with a fuzzy blanket and bowl of popcorn watching nature documentaries. A warm sense of comfort burned in his chest as he felt a longing to sit beside her in that image. He nearly typed out a response asking to join her when another text popped up, reminding him of his original plan.

Ellie: What did you have in mind?

Sullivan: Can I take you to dinner? I can get my brother to watch Charlotte for the night.

He held his breath as those three dots appeared. Staring, he waited, wondering if he'd taken the right approach, asked the right way. It had been years since he'd asked a woman out. Texting the question was probably not the best way to do it. Shit! He should have called or sent her flowers or something. A text? *Way to woo the woman, Sullivan.*

Inwardly cringing at his own stupidity, a breath of relief left him when her reply appeared.

Ellie: I'd love to.

"Yes!" He pumped his fist in the air, grateful for his private office, where no one could witness his unsophisticated reaction.

Sullivan: Send me your address and I'll pick you up. Does 6:30 work for you?

Ellie: Sounds perfect.

She signed off, stating she needed to feed someone named Bill. He supposed that was a bird. Weird name for a bird, but he didn't really care about that right now. *She said yes!* He had a date. Holy shit, he had a date! He hadn't been on a date since...he couldn't even remember. He went out with his brother and some buddies when his housekeeper offered to watch Charlotte, but he hadn't gone out on an actual date with a woman since before his marriage.

Picking up his cell again he hit the number for his brother without even thinking about it. The moment his brother answered words spewed out of his mouth like lava from an erupting volcano.

"I have a date."

"Sullivan?"

"Yes, it's me. Who else would it be?"

"I don't know, but since I haven't heard the word *date* come out of your mouth in almost a decade, I figured it wasn't my big brother."

He could really do without the sibling heckling right now.

"Gavin, focus. I have a date."

"So you've said, but I still can't believe it. Who's the unlucky lady?"

They made phones you could wear on your wrist, video call to see the person's face, hell he'd seen some that could work underwater these days. What he really needed right now was a phone that had a button you pushed, and it would automatically smack the other person on the line. Right upside the back of their head. He'd pay good money for a phone like that right about now.

"Don't be a dick."

"I'm surprised you have a dick."

"Hanging up now. Thanks for all your help."

"Wait! Wait." His brother laughed. "I'm sorry, really. I'm happy for you, big brother. I've been telling you to get out for ages. So, what do you need?"

Debating whether he should hang up on his immature ass of a brother—but then who would watch Charlotte?—he sighed and explained. "First off I need you to watch Charlotte on Friday night."

"Done."

That was easy. Not surprising. Gavin loved being an uncle. He was always game to spoil his niece. Speaking of spoiling, Sullivan would have to reiterate the "no candy after six" rule. Not that Gavin would follow it, but it still needed to be said. He had to portray some authority even if the troublesome twosome ignored his every edict.

"What else?"

Here was the tricky part. He hated to admit it, but he needed some advice. As his brother so rudely pointed out, it had been a while since he'd been in the game. This date was too important to mess up. Ellie deserved an amazing night. Something told him ordering mac and cheese and watching dinosaur movies wouldn't sweep her off her feet. What worked for an eight-year-old girl would not appeal to a twenty-eight-year-old woman. He didn't think.

"I need some…" God, he hated to confess this. "Tips."

"Tips? Like restaurant recommendation? Ideas for after dinner? Ways to make Ellie fall into your arms and spend the night riding you like a bronco at the county fair?"

"Yes, I mean no! I—wait, how do you know I'm going out with Ellie?"

"Dude," his brother chuckled. "You haven't shown any interest in a woman since Claire left. You met this woman a few weeks ago and you talk about her nonstop."

"I do not."

"You invited her to your daughter's birthday party."

"Charlotte wanted her there."

"You barely strayed five feet from her the entire day. You like her."

He didn't know why he was arguing with his brother about this. Of course he liked Ellie. So why did it bother him so much that Gavin had noticed?

"Are you going to give me advice or not?"

"Are you going to admit it's Ellie?"

"Yes! Fine, yes, I'm going out with Ellie, and I want her to have a fantastic time, but I'm a little rusty in the impressing women department, so give me your best recommendations, please. Happy?"

"Ecstatic."

Oddly enough, his brother did sound overjoyed about the situation. Maybe Gavin was just happy he was the brother with more knowledge, for once.

"Okay, here's what you need to do."

CHAPTER 17

$\mathcal{A}$fter another fifteen minutes talking to his brother, he had a list of restaurants, after dinner activities, and a suggestion for a very public make out point and zero clothes. He would be ignoring that last one. The lack of clothes idea he liked, but Sullivan had never been much of an exhibitionist. His brother, on the other hand…

"Dr. Green?"

The door to his office opened and Chuck, one of the RNs, popped his head in.

"Yes?"

"Your first appointment is here. Mrs. Wilkins. Room six."

"Thanks, Chuck. I'll be right there."

Time to start the day. Good thing he handled all that business because from here until he went to pick up Charlotte, his day would be jam-packed with patients, charts, and the general chaos that came with the medical health profession.

He left his office, heading down the hall to room six. Knocking softly, he announced himself before entering.

"Hello, Mrs. Wilkins. How are you today?"

The elderly white woman on the table gave him a wide smile. "I'm doing okay, Dr. Green. But I have this tiny tickle that won't go away."

"Let's have a quick look."

Stepping up to the in-room sink, he washed and dried his hands before moving to the exam table.

"Has your grandson been smoking in the house again?"

He knew he wasn't supposed to have favorite patients, but he really liked Mrs. Wilkins. She reminded him of his late grandmother. They were both sweet as apple pie, which was why he worried about her. Mrs. Wilkins would never turn anyone away. Recently, her wayward grandson had come to live with her after getting kicked out of three different relatives' homes. The guy was in his early twenties and apparently liked to party far too much. He wasn't a bad kid, per se, he just needed to screw his head on straight. And he also needed to stop smoking around his asthmatic grandmother.

"Oh no. Derrick is a sweet boy. He promised me he quit those death sticks. He knows how I feel about them after what they did to his grandpa."

Mr. Wilkins had passed away ten years ago from stage four metastatic lung cancer. The man had smoked like a chimney since the day he turned fourteen. A shame more people hadn't known of the dangers of smoking back then. Then again, people knew now, and they still smoked. He'd bet his medical degree "Sweet Derrick" was still sucking on cancer sticks. The sad truth was smoking was an incredibly hard habit to break.

He placed his stethoscope in his ears, instructing Mrs. Wilkins to take a few deep breaths.

"Hmmmmm." He didn't like the sound of her lungs. Asthma was a tricky disease. It could change over time due to any number of factors. He often saw his asthma patients regularly. Especially the elderly patients like Mrs. Wilkins who had other health issues to contend with.

"Oh dear, it's never good when a doctor says *mmmmm*." The old woman chuckled. "Oops is also bad."

He couldn't fight a smile around her. "Don't you worry. It's nothing too serious, but I would like to order a new scan of your lungs."

No need to upset the patient. He'd review the scans and then discuss the proper steps to take. Hopefully nothing was wrong, and it was just this spring's ridiculous amount of pollen. Allergies had taken a steep rise in the past few weeks.

"You're the doc, doc."

He made a note on her chart. "Anything else you'd like to discuss today?"

"I'd like to ask who's responsible for that happy smile you had on your face when you walked in the door."

His hand slipped, pen streaking black ink across the signature box. Oh well, didn't look much different from normal. The stereotype was true where he was concerned. He had crappy handwriting.

"What? I'm always happy."

Wrinkled lips pulled into a grin. The mop of short, pure white curls shaking back and forth. "No, you're always pleasant. You have a wonderful bedside manner, Dr. Green. That's why everyone loves you. But I know the difference between a man's pleasant smile and his smitten one."

Smitten? Did people still say that? Eighty-year-old women did, apparently.

"It's a lady friend, isn't it?"

"Um—"

"I knew it!"

She clapped her hands together so hard Sullivan was afraid she might shatter the bones.

"I didn't say it was a...lady friend."

"You didn't have to." She shook a finger at him. "You have that twitterpated look about you."

Smitten? Twitterpated? Had he fallen into a time vortex?

"I might have met someone...special recently."

He didn't like to get too familiar with his patients, but they shared very personal information with him, trusted him with their health, their very lives. He had to give a little back. Plus, he found if he related to his patients, shared a little of his own life, they tended to be more honest with him and he could care for them better. Hard to treat someone when they lied about their habits or symptoms.

"Oh wonderful! Good for you, Doctor." She placed hands, covered in sunspots and freckles from a lifetime of enjoying the outdoors, over her heart. "I've been hoping for years that you would find someone sweet and kind and loving to take care of you and your precious little girl."

Ellie may be all those things, but Mrs. Wilkins was barking up the wrong tree. He and Ellie agreed to keep this thing casual. She understood he wasn't looking for anything serious. He didn't need anyone to care for him and Charlotte. They were doing just fine on their own. Speaking of Charlotte, he had no idea what to tell her about him and Ellie. Until this moment, he hadn't considered the impact of dating a woman his daughter considered a friend.

He'd have to talk to Ellie and make sure when they decided they were done having fun, it wouldn't come between her and Charlotte's friendship. His daughter needed a strong, smart female presence in her life, and he'd be damned if he was the one who took it away from her because his dick decided it wanted someone for the first time in years.

"It's nothing serious, Mrs. Wilkins. We're just taking things one day at a time."

"Well, don't be too loosey-goosey about it. We never

know how many days we've got. Have to live them all to the fullest."

He knew that better than anyone. Less than ten seconds of distraction took his parents away from him forever. As a doctor, he'd seen life snuffed out in moments without a damn thing anyone could do to stop it. He knew how precious every day was. That's why he was trying to enjoy this time with Ellie without complicating it with thoughts of a future he couldn't give her.

"You deserve your happiness, doc. I'm glad you found it."

Happiness.

Yeah, that pretty much described how he felt around Ellie. She was sunshine and laughter all rolled into one sexy package that made his blood boil and spirit lift. He didn't know if they were going to soar to the heavens or crash and burn, but damned if he wasn't excited as hell to find out.

CHAPTER 18

"*E*leanor Constance Clark, don't you dare wear jeans and a shirt tonight! You're going on a date you cannot dress in animal puns."

Ellie pulled the phone away from her face as her best friend's loud demand pierced her eardrum, causing a slight ring.

"Ouch!"

"If I don't yell, you won't listen."

She touched the screen to enable speakerphone so her eardrum wouldn't burst before her date and set the cell on her dresser.

"I have nothing else to wear," she complained, digging in her dresser drawers. "He's already seen me in the black dress you gave me. The only other date-ish outfit I have is my peacock dress."

The short skater style dress with a peacock-patterned print was her only concession to dressing up. It wasn't nice or fancy, but it sufficed when she needed to wear something formal, like at the zoo fundraiser dinner last month. Paired with her black lace shrug, the outfit could pass for fancy.

"Perfect! Wear that."

"But you said I couldn't wear animal puns."

"It's animal print, not a pun. And you look amazing in it. The blue and green hues complement your eyes. Really makes them pop."

She had no idea why people said that. She'd never noticed anyone's eyes *pop* because of a certain color they were wearing. Wasn't eye popping a bad thing? Something you should see an optometrist about?

"Okay, so the peacock dress. Do I have to wear heels?"

"Doll-face, you don't have to wear anything you don't want. You called *me* for advice and I'm just giving it. Take it or leave it."

That was certainly thoughtful considering Cam nearly shouted her head off five seconds ago when she suggested just wearing what she had on at work that day.

"Then I'll wear my black ballet flats."

"The ones with the bow on the toe? Those are adorable."

Perfect. Just what she wanted to be on her date with the most attractive man she'd ever kissed. Adorable. Ugh! For once in her life, her desire to be seen as sexy might override her love of comfort.

"I also have those silver heels from my cousin's wedding two years ago."

She'd worn them once, gotten the worst blisters ever, and shoved them as far back in her closet as she could, vowing to never again let them see the light of day.

"Ooo, those are hot. Are you sure you can walk in them?"

"I thought you wanted me to be sexy."

"I want you to be yourself. If he doesn't like you the way you are, then he's not worth it."

She opened her tiny closet door, getting down on her hands and knees to shove piles of old schoolwork and

153

worn-out textbooks out of the way. Geeze, she really needed to throw a lot of this stuff out. She graduated years ago.

"A date is a chance to put your best foot forward," Cam continued as Ellie carefully dug through years of crap to find those damn shoes. "But you don't want to give a false impression of yourself. That's why an animal print dress is perfect for you. And if you want to wear the heels, then I say go for it, but if they're going to make you feel uncomfortable all night, flats are great too. He'll like you for who are you, not what you wear. Trust me."

She wished she had her friend's confidence.

Cam had a good point. Besides the one time at speed dating, Sullivan had only ever seen her in her everyday wear and a sopping wet, smelly zoo uniform. He kissed the ever-living daylights out of her when she was wearing her elephant pun shirt. Heels or flats, she didn't think he'd care. Not like she could find the torture shoes anyway.

Falling back on her butt, she huffed out a breath of frustration.

"I just really, *really*, want tonight to go well. I like this guy, Cam. A lot."

"I know, and he likes you."

She laughed. "How do you know that?"

"He better," her best friend's voice came out stern over the phone line. "Or I'll hunt him down and smack him upside the head for not realizing he could have had the best woman in the entire world."

Damn, she really loved her best friend.

"Now stop talking to me and go get ready. Isn't he going to be there soon?"

No. She still had—

Shit!

A quick glance at the screen of her phone revealed she'd

been talking to Cam for twenty minutes. Which meant she only had fifteen to get ready.

"Crap! I gotta go. Thanks for listening and all the advice."

"Anytime. You have fun tonight. Don't do anything I wouldn't do."

She snorted, smiling even though her friend couldn't see it. "That's not much."

"True, but it makes for some great stories."

That it did and, boy, did Cam have some funny ones.

"Knock his socks off, sweetie. Love ya!"

"Love you too."

She waited, staring at the screen until Cam ended the call. Then she whirled like a tornado around her room. Thankfully, she'd already taken a shower the moment she'd gotten off work, so she didn't smell like bird poop. Makeup had never really been her thing, but she put on mascara and lipstick occasionally. This occasion called for it. A bit of eye shadow and blush, too. She could never get the hang of the amazing contour thing Cam did, but the soft rosy cheeks, smoky eye, and dark red lips weren't so bad if she said so herself.

Grabbing her blow dryer, she finished drying the two braids she weaved her hair into after her shower. Giving them one last blast of hot air, she removed the ties and ran her hands through her strands to get perfect soft beachy waves. A neat trick she'd seen online.

She slipped the peacock dress off its hanger and carefully pulled it over her head. The stretchy fabric felt silky against her skin, completely comfortable. Unlike the scratchy lace underwear and matching bra she'd secretly bought at a mall in Denver two days ago. It had been ages since she'd been on a date. She didn't know the protocol as far as when jumping into bed was appropriate, but she wanted to be prepared. Just in case. Anyway, Cam would say *screw appropriate and do what you want.* Since what she wanted was Sullivan, she planned to do just that. Hence the sexy, uncomfortable underwear.

Beauty can be painful, dear.

Her mother's words. She'd never agreed with them. Why did you have to endure pain to be beautiful? It didn't make sense. But she had to admit, she felt…powerful knowing she had a sexy secret under her clothing.

Just as she slipped her feet into her black flats—because, yes, the heels were sexy but tripping on three-inch spikes and breaking her neck wasn't—her doorbell rang. With one last glance in her dresser mirror, she wished her reflection luck and hurried to the front door. She swung it open to reveal Sullivan standing there, flowers in hand and a smile on his face.

He brought flowers!

Had a man ever bought her flowers before? She couldn't remember the occasion ever happening.

"Wow, you look amazing."

Heat crawled up her cheeks. "Thank you. You don't look so bad yourself."

His grin widened at her attempt to be casual. She'd tried to sound cool and aloof, like Cam would, but the breathy tone belied her casual words. Could anyone blame her? The man looked like a walking advertisement for arousal issues. Can't get things started in the bedroom? No need for Spanish fly or horny goat weed. One glance at Dr. Sullivan Green and the engines would rev all night.

Hers certainly was.

She'd noticed he always dressed a bit more formally than she did. Due to his profession, she assumed. But tonight, he had on a pair of dark washed designer jeans and a long-sleeved V-neck shirt that molded to his chest like a second skin. He'd pushed the sleeves up in deference to the warm spring they were experiencing, exposing a pair of delicious looking forearms. Ellie had never thought of forearms as sexy, not until this very moment.

The slight blond stubble on his face gave him a roguish appearance and the dark charcoal color of his shirt made his green eyes sparkle and…pop. Now she got it!

"These are for you."

He held out the bouquet of multicolored daisies. She took them, her fingers brushing against his, sending a thrilling shock of desire straight to her core.

"Thank you. They're beautiful." Bringing them to her nose, she inhaled their sweet fragrance. "Would you like to come in while I put them in some water?"

"I'd love to."

He stepped inside, closing the door behind him. She moved to the small kitchen, taking down the only vase she owned and filling it with water.

"I like your place."

A sudden wave of embarrassment crashed over her at his words. She'd been so excited to see him, so happy to receive flowers. She'd completely forgotten how tiny her apartment was compared to Sullivan's beautiful, spacious house.

"I know it's not much, um, there's just me, so I don't need a big place or anything and—"

Suddenly, he was behind her. His arms encircling her, hands covering her own as they fussed with the flowers already perfectly arranged in the vase.

"Ellie. I really do like it. I didn't always live in a five-bedroom house, you know. When I was in med school, I lived in a two-bedroom apartment with five other guys. It was crowded, dirty, and the smell could knock out a bear at fifty paces."

She chuckled, leaning back into his warm embrace. "Did you know bears are suspected of having the greatest sense of smell in the animal kingdom?"

Wrapping his arms around her waist, he squeezed with a soft laugh. "You, Ellie Clark, are one of a kind."

Warm lips pressed against the sensitive spot on the back of her neck just below her ear. She tried and failed to suppress a moan. His arms tightened around her, mouth moving against the shell of her ear, creating wonderful sparking sensations to shoot across her entire body as he whispered.

"If you're hungry, we better leave for dinner now."

Oh, she was hungry all right, but she doubted the restaurant they were going to would serve what she wanted. Naked Sullivan Green. Just as she was about to suggest they skip dinner and head right to dessert, her stomach let out a loud grumble.

Dammit, would the floor just open up and eat me now!

Why had she skipped lunch? Oh right, because she had a hot date tonight and she'd been too nervous to choke anything down.

"Come on," he said with a laugh, taking her hand and heading to the door. "Let's get you some sustenance."

Perfect way to start a date. Letting her stomach do the talking. She'd have to watch what she ate tonight. No cruciferous vegetables. She didn't want other body parts talking to Sullivan later on. Just the thought made her want to crawl into a hole and die.

As Ellie pulled the door closed, she glanced over to her small kitchen, noting that all the stove lights were off. Of course they were. She hadn't cooked anything today, but the irrational fear of her apartment catching on fire while she was out caused her to do the check every time she left.

"Off, off, off," she mumbled under her breath, counting the stove, toaster oven, and small coffee pot on her counter. Pulling the door closed, she noticed Sullivan staring at her from the corner of her eye.

Dammit!

She must have been mumbling louder than she thought. Not wanting to ruin what had started as a perfect date, she ignored the question in his eyes and focused on locking her door. Sliding the key into the lock, she turned it and paused. Oh, how she wished she could simply pull the key out and drop it into her purse like any other person. But just the thought of not relocking the door another two times had her heart racing. And not in a good way.

The cold metal key dug into her finger as she squeezed, trying to argue with her illogical fear, whispering if she didn't lock it three times, how could she be sure it was locked? And if it wasn't locked, someone would waltz in, hide in her closet, and murder her in her sleep. She knew that sounded ludicrous, but she also knew if she didn't perform her ritual, the anxiety would eat at her all night.

Things like this were why she never made it past a first date. Her OCD was a part of her, she could manage it, but it would always be there. She had to live with that. She understood why someone else might not want to.

"Ellie," Sullivan's soft, deep voice rumbled in her ear. "It's okay if you need to…check things."

She turned her head to glance at him over her shoulder. He smiled. His eyes filled with understanding.

"I've had a few patients with OCD. It's not something I treat, but I notice they do better when they're able to perform their…"

"Rituals."

He tilted his head at her blurted explanation.

"I call them rituals or compulsions. People call them different things. They just…they help ground me. Calm the anxiety. I just need to check to make sure everything is safe and secure, so nothing bad happens."

Leaning down, he brushed a kiss against her temple, warm breath caressing her cheek as he spoke.

"Check away, honey. I'm right here, ready whenever you are."

She hesitated. "It's just that, they...my compulsions, bother some people. Some of the men I've gone out with think it's weird or annoying. They can't understand why I don't just stop, but I try and—"

"Ellie," he interrupted her. "I'm not those jackasses. I might not understand what you're going through, but I'd never assume it's as easy as flicking off a light switch. The brain is the most complex organ in the human body and no two are alike. Doctor, remember?" He chuckled.

Feeling an immense weight lifting off her shoulders, she turned the key and jiggled the doorknob twice more. Slipping the key from the lock and dropping it into her purse without a hint of anxiety, her ritual performed to completion.

Tears of relief gathered in her eyes at Sullivan's understanding, but she blinked them back. Her chest filled with an entirely novel sensation. Gratitude. No one except Cam and her therapist had ever accepted her rituals with no form of judgment, but Sullivan did. He might not fully understand, but he didn't judge her for them. He didn't know how much that meant to her.

CHAPTER 19

They headed out to his car, which was the nicest vehicle Ellie had ever been in. She didn't know what it was. She wasn't a car person, but it started with the push of a button and for the life of her, she couldn't hear the engine make one peep of sound. Such a difference from her fifteen-year-old bucket of rust with over two hundred thousand miles on it and a muffler that announced to people a state over she was driving by. She really needed to replace the old girl, but it still ran and until her student loans were paid off, that was all that mattered. She'd get a new car in, oh, another twenty years.

The drive to the restaurant was short. Sullivan had chosen a local place that specialized in new ways to serve old classics. Sunlight was a smaller suburb of Denver, so they received some of the hipster spillover. She'd never been to Ipsum, but she'd always wanted to try it. Hopefully, they served the food on plates and not shovels. The food industry could be weird sometimes.

When they arrived at the restaurant, they were seated right away, as Sullivan had made reservations. Again, she couldn't ever remember a date making actual reservations. He even pulled out her chair. Much more of this, and he would ruin her for other men.

Yeah right, like he hasn't done that already. Don't forget, this is just for fun.

Her smile dropped a bit at the reminder. Sullivan made his position on long term very clear. She had to be careful not to get stars in her eyes where he was concerned.

The server came by to drop off water for each of them. Ellie took a sip, tapping her straw three times. Sullivan smiled, but said nothing, ignoring it as if everyone in the world drank that way. Her heart swelled a little more. This wonderful, understanding man was taking up far too much room in the pounding organ. She really needed to find a way to wall off the silly thing.

"So, tell me what it takes to be a zookeeper?"

She told him about school and how she never liked any subject except for biology. Combined with her love of animals, that led her to study zoology at university. Oddly, she found herself talking on and on, something she rarely felt comfortable doing around anyone. But with Sullivan...there was just something about him. A sincerity. He really seemed to care about what she had to say. He made her feel comfortable, wanted. And not just sexually—though he had made his desire clear on that front. When she was with him, she felt accepted for who she truly was. He had no idea how much that meant to her.

"And how about you?" she asked after talking about herself so much that their food had arrived. On plates, thankfully. "Is it really as hard as they say? Becoming a doctor?"

"Harder." He laughed, digging into his artisanal deconstructed Cobb salad.

She ate her meal, listening with fascination as Sullivan

described the long days and even longer nights on his path to working in the medical field. After dinner, Sullivan suggested taking a walk through the downtown area. Sunlight wasn't as big as Denver, but it had a charming downtown with historic buildings, some dating back to the gold rush era.

They walked along the sidewalk, enjoying the brisk evening air. Sullivan held her hand in his and she couldn't stop the big, goofy grin from taking over her face. The night was perfect. Absolutely perfect.

"Hey, look."

They stopped, and he pointed to the end of the road where an old, abandoned lot was currently filled with lights, music, and carnival rides. The shouts and laughter of people drifted in the air, advertising the excitement of the event.

"It's the Spring Fling Faire. I didn't realize that was this weekend." He smiled, the dent in his cheek making her heart stop. "Want to check it out?"

"Sure." Like she'd say no to anything this man asked of her. Not tonight.

The street fair was in full swing. Sullivan purchased some tickets from the booth. Normally, all the loud noises and crowds of people made her feel anxious, but with Sullivan holding tightly to her hand, Ellie felt calm and safe. Amazing. They played a few games, losing terribly because those things were all rigged in her opinion. The smell of cheap beer and starchy fried food filled the air, mixing with the boisterous bluegrass music being played by a band of older men and women on a stage a few yards down. It was loud, smelly, and crowded. And to her surprise, Ellie was having the time of her life.

"Oh wow," Sullivan pulled to a stop, his head tilting up. "I haven't been on a Ferris wheel in ages."

The lighthearted mood slipped from her grasp as Ellie's

heart stuttered to a stop. She glanced up at the large wheel full of swinging seats of couples. Terror gripped her hard and fast. In her mind, she saw a vision of her and Sullivan sitting in one of the chairs. They rose to the top, but she shifted in the seat, causing the lock to open and as they swung, they slipped out, falling to their death on the harsh pavement below, blood spilling out of their cracked skulls.

She sucked in a harsh breath, closing her eyes on the image. But she couldn't stop it from playing out, over and over again, in her head. Why? Why did her brain do this to her? She knew it was an irrational thought. Something that would never happen. But still. The dark voice whispered that it could happen, and it would be all her fault.

Don't check the food and the birds will get sick and die all because of you.

Don't check the locks and someone will break in and kill your family all because of you.

Don't let them hang up first and it will be the last time you'll talk to them. They'll die and it will be all your fault.

She hated that voice. Hated that it wasn't a voice at all, but her. The monster who lived inside her brain.

"Ellie."

He said her name softly, but it broke through her fog of fear. Sullivan placed a gentle hand on her chin, turning her head until she gazed into his beautiful, understanding eyes.

"We don't have to do anything you don't feel comfortable with."

Damn, there is no way this man could be this perfect. He was so considerate and here she was ruining a wonderful night. No. She wouldn't allow it. She was stronger than this. She'd worked hard to get where she was, and she'd be damned if she let her fears ruin a perfectly lovely evening.

"It's okay. Let's do it."

He furrowed his brow. "Are you sure?"

"Yes."

Squeezing her hand, he gave her a soft, but thorough kiss and led them to the Ferris wheel. After handing the ride operator some tickets, they slid into a seat. Her heart raced, unfortunately not from the proximity of the sexy man next to her. The operator locked them in. She knew because she'd watched very, *very* carefully. As they rose into the air, she let out a small squeak. Sullivan wrapped an arm around her, pulling her close to his side. She snuggled into him, not ashamed to admit she needed some of his strength right now. They rose into the air, or she assumed they did, her eyes were shut tighter than Bingo's when he needed his eye drops.

The slow swing of the chair as they rose in the air made her stomach drop. When the motion stopped, she slowly opened her eyes. They were stopped at the top. A breath of awe left her as she gazed upon the city lights, twinkling like a million stars scattered along the ground.

"Wow."

"Not so bad, right?" Sullivan said softly, holding her tight.

She turned her head to smile at him.

"Not so bad at all."

Sullivan stared at her for a moment, his gaze roaming over her face. Seeing what, she had no idea. But a small smile ticked up the corner of his mouth.

"You really are an extraordinary person, Ellie."

She had no idea what to say to that. Thankfully, he didn't expect her to say anything. Instead, he leaned in and took her mouth in a soul searing kiss that made her forget she was dozens of feet in the air in a contraption that was broken down and carted back and forth across the country. She dug her nails into his shoulders, not because she was afraid of falling, but because she was afraid if she didn't alleviate this deep, burning need inside her, she just might explode.

"Hey, lovebirds," a rough, rude voice interrupted them. "Ride's over."

Sullivan pulled away to glare at the ride operator. "Couldn't let us go another round?"

The large man shrugged. "You should have slipped me a twenty beforehand."

A twenty? Did people actually do that? She thought it was just something that happened in those Rom Com's Cam liked to watch. Didn't matter. What she wanted to do with Sullivan couldn't be achieved on a rickety Ferris wheel. Not unless they wanted to add risk of death to their date night, and she didn't.

"Come on," she said, rising from the seat as the operator unlocked the safety bar. "Let's go."

Sullivan followed her lead as she headed out of the fair-grounds and back to his car. The things she wanted would be dangerous on a carnival ride high in the sky. But if she played her cards right, she and Sullivan would be achieving a different kind of high in her bedroom tonight. The kind with no loud music, bad smells, or crowds of people. This high involved only two people and if kissing this man was anything like making love to him, she'd be in the stratosphere by the end of the night.

CHAPTER 20

They drove back to Ellie's place in relative silence. Sullivan gripped the steering wheel so tight his fingers ached. His body was on fire, every muscle tight and screaming for release. The sexual tension hung like a thick cloud in the car. Choking out all other rational thought. The vision in his mind had tunneled to one thought.

Ellie naked, screaming his name as they drove each other out of their minds with pleasure.

Yeah, that sounded good to him. He thought she was on the same page, but he wouldn't assume. The moment he stopped this car, he would make sure his intentions were clear and allow her to decide on their next move. As badly as he wanted her, he never wanted to engage in any activity where both parties weren't one hundred percent on board.

As they pulled up to her complex, the atmosphere in the car was so thick you could cut it with a knife. He turned off the car, getting out to open her door. No matter what happened, he was walking her to her door. The evening could end with a handshake—preferably not. A kiss—yes, please. Or an invitation inside—oh, hell yes! But first, he would make sure she got inside safely. That was just good first date etiquette.

She slipped her hand into his as they entered her apartment building and headed down the hall to her place.

"I had a lovely time tonight, Sullivan."

"Me too." And he hoped to continue it.

They stopped in front of her door. Ellie pulled her keys from her small purse, fiddling with the metal objects as she stared down at the ground.

"So, um, is Charlotte waiting up for you?"

Her head tilted up, dark brown eyes peeking at him from under her lashes. His body tightened to the point of pain, but he held it together.

"If I know my brother, she's passed out on the couch from a candy coma. Probably doesn't even miss me."

She smiled. "I find it hard to believe that anyone wouldn't miss you."

She'd be wrong. Claire certainly didn't miss him. He brushed off the negative thought. He didn't want to think about his ex-wife or her abandonment. Right now, all he wanted to do was take Ellie inside and worship every inch of the creamy soft skin that had been tormenting him the entire evening.

She turned, fitting the key into the lock, and opening the door before turning back to him to ask, "Do you want to come in for some...coffee?"

Lifting his hand, he set his palm against her jaw, cupping her cheek, and rubbing his thumb against the smoothness he found there.

"I would love to come in, but I don't want any coffee."

Brown eyes widened, stark need staring directly at him from their depths. "Wh-what do you want?"

He lowered his head to brush his lips against hers in the

barest of kisses. A teasing hint of the tightly leashed need raging within him.

"You, Ellie. I want you. What do you want?"

He held his breath, waiting, hoping, praying...

"You. I want you too, Sullivan."

Hell yes!

Putting his other hand on her waist, his mouth came crashing down on hers in a desperate kiss as he moved them both inside, slamming her door with his foot. Ellie reached around him, and he heard the deadbolt being locked once, twice, and a final third time. A smile curved his lips as he continued to kiss her. He knew she thought her rituals upset others, but they were such an intrinsic part of this fascinating woman. They didn't bother him in the slightest. The only thing he hated was how embarrassed she seemed to be by them.

Ellie was amazing. She should never feel an ounce of self-doubt. And Sullivan was going to make damn sure she felt nothing but the ultimate pleasure tonight.

They stumbled as they walked, mouths fused, hands caressing, clothes flying. He thought he heard a tiny rip as she pulled his shirt over his head, but he couldn't find it in him to care. Ellie could rip every single item of clothing he owned so long as it meant she'd cover his naked body with her own.

"Bedroom?" he asked between deep, drugging kisses.

"On the right."

Her place was so small there were only two doors beyond the living area and tiny kitchen. A bathroom on the left and the Holy Grail on the right. Scooping her up into his arms, he made a beeline for the bedroom. He set her on the bed, grabbing the hem of her dress and lifting it up over her head as he placed her on down the soft green comforter.

"Hot damn, woman."

His brain had shut down. Simply turned off and left his head. Because Ellie lay sprawled on the forest green bedspread in nothing but a pair of black lace panties and matching bra. Used to her adorable and comical animal T-shirts, tonight's dress had been a stunning surprise. What lay under the dress was knocking the air right out of him.

"Do you like it?"

Like it? If he liked it any more, he'd be embarrassing himself in his jeans. The woman looked like temptation personified. If lust truly were a deadly sin, one look at Ellie in black lace and the entire world would be dead in a heartbeat.

Scratch that.

He didn't want anyone looking at Ellie but him. He knew he had no right to put that claim down, but his inner caveman didn't care. It wanted Ellie all to himself and vice versa. He didn't care what other people did in the bedroom. That was their business and the people they shared it with. Sullivan didn't share.

"Sullivan?"

Uncertainty crept into her voice. He kicked himself for just standing there, staring without saying a word.

Way to be suave, man.

Time to step up his game.

ELLIE FELT HER BRAVADO SLIP. A moment ago, her head had been swimming with lust, desire, need. Sullivan had all but consumed her the moment she told him she wanted him. *Like he could ever doubt it. The man had looked in a mirror recently, right?* For once in her life, she felt like a bona fide sex kitten instead of an insecure dolt fumbling around, pretending to know what she was doing. She'd had sex before, even good sex upon occasion, but it had always come with a bit of doubt and awkwardness. She guessed tonight would be no different.

"You, Ellie Clark, are the sexiest, most beautiful woman I have ever laid eyes on."

Oh. Oh my!

That certainly went a long way to boosting her confidence.

"Really?"

"Honey, the only reason I'm standing here frozen is I'm afraid if I don't take a minute to cool down, I'll embarrass myself and let you down."

Her heart melted a little at his words, awkwardness dissipation into the air, replaced by confident desire. "You could never let me down, Sullivan."

Those delicious lips curved in a sexy, dent revealing grin. "I will do my best not to, honey. I swear."

He placed a knee on the bed, leaning close.

"Wait," Ellie put her hand on his chest. His bare, hot, hard, deliciously sexy chest. "Don't you want to finish taking your clothes off?"

"No. First, I want to take care of you and if I take my pants off, I won't be able to hold back."

"Oh, you don't have to worry about that. I'm usually a one and done kind of girl." She'd heard of women having multiple orgasms, but she'd never experienced them before.

"Now that sounds like a challenge," he murmured, his lips pressing against the side of her neck.

She moaned in delight, but she didn't want to disappoint him. "Sullivan, really, you don't have to—"

"I want to, honey. Please?"

Far be it from her to deny a man who wanted to pleasure her body. She supposed she could always fake the second orgasm. Just so he wouldn't feel bad.

"Please away."

He chuckled, the vibrations of his lips against that soft spot behind her ear zinging straight down between her legs.

His mouth traveled down her throat, across her clavicle, and down between her very modest cleavage. Now was usually the point she felt anxious, seeing as how she really had nothing to offer in the chest department, but Sullivan's hands came up, cupping her breasts, gently massaging them in a way that made her cry out. Normally guys just pulled and tugged, as if boobs were their personal fun bags, but not Sullivan. He squeezed and caressed, listening to her moans and cries, finding out what she liked, what excited her. And that seemed to get him excited, too, if the hard bulge against her stomach was anything to go by.

Just as she thought it couldn't get any better, his tongue traced a path between her breasts. Encircling first one nipple and then the other through the lace fabric. Her hand flew behind her back as she hastily tried to unclasp the uncomfortable but sexy underwear.

He chuckled. "In a rush, honey?"

Yes, dammit! She'd never been in a rush before, but right now, she felt as if she didn't feel Sullivan on her bare skin right this very moment she'd explode. He didn't wait for her answer but reached around to help her get free of the bra, tossing it across the room...somewhere. Who the hell cared where the damn thing went?

"Beautiful," he murmured before his mouth came down, latching onto her right breast.

She cried out as pleasure assaulted her, fireworks exploding behind her closed eyes. Her hips thrust upwards of their own volition, colliding with Sullivan's hard body. He ground himself against her, allowing her to ride him as the pleasure wave crashed over her.

"Holy...." But she couldn't finish that sentence because she'd never had an orgasm from simple breast stimulation.

There was nothing simple about that.

True, but now a tiny nugget of guilt wormed its way inside. She didn't even have her panties off and she'd already come. Not a sex kitten after all.

"One down," he chuckled against her breasts. "Two to go."

Two? He had to be joking. All thoughts of joking flew out the window as his hand traveled down her stomach to her hips, pulling her closer as he undulated against her. The movement on her sensitive nerves was almost too much. Pleasure with just the hint of pain. But then she felt his hand slip in between them. His thumb gently rubbed in small soft circles right above her clitoris. Her panties still lay between them, and she suddenly wished she had magic that could make them vanish with a thought. She needed to feel him, feel Sullivan against her skin.

As if he read her mind, his thumb slipped beneath the waistband of her panties. His mouth continued its worship of her breasts as his fingers slid in beneath the black lace. The concentration of feeling on her senses was almost too much. She couldn't believe what was about to happen. Sullivan plunged two fingers inside her, continuing with his ministrations on the other parts of her body. In a matter of seconds, she was flying high again. Experiencing her very first multiple orgasm. As she cried out, she heard the faint tear of fabric.

"I'm sorry," his voice was so deep and rough it sounded like the growl of Benji, their Bengal tiger. "I'll buy you a new pair."

It dimly registered in her lust-addled brain that he had torn her underwear off her body. Who cared? That scrap of lace masquerading as an undergarment was uncomfortable anyway. Now she lay fully naked—having lost her shoes somewhere on the journey from the door to the bedroom. The time for proving points was over. Because somehow, astoundingly, even though she'd gotten off twice, her body still craved more. It craved him. Sullivan. All of him. And she'd never been good at denying a craving.

"Now, Sullivan!"

"Now," he agreed, pulling away to shuck off the rest of his clothing.

He grabbed something from the pocket of his jeans as they fell to the floor. A square foil packet. At least one of them still had enough brain cells to remember protection. She certainly had been thinking of nothing but getting Sullivan inside her right now.

He donned the condom, laughing as she reached up to grasp his shoulder and pull him on top of her.

"Eager?"

"Desperate." Sad to admit? Maybe, but right now, she didn't care. She wanted Sullivan, and she wanted. Him. Now.

He eased between her legs, placing the blunt head of his cock at her entrance. The first inch made her cry out. He paused, staring down at her.

"Are you okay?"

She couldn't hold in the moan, so she didn't even try. "Yes. Oh, Sullivan, you feel amazing."

"No. That's all you, sweetheart."

His lips came down on hers as he thrust fully inside. He held himself still for a moment, allowing them both to feel the awe and rapture of their joining. Then he moved in slow, deliberate strokes. It took her a moment, but she matched his movements. Every thrust had his pelvis connecting with her clit, sending bolts of pleasure streaking through her body. Her heart raced, blood pounding in her ears. The world seemed to disappear. There was only them, Sullivan and her, connecting, twisting together not only physically, but on a whole other level as well.

"Ellie, I'm close," his breath panted harshly against her lips.

"Me too."

At her words, his hand snaked down between them. He rubbed in those soft slow circles again, right where she needed. His pace increased, thrusts getting harder, faster until the tightness coiled insider her couldn't handle any more pressure and she broke into a million tiny pieces of pure gratification. He wasn't far behind. His entire body stiffening as a loud groan escaped his lips.

Sullivan collapsed, rolling to his back, and taking her with him so she sprawled on top of him, still connected in the most intimate way.

"Holy hell, woman. I think you killed me."

She killed him? Who was the one who just experienced not one, not two, but *three* orgasms! But let the man think whatever he wanted. Because she didn't have the energy to argue. All she could do was smile. Sex kitten? Hell no, she wasn't a sex kitten. Eleanor Clark was a verified sex goddess!

CHAPTER 21

*S*ullivan buried his nose in the softness of Ellie's silky strands, inhaling their sweet fragrance. Despite the vigorous workout he'd just put it through, his body hardened again. As desperately as he wanted to stay here and continue making love to her for the rest of the night, he couldn't. He had to get back home.

"Hey," he murmured, kissing the soft spot behind her ear that made her sigh in pleasure. "You asleep?"

"Mmmmm," Ellie moaned. "No. I'm in an orgasm-induced coma."

He chuckled. "Funny, in all my years of medical practice, I've never seen anyone in a coma talk."

"Sex coma. They're different."

"How so?"

She turned in his arms, those deep brown eyes sparkling. "A sex coma only puts your worries and stress to sleep. Everything else is awake and…amazing."

He leaned down to brush his lips against hers. He'd meant it to be a soft, sweet kiss, but in moments it turned hot and heavy. Touching this woman sparked something inside him, something that burned for more. One gentle caress would never satisfy. Like the jingle for those chips he loved as a kid. One taste of Ellie was never enough. It simply made him hunger for more. He could gorge himself on the woman and he suspected he still wouldn't be sated. She'd created an endless well of need within him and every moment he spent with her took him deeper and deeper until the only light he saw was her.

Unfortunately, as much as he wanted to stay, there was another light in his life. One he needed to get back to. He pulled away, using every ounce of self-control he had within him.

"You are amazing, and tonight was…I don't even have words. I hate to leave, but—"

"You have to get home to Charlotte," she said with a soft smile, proving she was not only magnificent, but understanding, too.

"Yeah. I wish I could stay."

She shook her head. "No, you don't. Cam used to complain all the time when we roomed together in college that I snore like a lumberjack."

He frowned. "Have you ever seen a doctor about that? Snoring could be a sign of sleep apnea. It's a very serious cond—"

She placed a warm palm over his mouth, effectively cutting off his worry mid-sentence.

"Yes, Dr. Green, I have, and it's not an issue. I have a slightly deviated septum. One day I might need surgery to fix it, but it's nothing serious."

He chuckled. "Sorry. Sometimes it's hard to turn off the doctoring." Especially around people he cared about, and he was coming to find he cared about Ellie. Deeply.

"I understand. You wouldn't believe how hard it is for me to watch animal cartoons and not shout at the TV how inaccurate the animal's characteristics are. I know they're kid shows, but clownfish do not raise their babies, let alone cross the ocean to find *one* offspring."

He threw his head back and laughed. He couldn't help it. This woman made him smile from his very soul. "Fair enough, but please, whatever you do, don't point that out to Charlotte. That's one of her favorite movies."

"I'd never do that." Her face pinched in disbelief. "Besides, I didn't say it wasn't a good movie. Just biologically inaccurate."

"You are one of a kind, Ellie Clark." He kissed the tip of her nose, too afraid to touch those tempting lips again. Charlotte was—hopefully—asleep by now, but he needed to get home. "I'll call you tomorrow?"

She nodded, a satiated smile on her face. He took immense satisfaction knowing he was the one who put it there. Slipping out from under the covers, he walked around the room, gathering his clothes. A small squeak sounded from the bed, and he turned to see Ellie's hand covering her eyes, but if he wasn't mistaken, he could see a bit of dark brown iris peeking out from between her fingers.

"Problem?"

"You're naked!"

He glanced down at himself, then back up to her with puzzlement. "Um, yeah. I have been for the past few hours. Did you not remember ripping my clothes off me the moment we stepped foot inside?"

Her hand flew down to the bed, one dark eyebrow arched. "I did not rip your clothes off."

Grinning, he winked. "A goal for next time."

A beautiful pink blush crawled up her cheeks.

"We'll see." She let out a small giggle. "I'm not used to naked men parading about my bedroom."

And why did that give him a rush of pleasure? He wasn't

an innocent virgin—obviously, he had a kid—and he knew Ellie wasn't either. When people were safe about it, sex could be a very healthy and important aspect of life. So why did it please him to know he was one of the lucky few to grace Ellie's bed?

"Does it bother you? My being naked?"

The sweet pink tongue that had tormented him less than an hour ago came out to slide along her bottom lip. The sight made his body harden and his cock stiffen. Damn appendage. He did not have time for round two. Round three, technically.

"No. I must admit, the view is spectacular."

"Sweetheart, you've got to stop looking at me like that." Or he might be tempted to call his brother and ask him to watch Charlotte until morning.

"Then put some clothes on, though I can't guarantee that'll stop me since I now know what you look like underneath them."

He laughed as he slipped on his boxers and jeans. He couldn't remember the last time he'd been so charmed by someone. His shirt had been flung across the room, the dark grey material hanging precariously on the corner edge of her dresser. He grabbed it, shoving it over his head as he noticed there was a small tear at the back of the neck. A huge grin split his lips. See? He hadn't been the only eager party on the path to naked town.

Sitting on the edge of the bed, he shoved his feet into his socks and shoes. Now came the hard part. Actually leaving. Damn, he didn't want to. This was strange. He'd never had trouble leaving after sex before. Over the years, he'd been too focused on Charlotte and his job to do much dating. The intimate times he'd had had been few and far between, casual hookups where everyone involved knew the score. But every time he'd had no issue getting up after and leaving a woman's bed. But those beds hadn't been Ellie's.

Dark brown eyes, so deep he could drown in them—a delicious death by chocolate—stared up at him.

"You better go," she said with a hint of a smile on her face.

"I'm going."

"Really? Because from here, it looks like you're debating whether to take your clothes off again and test out the stability of my bed frame."

Minx. She was teasing him, testing him. And damned if he didn't want to do exactly that.

"Sullivan." Her face softened. "You have to leave."

He did. And he couldn't believe it was Ellie who had the mental fortitude to push him out the door. She was the reason he wanted to stay, and she was the one pushing him to leave, knowing he had to go. A unique situation, to be sure.

"I'll call you tomorrow," he promised, leaning over to place a soft kiss on her lips, remembering to keep it brief in case he forgot himself and pinned her down to worship her amazing body for the third time tonight.

She walked him to the door, and he waited until he heard the click of her lock. He stood listening as the lock clicked twice more.

"Goodnight, Sullivan," her soft voice filtered through the door, making him realize she knew he was still standing there.

"Night, Ellie."

A tender smile lifted his lips. His body might be sated, but for the first time in…ever, he also felt something more. Humbled. Ellie didn't hide herself or her compulsions with him. She allowed him in. Knowing she felt safe being her true self in his presence made him feel like he could kill a lion with his bare hands.

He winced. Bad analogy. Ellie wouldn't be so fond of him if he harmed the animals she loved so fiercely.

Slay a dragon. Yeah, that was better. Fiercer and fictional.

Knowing he'd already hovered at her door too long, he turned and headed out of her apartment building to his car. The streetlights lit up the dark night sky, giving him plenty of visibility for the short drive home. He ran into zero traffic, not unusual considering it was past midnight and most places in Sunlight rolled up the sidewalks around ten.

He pulled into the garage, fully expecting to see Gavin and Charlotte sacked out on the couch watching something he'd expressly told his brother his daughter wasn't allowed to watch—last time it'd been an old school creature feature that had given her nightmares for a week, he'd given his brother a huge lecture about that one—so color him surprised when he came in the living room to see Gavin, sitting on the couch alone watching late night stand up.

"Charlotte in bed?"

His brother turned at his question, a can of soda halfway to his lips. "Oh, hey, man. Yeah. She sacked out around nine during a marathon of Curious George. I put her in bed, and she hasn't made a peep since."

"Curious George?"

Gavin snorted. "Yes, oh skeptical one. Like I'd let her watch anything else after last time. She asked for another Godzilla movie, but I convinced her they hadn't made any more yet."

His brother had expressed regret after Sullivan told him about Charlotte waking up in the middle of the night crying about the big lizard stomping on all her dolls. He knew Gavin just wanted to be a fun uncle and give Charlotte whatever she wanted, but sometimes his brother forgot how impressionable young kids were.

"How did you survive hours of an inquisitive cartoon monkey?"

Gavin held up his cell. "Stone Blaster. Got the high score on the leader boards."

He chuckled, coming around to join his brother on the couch. Gavin turned off the TV, taking a sip from his soda.

"So. how'd the date go?" He glanced at the phone, still in his hand. "I mean, it's past midnight, so either you scored big time, or she kicked you to the curb after ten minutes and you've been sulking in your car for the past few hours to avoid the humiliation of defeat."

He glanced sideways at his brother. "Dating isn't a game, Gavin."

"Hell, yeah it is. It's a team sport, so you either win together or both lose. Although." He sat back with a meaningful gleam in his eyes. "Sometimes losing can be winning."

"It's late. I'm exhausted, and you are not making one ounce of sense."

"Ah ha!" One finger pointed at him while the rest still gripped the aluminum can. "You're exhausted. So it *did* go well."

A statement rather than a question, but a smile curved his lips as he lay back against the couch cushions. "It went better than well." Amazing, stupendous, life-altering would be a more appropriate description of the evening he'd just experienced.

"About damn time, man." Gavin slammed a hard hand down on his shoulder in congratulations. "Shit, I didn't think you'd ever get serious with another woman after Claire."

He didn't want to talk about Claire. He didn't even want to think about his ex-wife in relation to Ellie. They were two entirely different people. He'd loved Claire, or he thought he had, at one point in their lives. But that love had faded, died, snuffed out the moment his ex-wife decided she preferred the oblivion of drugs and booze to honest communication. Then she'd run before even giving him a chance to help her.

She didn't want help. That's why she left. She didn't want help. Or you. Or Charlotte.

And just like that, a dark cloud settled over his euphoric mood. He could forgive his former wife a lot of things, but one thing he could never understand was how she could abandon Charlotte. Up and leave without sending a single card, making one phone call, checking in on the baby she created with him. No. He would never forgive Claire for abandoning their daughter. And because of that, he'd been reluctant to start any relationship.

How could he guarantee another woman wouldn't leave and hurt his daughter when her own mother had done just that?

How could he guarantee he wouldn't fail again?

"We're not serious," he denied, an unpleasant taste coating his tongue as the words fell out of his mouth.

"Could've fooled me."

He glared at his brother. Sitting smugly on *his* couch drinking *his* soda, telling Sullivan he knew *his* life better.

"We're just…seeing how things go."

"Taking it one day at a time?"

"Yeah." Ellie knew the score. She agreed this wouldn't turn into anything long term.

Gavin snorted. "Famous last words before the mighty fall."

Dammit, he'd had one of the best nights in a long time and now his brother had gone and…dimmed the glow by bringing up his ex and relationships and shit. His post-orgasmic high had turned into a dull, pounding headache.

"Don't you have somewhere to be, jackass? Like your own home?"

Downing the rest of his drink, Gavin rose, stretching his

long limbs. "Yeah. I do. You're welcome, by the way, for watching Charlotte while you could get your freak on."

"There was no freakiness involved tonight." Just mind-blowing, body-melting, earth-shattering sex.

"Then you're doing it wrong." His brother shook his head, making his way to the front door.

"Thanks for tonight, Gavin." He appreciated the help his brother handed in raising Charlotte. Especially in the first few years of her life. Without Gavin, he didn't know if he would have made it through those difficult times.

His brother nodded, placing a firm hand on his shoulder. "Anytime. You know that. I love Charlotte and you're alright too, I guess."

Rolling his eyes, he embraced his little brother before shoving him out the door.

"Go get some sleep, jackass."

Giving a middle-fingered salute, Gavin got in his car and drove off. Once he'd closed and locked the door, Sullivan headed up the stairs to check in on Charlotte. Her bedroom door was cracked open, as she preferred. He glanced in, heart catching as the small shaft of light from the hallway fell across her angelic sleeping face. It hurt to look at her sometimes. He loved her with every ounce of his being. Even when she misbehaved or threw a tantrum—he wanted to put her in her room and down a tumbler of scotch in peace, but he still loved her.

She was his world from the moment she'd come screaming into it.

"Daddy?"

Her sleepy voice came from the dimly lit room.

"Yeah, Angel. It's me. I'm sorry. I didn't mean to wake you up."

He slipped into the room, coming to kneel at the side of her bed. One tiny fist rubbed at sleepy eyes. He noticed she was wearing her Wonder Woman pajamas. Uncle Gavin's influence, no doubt. His brother still loved superheroes and shared that love with his niece. Sullivan didn't mind. Wonder Woman was awesome.

"Did you have fun with Ellie?"

"How did you know I was with Ellie?" He hadn't told his daughter about his date—he'd chickened out, honestly and simply said he was going out.

"Uncle Gavin told me. He said you and Ellie went out on a date. Does that mean you kissed her?"

He was going to kill his brother.

"Yeah, I was with Ellie. We had a very nice night."

"Are you going to get married? Is she going to be my new mommy?"

Out of the frying pan and into the fire. First, his brother grilled him and now his daughter. Couldn't a guy just enjoy a nice evening with a lady friend anymore without it turning into wedding bells and happily-ever-afters?

"Whoa, slow down there, Angel. Ellie and Daddy are just friends." Not true. They were more than that. What exactly, he didn't know, but he knew one thing for sure. Charlotte came first.

"I like Ellie, Daddy."

"I do too."

He did like Ellie, a lot, but marriage was something never wanted again. He'd already failed one wife. What's saying he wouldn't do it again? He didn't want to put Charlotte through the pain of losing another mother.

He and Ellie were just having fun. They'd agreed. It wasn't more than that. It couldn't be.

"I'm tired again, Daddy," Charlotte sighed, snuggling El the elephant in close to her chest.

"Go to sleep, Angel."

He bent down, placing a soft kiss on her forehead as he

tucked the wayward covers around her. She was asleep again in moments. He quietly made his way out of her room and into his own. As he started his own bedtime preparations, his phone buzzed with an incoming text. Grabbing his cell, a smile tilted his lips as he read. The dark cloud that had settled over him lifting with each word.

Ellie: Tonight was wonderful. I can't remember the last time I had so much fun. Thank you.

He sat on the bed, reading the text over, allowing the warmth and happiness from earlier to soak back into him.

Sullivan: I should be the one thanking you. Tonight was incredible. You're incredible.

She signed off with a kissing winky face emoji. Sullivan stared at the phone, mind whirling with all the events of the night. He knew he was in dangerous territory, that things could go south quickly with all the obstacles in front of them, but right now, in this moment all he could do was look back over the night and take delight in every minute of the imperfect perfection.

CHAPTER 22

he harsh ring of the phone interrupted the lovely very naughty dream Ellie had been enjoying. The only thing to drag her out of her perfect slumber where she was currently licking her favorite ice cream—mint chocolate chip—off Sullivan's lean and deliciously sexy body was the knowledge that the person on the other end of the line would be Mr. Sexy Ice Cream Cone man himself.

With a smile on her lips, she slapped her hand on top of the nightstand until she encountered her cell. Without glancing at the caller, she brought the phone to her ear.

"Good morning, sexy."

"My gracious, no one has called me that since your father tried to butter me up when he wanted to buy the fifth wheel."

Horror washed over her like a bucket of polar ice melt. She jackknifed up in bed, pulling the covers up even though her mother was on the phone and not in the room. "Mom?"

"Well, of course. Who else were you expecting to call you so early on a Saturday morning?"

The man who'd given her multiple orgasms last night, who promised he'd call tomorrow.

Yeah, but he didn't promise to call at—she glanced at the clock, red lights blinking six-thirty in the morning. Ugh! He probably wasn't even up yet. *She* shouldn't even be up yet. Ellie should still be snuggled under the covers, licking the delicious dairy confection off dream Sullivan. Instead, she'd answered a call from *her mother* in the most embarrassing way possible.

"I, um…" She had no idea what to tell her mother. Anything but the truth, that was for sure. If her mother found out she'd gone out with Sullivan, the woman would have their entire wedding planned by noon. "What's up, mom?"

"What's up? I know avoidance when I hear it, Eleanor Clark, but for the moment I'll allow it because I have some important news."

Immediately, her mind filled with the worst news. The dark voice whispered every tragedy imaginable. Her father died. Her brother killed his ex and was now on the run. Her parents' house burned down and now her parents would have to come live in her tiny one-bedroom apartment with her.

Somehow, every single scenario could be traced back to her. She wasn't careful enough the last time she put the Christmas decorations away, and they all came crashing down on her father's head, cracking his skull. She hadn't been there enough for Oliver, and he'd come undone, flying into a murderous rage. The air freshener she'd bought when her mother asked her to pick one up from the store last dinner night had been a faulty brand and burst into flames, consuming everything in its path.

To anyone else, thoughts like this would be irrational. And they were, she knew that, but she couldn't stop them from filling her mind. Logically, she could tell herself it wasn't her, it was the OCD, the mix-up in her brain caused by her neurodivergence. She *knew* that, but logically knowing something didn't help it go away. Instead, she practiced the exercises Dr. Mitchell taught her. Addressing each fear and acknowledging it wasn't true, the dark voice lied. Her hand came up to tug her earlobe, the familiar sensation soothing her jagged nerves until she could open her mouth and speak without having a panic attack.

"What news?"

"Your brother is moving back home."

"Oliver's moving back in with you and dad?"

Her mother laughed. "Oh heavens no. But he is moving back to Sunlight."

Oh.

See, nothing horrible. In fact, having her brother move back from Denver sounded pretty great. Even though he had only been a forty-five-minute drive away since he married his now ex-wife, they hadn't seen each other much in the past few years. Honestly, she kind of missed the big lug.

"That's great!"

"It is. After the horrible mess with Janice and the condo, he's decided a change of scenery is in order, and your father and I agree."

From her mother's updates, she knew her brother had given the condo to his ex in the settlement. She could understand him not wanting to live there after he came in one evening and found her in their bed with her boss. She'd never been overly fond of Janice, but after that incident, she hated the woman simply for breaking her brother's heart. The guy might be a big, badass firefighter, but he was a cinnamon roll on the inside, all gooey and soft. Discovering his wife cheating on him had crushed her brother.

I should call him more often. I'm a terrible sister.

That wasn't entirely fair. Oliver had been incommunicado for the past three months. His crew was helping the

California fire department to help with the raging wildfires they'd been battling up north. He barely had time to call their mother for updates, let alone cry on his baby sister's shoulder about his broken marriage.

Not that he would cry. He was a sensitive guy, but she didn't think she'd even seen her brother cry.

"When's he moving back?"

"As soon as he gets released from duty in California."

A faint beep sounded, followed by the clinking of ceramic on a hard countertop. Based on her mother's morning habits, Ellie would say coffee would be poured into her mother's favorite mug in less than two seconds. The soft sound of liquid being poured confirmed her suspicions.

"He put in for a transfer to Sunlight fire department last month and the approval just came in last week. As soon as the situation out west is under control, he'll be moving back home."

"That's wonderful, mom." But did it really warrant a wake-up call before seven on a weekend?

"It is wonderful, and your father and I were hoping, since Oliver is so busy saving the west coast, if you could help keep an eye out for available apartments in town?"

Her mother was lying on the hero stuff a bit thick, but she got the drift. Oliver had nowhere to live and she'd bet the last fifty dollars in her checking account he would rather sleep in his car than move back in with their parents. They were great parents but tended to be a bit...overly involved in their children's lives.

"Sure, I can do that. In fact, I think one of my neighbors is moving out. I'll ask the super if her place has been rented yet."

Might be nice to have her brother so close by. It would certainly go a long way to soothing her guilt over being a crappy sister lately.

"Oh wonderful! Thank you, dear." Her mother's cheerful tone turned serious as she asked, "Now tell me about this morning caller you were expecting? The, how did you put it? Oh yes, *sexy* one."

Crap! She'd hoped her mother had forgotten about that. *Dream on.* Her mother had a mind like a steel trap. The woman never forgot *anything.*

"What? Oh, nobody really."

"Nobody?" her mother scoffed. "Do you mean to tell me you call everyone who rings your phone *sexy*? Even solicitors."

"Solicitors don't call. I put my number on the do not call list."

"Don't be smart with me, Eleanor."

She sighed, seeing no hope of hiding anything from her bloodhound of a mother. "I went on a date last night and he said he'd call, so I thought it would be…him."

"A date? With who? Where did you go? What does he do? How long have you been seeing each other?"

The rapid-fire questions exploded in her brain. If she was going to have this conversation with her mother—and it looked like there was no avoiding it—she needed her own mug of coffee. Throwing off the covers, she plodded her way to the kitchen.

"Sullivan Green. We went to dinner and the Spring Fling Faire. He's a doctor, and last night was our first date."

She answered each question as she scooped the dark, coarse coffee grounds into the machine, filled it with water, and pressed the start button. Within seconds, the rich fragrance of caffeinated heaven filled her little kitchen. She grabbed a mug from the cabinet and stared as the dark liquid filled the tiny carafe.

"Dr. Green? Isn't he the man of that young girl you—"

"Yes, mother. He's Charlotte's dad. She's kind of

191

taking a liking to me and invited me to her birthday party and, well, Sullivan and I hit it off and he asked me out."

"Oh darling, that's wonderful!"

It was pretty wonderful. She couldn't remember a time she'd felt this happy.

"Now just be sure you don't go spoiling things with your…issues."

There went all her warm and fuzzies. Leave it to her mother. She knew her mom didn't mean to intentionally hurt her, but comments like that…did. No matter the intent. Her *issues,* as her mother called them, weren't spoiling anything. Sullivan, amazingly enough, seemed fine navigating her anxieties and rituals. Could be because he was a doctor and understood mental health. Then again, he *was* a doctor, so how long would it be before he saw her as less of a woman he found desirable and more of a patient he needed to fix?

No. She couldn't let thoughts like those enter her brain. That was just the OCD talking…right? Dammit! Now her mother had gone and made her doubt. Doubt was never a good thing for Ellie. She lived with it constantly as her bedside companion, and now it seemed to find its way *inside* her bed.

Sonofabitch!

"Are you bringing him by for a family dinner soon? I'd love to meet him and his adorable daughter. What did you say her name was again?"

"Charlotte and I'm not sure. I'll have to ask what their schedule is." They were supposed to be keeping this thing fun and easy. Dinner with her parents sounded like the exact opposite of that.

"Oh yes, of course. Schedules are very important with children." Laughter filtered over the line. "I remember you used to pitch an absolute fit if we didn't make it home in time for you to get to bed."

No, she used to have panic attacks when she fell asleep in the car and woke up in her bed because she hadn't performed her door locking ritual and she feared the robbers would break in and kill her entire family because of it. She loved her mother, but she really wished the woman would educate herself on her daughter's condition instead of burying her head in the sand and pretending everything was fine. Everything was not fine, but that was okay. Things could be messy and scary as long as you stood up and faced them. Maybe her rituals seemed excessive, but they helped her cope and didn't hurt anyone. Why couldn't her mother just see that?

She learned how to manage her OCD over the years and —though she still had to remind herself to not listen to the dark voice daily—she was perfectly fine. Great, even when not talking to her mother.

"Let me know what Sullivan says, dear. I have to run. Your father will be up any moment, and he promised to take me to the nursery today to look at saplings for the backyard. Bye now!" Her mother said her goodbyes, with no thought as to the impact of her words on Ellie's psyche. Then again, Ellie didn't do a very good job of confronting her on it.

"Bye, mom."

"Email your brother apartment listings if your building doesn't end up having a spot."

"I will."

"Love you."

"I love you too."

She held the phone to her ear, waiting until her mother hung up. Once the dial tone clicked over, she set her phone on the counter. So much for her morning mood. The coffee beeped, indicating it had finished brewing. A few minutes too late, in her opinion. She could have used the stimulant boost about five minutes ago. As she poured a cup, her cell rang again. Not wanting to embarrass herself twice so early in the morning, she glanced at the ID before answering.

Oh sure, now he calls!

"Hello."

"Hi sexy."

She chuckled as Sullivan used the same greeting she had twenty minutes ago. At least he used it on the right person.

"Something funny?"

She snorted. "So many, many things."

Blowing on the steaming coffee before taking a small sip, she sighed when the rich and slightly bitter flavor hit her tongue. Normally she'd put a boatload of cream in it, but after that call with her mother, she needed the full octane stuff.

"Wow, barely seven in the morning and it sounds like you've already had quite the day."

"I just got off the phone with my mother, so you could say that."

Her mind reminded her that Sullivan's parents were both deceased. He'd shared the sad story last night over dinner. How he lost them to a random car accident and had to fight hard to take over guardianship of his brother. How selfish of her to complain about her mother when he would probably do anything for just one more day with his.

"Oh, Sullivan, I'm sorry I didn't mean—"

"Sweetheart, it's fine," he interrupted. "I remember how frustrating it can be talking to a meddling mother. I miss my parents, but that doesn't mean I forgot how tiring they could be. Parents can be a handful. Charlotte reminds me all the time with daily eye rolls. They're going to get stuck in the back of her head one of these days."

She laughed along with him.

"What did your mother want so early in the morning?"

"My brother is moving back to town, and she asked me to look for a place for him."

"He's a firefighter, right?"

She'd shared a little about her brother at dinner the other night when they were talking about their families.

"Yup, he's transferring to the station in Sunlight. It'll be nice to have him back home."

Sullivan laughed. "You say that now but wait until you come home and find out he's let himself in and eaten the last of your secret chocolate stash."

She giggled, knowing Sullivan was speaking from his own brotherly experiences. Oliver was miles away from Gavin personality wise, but she made a mental note to hide the gummy bears in her cabinet. They were her and her brother's favorite.

They talked for a few more minutes until the sound of Charlotte calling out for him came over the line.

"Your biggest fan is awake, and she'll be demanding pancakes and princess movies in less than two minutes."

And he'd come through on every one of those demands, she had no doubt. He was a good dad, a sucker, but a good dad. Even as he doted on Charlotte, his little girl was sweet-natured and loving.

"I better let you go then."

"Yeah, Wanna come over tomorrow for dinner? Around six?"

Dinner? At his place? Did that mean Charlotte knew they were…spending time together?

"Um, sure."

There was a slight pause before Sullivan asked, "That didn't sound very encouraging."

"No," she rushed to say. "It's not that I'm not excited to come over, it's just…Charlotte. Does she know…"

"Ah," Sullivan's deep voice carried over the line with

understanding. "She knows we're friends and…spending time together."

That sounded like an appropriate explanation for a kid. She guessed. Other than camp days at the zoo, she hadn't interacted with children much before Charlotte. Since Charlotte was Sullivan's kid, she deferred to him on what to tell the young girl about their relationship.

"Okay then, it sounds lovely. I'll be there."

"Great. And, Ellie?"

"Yes?"

She held her breath for what seemed like an eternity, but in actuality was probably only a few seconds.

"I had a great time last night." His voice deepened. "A really great time. And I can't wait for a repeat."

She pressed the phone to her ear, wishing she could melt through the line and press her lips against his like she'd done last night. "Me too."

"Bye, Ellie."

"Bye."

She held the cell to her ear, listening as Sullivan hung up, breathing in the rich aroma of the coffee still wafting from her mug, enjoying the warm sensation filling her heart as his words played over and over again in her mind.

I can't wait for a repeat.

Oh, there'd be a repeat and another and another and another. As many as he wanted because as far as Ellie was concerned, Sullivan Green was the most amazing man she'd ever met, and she was going to enjoy the time they had together. No matter how it all played out, she was going to do her best to silence the dark voice, because she deserved to have a little happiness in her life. And Sullivan? He made her happier than she ever thought possible.

CHAPTER 23

"*H*ot date?"

Surprised by the loud question in the previously silent room, Ellie almost dropped the fish bucket she'd been scrubbing in the large industrial sink at Cam's question. Her fingers gripped the edge at the last minute, saving the squeaky-clean metal container from crashing to the ground.

"Why would you think that?"

Her friend smiled. "I've never seen you perform your end of day duties so quickly before, so I figure there's a fire somewhere or you and Sullivan have something planned that involves zero clothes and an assortment of fun toys. Since I don't hear any sirens…"

"No." Heat rose on her face at the mention of *toys.* There'd be games tonight, but not the kind her friend pictured. "It's puzzle night."

"Sounds exciting."

It was. To her, at least. Two weeks had passed since she and Sullivan had officially started seeing each other. The best two weeks of her life. They'd only managed to squeeze in a few nights of alone time between their jobs and his duty as a father, but every moment she spent with Sullivan was wonderful. Charlotte had insisted Ellie come over every Sunday for dinner and Friday for puzzle night. Ellie was discovering she was as big a sucker as Sullivan. She couldn't say no to anything the sweet little girl asked of her.

"We're doing an elephant puzzle tonight."

Cam laughed. "Of course you are."

Charlotte seemed to grow more obsessed with the large animals every day.

"Why don't you head on out? I can finish up around here by myself."

"Oh no, I couldn't ask you to do that."

Her friend reached out, grabbing the wet bucket from her hands. "You're not asking, Ellie. I'm offering. Go. Have fun at puzzle night with your boyfriend and his daughter."

Boyfriend.

Such a strange word to use. It felt so juvenile. It didn't even come close to describing the way she felt about Sullivan, but what else was she supposed to call him? Lover? That sounded too much like those characters on one of her mother's soap operas. *Man she was dating* was too much of a mouthful. She supposed Cam had it right. Sullivan was her boyfriend, as silly as it sounded to her.

She had to admit, it evoked a sensation of butterflies fluttering about in her stomach every time she thought about it, like the first time she'd seen Taylor Lautner. The strange awareness low in her gut that conjured something inside she hadn't felt before. But Sullivan wasn't some schoolgirl Hollywood crush. Her feelings for him were stronger. Deeper.

"You're sure?" she asked again, desperate to leave, but not wanting to shirk her responsibilities simply because she was excited for puzzle night. Something she'd never, in a million years, thought she would find exciting.

"Yes. Now go while I'm still in a generous mood."

She snaked her arm around her friend's waist, giving her a side hug since their height disparity made front hugs a face full of Cam boobs for Ellie.

"You're always generous because you're an amazing friend, and I love you."

"Love you too, Doll-face. Now get."

"Yes, ma'am."

Without another word, she headed out the back of the aviary and to the employee parking lot. She'd need to stop at her place for a quick shower. Bill had aimed with amazing accuracy today during feeding time. Dang macaw landed a perfect poop streak down the front of her shirt. She'd cleaned it up, but working with animals always made a person smell. No matter how hard she tried to stay clean, the smells hung in the air, permeating clothing, hair, and skin.

Luckily, she had a special soap at home that washed all the stink away. She never minded it much. By now she was used to animal smells, but other people weren't as desensitized. And no one was as honest as an eight-year-old. Last Friday night she hadn't had the time to shower before heading over and sweet Charlotte asked Ellie why she smelled like sour milk. Sullivan had been embarrassed, but she just laughed. She had smelled like sour milk. The kid was just being honest. Ellie appreciated honesty.

Thanks to Cam, tonight she would be *sour milk* free.

After a quick shower and change of clothes, she grabbed the brownies she'd made last night and hopped back into her car. Thankfully, there was no traffic on the way to Sullivan's and she parked by his house just as his fancy electric car pulled into the driveway.

"Ellie! Ellie!" Charlotte came bursting out of the car, waving her arms wildly in the air as if Ellie wasn't five feet away.

"Hey, sweetie."

She grabbed the brownies from the passenger seat, locking her car and checking the handle three times before bending down to open her arms for the launching hug she knew she was about to receive.

"Oof!" She stumbled a bit on the tips of her toes, staying upright in her squat as Charlotte's arm flew around her neck.

"Charlotte!" Sullivan sighed as he shut the car door his daughter had left open in her excitement. "Can you let Ellie get into the house before you overwhelm her with your enthusiasm?"

"It's fine," she laughed, rising to her feet, and juggling the little girl on one hip and the chocolate dish in her other hand.

Sullivan shook his head with a smile. "You get off early?"

"Yeah. Cam practically pushed me out the door when she heard it was puzzle night."

"I think I'm a fan of your friend."

"Me too."

He held up the plastic sack in his hands from Charlotte's favorite restaurant. The one they'd run into each other at a month ago. The familiar writing on it letting her know what was inside even before the delicious aroma of herbs and sauce hit her nose.

"I brought dinner."

"I brought dessert." She lifted the pan.

"Yay!" Charlotte squealed. "Spaghetti and meatballs. And brownies. My favorite!"

Sullivan chuckled at his daughter, motioning for Ellie to lead the way inside. They set up dinner on the kitchen table, going around and discussing their respective days. Charlotte was doing better with her bully problems. Since the incident at the penguin pool, she'd become a bit of a school celebrity, as she told it. Her class had a section on animals and apparently the kids had taken to asking Charlotte questions since she seemed to have firsthand knowledge of all animals with her one experience.

"We're learning about piemates this week and Sarah said if we go see them at the zoo no one could fall in 'cause there's glass all around."

Sullivan paused with a fork full of spaghetti Bolognese halfway to his mouth. "Piemates?"

Ellie chuckled. "I think she means *primates*. Right, Charlotte?"

"Oh, yeah. Primates. You know, Daddy. Monkeys."

"Not just monkeys, but apes and lemurs. Even humans are classified as primates."

Green eyes grew impossibly wide. "So, Uncle Gavin is right? I am a monkey?"

Sullivan let out a heavy sigh. "That ridiculous nickname. I am going to strangle my brother."

She held in her laughter at the exasperatingly muttered words leaving Sullivan's clenched jaw.

"You're not a monkey, sweetie." She assured Charlotte, patting the child's hand. "We're just all classified in the same order."

"What's order?"

Oh boy. How did she explain this without getting too technical? She didn't want to bore an eight-year-old, but she believed in relaying proper information. How the heck did teachers do this? They were completely underpaid, in her opinion.

"Well, order is a term scientists use to classify living things that have things in common." At Charlotte's confused expression, she tried again. "Okay, so you know how humans have hands and feet. We have hair and babies, not eggs, so that makes us mammals. Well, monkeys have that too, so they're also mammals and they look a lot like us."

"Soooo we're family?"

"In a way, yes."

"Cool." She grinned, mouth covered in red sauce from her dinner. "I can't wait to tell everyone."

Ah, so that's why Charlotte had become the go-to for animal questions. She'd been relaying Ellie's animal knowledge. At least someone was getting good use out of it. Whenever she talked about animal facts around other people—her family, former dates—their eyes glazed over, and they lost all interest. Who knew all this time all she had to do was impart her education to an elementary student?

"Everyone thinks it's super cool I know the Zooperhero."

"The what now?"

Sullivan grinned, taking a bite of his dinner. Had he heard this term before? She didn't quite know what to make of it.

"Zooperhero. It's what the kids at school call you because you saved my life and you're a zookeeper, so that makes you a superhero. Zooperhero."

Moisture gathered in her eyes, making it impossible for her to see. She blinked back the tears. She didn't want Charlotte to think she was crying out of sadness.

No one had ever thought she could do much of anything. All her life, people had discounted her and her abilities. Even her own family had seen her OCD as a stumbling block in life. Asking her to hide it away or ignore it as if that would solve anything. No one had ever considered her anything close to a hero. Not until one little girl fell into the penguin pool and into her heart.

She glanced over to see Sullivan staring at her, a warm, understanding expression on his face.

"Zooperhero Ellie. You should get that on a T-shirt. It suits you."

Oh damn, now there was no holding back the tears. Having the adoration of a little girl was one thing, but to have a wonderful, sexy, smart, successful man she adored think she was some kind of wonder being? It was almost too much.

"Ellie, are you okay?"

Oh shoot, Charlotte had seen the tears. Sniffing, she wiped her cheeks clean with the back of her hand. "I'm fine, sweetie."

"Did you bite your tongue? Sometimes I eat too fast, and I bite my tongue. It really hurts."

"No, I just had something in my eye."

"You should have Daddy look at it. He's a doctor. It's his job."

She couldn't stop the smile at the child's endearing words. "I'm fine now but thank you."

They finished up dinner and took dessert into the living room, where they would put the puzzle together. The two-hundred-jigsaw pieces that created a beautiful picture titled *Elephant Water Fun* had been a birthday gift from Gavin. She assumed it would be difficult for a child of Charlotte's age, but as she discovered last week, Charlotte had a very advanced skill with puzzles.

The three gathered on the floor around the solid oak coffee table, spreading out the pieces and searching for the corners and sides. Sullivan had placed the box top at the end of the table so they could all see what the picture was supposed to look like.

"I like this," Charlotte stated as she sifted through the mass of jagged pieces, carefully inspecting each one she picked up.

"Me too."

"They're cool because it looks all wonky, but then the pieces all go together and make a picture. I like it better than coloring. Coloring you already see the picture. That's boring."

She'd never thought of it that way, but the kid had a point. There was a bit of a thrill when putting together a puzzle. Even if you knew what the final picture would look like, the moment you dumped the pieces out of the box, it just looked like chaos. But in that chaos and all those seemingly broken pieces was a perfect picture, just waiting to be put together.

A hush fell over the room as they all concentrated on the project in front of them. She was so focused that when Sullivan's phone pinged with a text message, she jumped in surprise. Glancing up, she saw him pull out his cell and frown.

"Excuse me, I need to make a call."

Charlotte barely paid attention to her father. One hand gently picking up puzzle pieces and placing them in their appropriate piles, the other—not so gently—shoving huge chunks of brownie in her mouth.

After a few minutes without Sullivan's return, Ellie got a sinking feeling in the pit of her gut. Putting on her biggest smile, she tapped Charlotte on the shoulder.

"You want some milk to go with that brownie?"

"Yes, please."

The child didn't even look up from her sorting. She really took her puzzles seriously. Shaking her head with humor, Ellie rose from the ground and headed into the kitchen after Sullivan and the promised milk. She found him with his head down, hands braced against the sink.

"Hey." Not knowing what was wrong, but sensing his distress, she came up behind him, wrapping her arms around his waist in a comforting hug. "You okay?"

His large hand came up to pat the hands she had secured around his waist.

"Yeah. That was the on-call doctor at my practice. One of my patients took a turn for the worse recently. She has asthma, but it's been getting worse. I did a scan a few weeks back, and we found some tumors. I was hoping they were benign, but it turned out to be lung cancer."

"Oh, that's horrible." Ellie's great aunt died from breast cancer. It was a horrible disease. In any form it took.

Sullivan sighed. "She was going to start chemo, but I just received a call that she decided to forgo treatment."

Why would anyone do that? Ellie didn't have the easiest life, but she couldn't imagine not fighting for it tooth and nail if she had even the slimmest possibility of survival.

"Her husband was a lifelong smoker. Lost the battle to lung cancer a few years back. I guess she decided not to go through what he did. She's eighty-eight. I suppose she feels it's her time."

How horrible. To make such a tough choice couldn't have been easy for the woman. And poor Sullivan. It was his job, no *his purpose*, to save people. Logically, he couldn't save everyone. She knew he tried his hardest to make sure all the people who came to him for help received it. It must kill him to think he failed this patient. But he hadn't failed her. The woman made a choice. Was it the right one? Who knew? It was her life and only she could say, but Ellie could feel how much this decision pained Sullivan.

"You did all you could to help her," she whispered against his back, placing a soft kiss between his shoulder blades, trying as hard as she could to infuse comfort into the man she held. The man she knew was hurting.

"I know. And it's Mrs.—it's her choice to decline treatment. Unfortunately, it would only give her a few more years at most and there'd be pain and suffering with the treatment so I can understand her decision, but…"

"You can't beat death, Sullivan."

"I can damn well try."

His voice cracked, breaking her heart. This man, this

wonderful, loving man, cared so much about everyone around him. She held tight, knowing that as much as he cared about the people surrounding him, she cared for him more. Damn it all, she was seriously afraid if she looked deep inside, she'd have to admit she loved him. And how could she not? Sullivan was kind and smart, a wonderful father and brother, handsome as anything and a verified sex god in the bedroom. But best of all? He accepted her as she was. How could she not love a man like that?

"Do you need anything? Can I help?"

She had no idea what to do to make him feel better, but if there was anything, anything at all, she'd gladly do it.

He turned in her arms, his hands coming up to cup her face. Bright green eyes, filled with pain and longing, stared at her. His thumb brushed against her lower lip, and she placed a soft kiss on the digit.

"Can you stay? Tonight, after Charlotte goes to bed?"

He was asking her to stay over? They'd never spent an entire night together. She wanted to, badly, but she'd always been conscious of his daughter and the responsibility that lay within the dynamic of a single father. She never wanted to push any boundaries. But here he was, asking her to stay, needing her. How could she deny him? Simple answer. She couldn't.

"Yes. Of course, I'll stay."

His face broke into a beautiful smile, cheek dent and all. It made her heart soar to see the look of devastation replaced with one of joy. She'd done that. She put the happiness there, and that made her feel ten feet tall.

Still cupping her face, he dipped his head, covering her mouth with his lips in a searing, bone-melting kiss that had her forgetting everything, including her own name as he plundered her mouth like a pirate seeking buried treasure.

"Ellie! I'm thirsty."

They broke apart with a laugh.

"Your daughter has some timing."

"She does, at that."

Smiling up at him, she placed a hand over his on her cheek. "Are you okay?"

His grin faded but didn't disappear entirely. "I will be. Holding you tonight will help."

Yup. She loved him. Dammit. When had that happened? And what the hell was she going to do about it? He didn't want anything long term. They'd both agreed. What was she going to do? For now, she had a glass of milk to get. Then she would finish a puzzle and comfort the man she'd fallen for. Everything else could wait until later.

CHAPTER 24

Sullivan watched Ellie walk back to the living room with a glass of cold milk in her hand for his daughter. The dark cloud that settled over him the minute he got the message from Dr. Brinks had broken with a simple touch. Ellie's touch. Her compassion broke through the failure filling him at being unable to save Mrs. Wilkins. Like the sun shining through the gloom of a stormy day.

How had this woman come to understand him so well in such a short time? How did she know what he needed and give it so freely? And when was the last time Sullivan let himself lean on another person? He couldn't even remember. Ever since his parents had died, he'd had to be the strong one, the one in charge. First, he'd needed to look after Gavin and make sure his brother finished school, then he'd taken care of Claire and later Charlotte. He'd been taking care of the people he loved for a long time.

But who takes care of me?

Ridiculous. He was a grown ass man. He didn't need looking after. But he had to admit, seeing the care and worry in Ellie's soft brown gaze glancing over him…damn, it hit a part of him he thought long buried.

Making his way back into the living room, he saw Ellie and Charlotte crouched over the coffee table, completely engrossed in the puzzle they were putting together. His heart clenched, and he rubbed at the unfamiliar pain. It hurt to look at the two of them, sitting together, smiling. But a good kind of hurt. The kind that let you know you had something special and if it was ever taken away, your life would never be the same. A thankful and cautionary warning to appreciate the moment and the people in it.

Sullivan hadn't been very good at appreciating things lately. He'd been too worried about making sure everything was going right, everyone was taken care of. But, as evidenced by Mrs. Wilkins's recent downturn, life rarely went smoothly no matter how hard one tried to keep it all together. Sometimes things broke, fell apart.

Like the elephant puzzle his daughter and girlfriend were currently giggling over as Charlotte tried to fit a piece into the wrong spot. The potential of something whole and beautiful was there, but you had to find the right pieces and place them in their proper spot. Fit the jagged and hollow edges together just so. It was the only way to make the picture complete. He gazed down at the two. One who'd been the center of his world since the moment he laid eyes on her and the other who he'd only recently come to know, but in that time had wrapped herself so tightly into his life he couldn't imagine it without her.

"Daddy, come help," Charlotte demanded, breaking him out of his profound musings.

"I'm coming, Angel."

He sat. Ellie's hand immediately came out to squeeze his in a reassuring gesture. Lifting their joined hands, he placed a firm kiss against the back of her knuckles, hoping she felt how much he appreciated and cared for her. And if she didn't, he planned on showing her later that night.

They sat on the living room floor eating brownies and putting together the puzzle, staying up an hour past Charlotte's bedtime to finish it. Normally Sullivan was very strict about his daughter's routine, but since tomorrow was Saturday and there was no school or work, he could be flexible.

"Are you going to tuck me in tonight, Ellie?" Charlotte asked as they cleaned up the empty brownie plates and milk glasses.

"Of course, sweetie."

"Yay!"

The past few nights Ellie had been over, she'd always stayed to tuck his daughter in at the girl's request. Tonight, Ellie would stay much later. At his request. Some people might frown on a single father asking the woman he was dating to stay over in the same house as his young, impressionable daughter. Those people could take their opinions and shove them. Ellie was an amazing role model for his daughter. He hoped she made an impression on Charlotte. And as for the reason for the sleepover? It wasn't like he would explain that to his eight-year-old.

Placing the dirty dishes in the kitchen sink, they all headed up the stairs, with Charlotte racing ahead. He wished his daughter would be this eager when he told her it was time for bed. Nope, the youthful enthusiasm was reserved for Ellie tuck-ins. He chuckled to himself, wondering how long it would last. How many nights of Ellie tucking her in before Charlotte saw it as old hat and started asking for drinks of water to delay the inevitable. A month? A year? Forever?

The word hit him like a punch to the gut.

Forever with Ellie.

He'd be lying if he said the idea hadn't popped into his mind once or twice. But always fleeting, like the dream of winning the lottery. Nice to imagine, but no one ever actually thought it would happen. That's how he viewed getting into another long term relationship. Another marriage. He couldn't risk it.

Then why have I been waxing on about Ellie all night long in my brain and thinking of permanence?

He had, hadn't he?

No. We agree to keep this thing light and fun.

If he were being honest with himself, it was fun, but it stopped being light long ago. He was in this deep. He hadn't meant for that to happen, but it did.

"Sullivan?"

He glanced up to see Ellie standing at the top of the stairs staring down at him, a worried expression on her face. When had he stopped moving? Man, he really needed to get his shit together. The impending death of a patient was always difficult for a physician, but coupled with tonight's realization of just how deep his feelings for Ellie were getting had really set him off kilter.

"I'm fine," he responded, forcing his feet to move. When he reached the landing, he cupped her cheek, placing a soft reassuring kiss to her frowning lips. "I promise. I'm okay."

"Daddy! I can't find my toothbrush."

Chuckling, he dropped his hand from Ellie's face, grasping her hand instead and linking their fingers together.

"Come on. We better go help her before she destroys the entire bathroom looking for the light up toothbrush that's where it always is. The mirror cabinet."

They helped Charlotte brush her teeth and hair. Or more accurately, Ellie did at his daughter's insistence. He stood back and watched, trying not to feel put out by being shoved over for the nightly routine. There was comfort to be had in watching his young daughter preen over the attention of Ellie. She'd had almost zero female influence in her young life. Ellie provided something to Charlotte that Sullivan never could, no matter how hard he tried.

Ellie had once been an eight-year-old girl.

After teeth, hair, and pajamas were taken care of, he read a bedtime story. About elephants, naturally. Then Ellie tucked Charlotte in, giving his daughter a kiss on her forehead.

"Goodnight, Charlotte."

"Night, Ellie. Thanks for playing puzzle with me tonight."

"My pleasure, sweetie."

"Night, Daddy."

"Night, Angel."

He leaned over for a hug and cheek kiss, returning it with an extra raspberry blow he knew would make his daughter giggle. He loved that giggle. It lit up his entire world. Rising from the bed, he took Ellie's hand once again and headed for the door. As he flicked off the light switch, Charlotte's soft voice rose from the dimly lit room.

"I love you, Daddy."

"Love you too."

"I love you, Ellie."

At the sharp intake of breath, he turned his head. The soft glow of Charlotte's star projector nightlight cast enough light in the room for him to see Ellie's eyes well up with tears. Her mouth dropped open, and it took her a moment to get any words out. When she did, they were filled with awe.

"I-I love you too, Charlotte."

Wonderful. Now two out of the three people in this house were an emotional mess. Good thing he hadn't denied Charlotte that second brownie or they'd be three for three.

"Now I feel the need to ask if you're okay," he said once they made their way into his bedroom and closed the door.

Ellie stared at him, dark eyes wide and watery. "I just I don't have a lot of people in my life who...she's...she's a great kid, Sullivan. Wonderful. You should be proud."

"I am. And she has excellent taste in people."

A blush rose on her cheeks. His heart skipped a beat at her beauty. Not simply her looks, but her inner beauty. She loved his daughter. It was clear on every interaction she spent with Charlotte. Here was a woman who had no cause to form a friendship with an eight-year-old girl, no reason to come over on Friday nights and do puzzles when she could be out at the bar with friends or whatever single young people did. Ellie didn't have to be nice to Charlotte just because she was seeing Sullivan. She did it because she truly cared for his daughter.

Dammit, if he wasn't careful, he was in serious danger of falling in love with this woman.

"Come here, Ellie."

He held out his hand, needing to get out of his head and into safer territory. Physical territory.

"You want to go to sleep?" she asked, a knowing twinkle in her eye.

"No, but I would like to take you to bed and memorize every single inch of you." Pulling her into his embrace, he lowered his lips to the shell of her ear, feeling her tremble in his arms as he whispered, "With my tongue."

"Yes, please." The words left her on a deep moan as her lips kissed the underside of his jaw.

Desire shot through him at the contact, a lightning bolt of passion that went right from his jaw to his groin. He immediately stiffened, cock going hard, pressing against his slacks insistently. Demanding to be satisfied. But no. Tonight wasn't about simply getting off. Tonight, he wanted to show Ellie how much he cared for her, how much it meant to him that she cared for him, his daughter. She had become an important part of their lives, and he wanted to let her know how much he appreciated that.

What better way to show her than to drive her out of her mind with pleasure?

He grinned, grabbing the hem of her T-shirt. Today's shirt was a duck laughing with the phrase *You Quack Me Up* on it. Damn, but he loved her sense of humor. Pulling the shirt up and over her head, he dipped his head down to take her lips. She opened for him eagerly, her hands tunneling into his hair, tilting his head so she had a better angle. He obliged, always happy to agree to any of this woman's requests.

They stumbled to the bed, kissing, touching, driving each other crazy. Had he ever craved a woman as much as Ellie? He didn't think so. He'd certainly never wanted one this badly after having her. For Sullivan, after a few times between the sheets, the passion died down. Even with his ex, the sex got stale quickly. But not Ellie. Each time they came together, he found it only increased his appetite for her. Every touch, every kiss ramped up his need to have her again, please her again.

When his hands came down to the button of her jeans, she suddenly pulled away.

"What?" The word panted out of him as Ellie had stolen all his breath. "What is it?"

"I didn't think…"

Her right hand came up to tug her ear. The motion causing a rock to sink in his gut.

"Ellie, whatever it is, it's okay. We can stop. We don't have to do anything you're uncomfortable with. You know that, right?"

Was it the location? Sex between them had always occurred at her place. Did having his daughter in the house make her nervous? He'd locked the bedroom door. Charlotte couldn't barge in. Perhaps it was simply the idea of making love with a small child just down the hall. He knew some people stayed away from single parents for that reason alone. Whatever it was, she could tell him. He wouldn't be angry. In pain, sure, but blue balls he could handle. Having Ellie upset and uncomfortable, that was unacceptable.

"I know, and I'm not uncomfortable. It's just…"

"What?" Not wanting to upset her more, but needing to reassure her, he stepped forward, cupping her face in his palms. "What's wrong?"

She frowned. "They don't match."

"What?"

"They don't match."

She'd lost him. "What doesn't match, sweetheart?" And why would something not matching be a problem?

Sighing, she glanced down at her feet and mumbled, "My underwear doesn't match my bra."

It took a moment for the words to register. When they did, a weight lifted off his chest and he couldn't stop the laughter that escaped him.

"That's why you stopped? Because you're not wearing matching underwear?"

She scowled, but the grim look had no effect. He was just so damn happy he hadn't done anything wrong. What a silly thing to be self-conscious about. He supposed women in undergarment ads always had matching sets, but real life was not an ad.

"I've always known when we were going to…ya know." She waved a hand toward the bed. "I had time to prepare and look sexy."

"Oh honey," he grabbed her hips, pulling her to him so she could see the effect she had on him. "You're sexy as hell. Matching underwear, non-matching underwear." He arched one eyebrow. "No underwear."

A ghost of a smile ticked up the corner of her lips, gradually growing until she threw her head back with an exasperated snort. "You mean to tell me I could have saved all that lingerie money and just worn my granny panties and still gotten you in bed?"

"As long as they're not your actual Grandma's panties, you could wear anything, and I'd still want you day and night." Hell, he'd even want her in hand-me-down underwear.

"Well then." Her hands went to her jeans, flicking the button open and pulling down the zipper. "It's a good thing the only thing I got from my grandma was her pearl earrings."

He grinned, pushing her hands away so he could tug the jeans down her legs. He followed them down, kneeling before her like a supplicant before a goddess.

Blue.

Blue panties and a white bra. They matched in a way. Didn't matter. It wasn't the clothing that had him awestruck. It was the woman who wore it. This generous, caring, loving, treasure of a person he'd been lucky enough to have come into his life. He promised her a thorough inspection of her body and he planned to follow through, starting with one of his favorite spots.

Ellie cried out as his tongue came out to tenderly touch the center of her. He chuckled as she shoved her fist against her mouth to muffle the cries, knowing the vibrations would only set her off more. She didn't need to worry about waking Charlotte. That girl could sleep through a hurricane once she was out. The hand not covering her mouth slammed down on his shoulder for stability. He kept up his ministrations, adding his fingers into the mix. It didn't take long before she was crying out with release.

Sullivan gently lowered Ellie to the bed, following her down, still fully clothed.

"This is going to be a lot harder if you keep your clothes on."

"Trust me, if I take my clothes off now, I'll be inside you in seconds and then things will most definitely *not* be harder."

She clutched at his shirt. "I like the sound of that."

Smiling, he gently lifted her hands away, setting them above her head on the pillow. "No. I promised you a very accurate and *detailed* map. And I'm a man of my word."

"So you weren't *lion* earlier?"

"Nope. I do what I say I will. I'm no *cheetah*."

Ellie groaned. "I can't believe we just used animal puns during foreplay."

"You started it, but I'll admit it is a bit *hawkward*."

She laughed, causing her breasts to thrust into his face. "Stop, stop. I—"

She gasped as his tongue swirled around one nipple and then the other.

"No, don't stop. Keep doing that. Yes, right there."

He listened to her commands, following through on his promise to map her body. By the time he finished, she was a quaking mass of need. Only fair. If Sullivan didn't get inside of her in the next five seconds, he might die of unsated lust. Quickly shucking his clothes, he grabbed a condom from the bedside table drawer and protected them both. Settling himself between her legs, he placed the blunt head of his cock at her entrance.

"Sullivan."

His name on her lips made him pause. Gazing up into deep, chocolate brown eyes, he felt himself fall just a little more. *Shit.*

"I just want you to know you make me feel..."

She didn't finish her statement. He saw a flash of panic in her eyes, but before he could ask, she'd pulled him down for a searing kiss. Over talking apparently, he felt the firm grip of her fingers on his backside. Again, willing to do whatever she asked, he pushed forward, plunging inside the heaven that was Ellie Clark.

She moaned in ecstasy, wrapping her legs around him, her heels digging into his ass as she met his fevered thrusts. It didn't take long for him. Touching her had primed him better than any foreplay he'd ever experienced before. He cursed himself for not holding back, not waiting for Ellie, but he couldn't stop the orgasm rushing over him. Reaching a hand between their bodies, he found her clit and rubbed with the slow firm pressure he'd discovered dove her wild. His mouth covered hers, swallowing her cries of completion with a long, deep kiss.

Exhaustion swept over him. He collapsed, rolling to his side to tuck Ellie into his arms.

"You're staying, right?" He knew he was in too deep with this woman, but right now, tonight, he needed her.

"Of course." She snuggled closer. "But we should really clean up before bed."

Right. The mundane afterward parts of sex they didn't show in the movies. Showers, bathroom trips, all the tiny annoyances of real life. He wished life was more like a movie and he could pause this moment forever. Just stay here with Ellie in his arms.

"Come on, before you fall asleep on me." She rose, tugging his arm.

He followed, realizing with a small bit of apprehension that he'd likely follow this woman anywhere. Once they'd cleaned up, he got Ellie one of his old shirts to wear to bed. They resumed their positions, her in his arms, snuggling up to his chest so perfectly it was like she'd been made to fit him. Two perfect puzzle pieces.

"Goodnight, Ellie."

"Goodnight, Sullivan."

As she drifted off to sleep, he heard the faintest whispered confession.

"You make me feel safe to be myself."

CHAPTER 25

ormally Ellie would never be so presumptuous as to sneak into someone's kitchen and use their coffee maker without their knowledge. But she desperately needed a cup this morning and Sullivan had looked so peaceful sleeping. She hadn't had the heart to wake him. Again. She might have woken the man once—okay, twice—in the middle of the night to repay the very thorough mapping of her body with one of her own.

He hadn't seemed to mind. In fact, he'd been very accommodating when she ordered him to grasp the headboard with his hands and let her have her way with him. Sweet Sullivan, always the gentleman.

Since she'd been to the house often in the past few weeks, she knew where the coffee beans were. As quietly as possible, Ellie spooned out enough grounds for a four-cup pot—she might be overreaching, but she wouldn't make a pot and not leave some for Sullivan—and filled the water receptacle. Now all she had to do was wait for the wake-up juice to brew.

"Did you stay the night?"

The innocent question in the soft, child-like voice made her jump about a foot. Turning around, Ellie grimaced when she spotted Charlotte, still in her jammies, hugging El to her chest.

"Oh, um, hi, Charlotte. I…ah…" What the hell did she do now? Caught in the act—well, not the actual act, thankfully—but caught after the fact by an eight-year-old. What did she say? "I, ah…"

"Charlotte."

The deep, masculine, sleep addled voice saved her from any pathetic excuse for a confession.

"Go get dressed for pancakes," Sullivan said with a smile, coming into the kitchen.

"Yay! Pancake day!"

The little girl squealed with glee and turned to race out of the kitchen, her heavy footsteps pounding up the stairs.

"I'm sorry," Ellie confessed once Charlotte disappeared. "I thought I could be gone before she got up."

Sullivan came to her side, wrapping his arms around her. His lips pressed gently against her temple. Despite exhausting themselves in bed the previous night, Ellie found her body still craved the man. Her nipples tightened and heat gathered between her legs.

Down body. Now is not the time.

"Don't worry about it. Gavin sleeps over all the time. She doesn't know you slept in my bed."

Right, because they were just having fun. It wasn't going to turn into something serious. A chill gripped her chest. She was afraid it was too late. Sullivan might still be under the assumption they were friends, casually dating and having a good time, but she feared her fallen heart didn't get the memo. This would only end in tears for her, she was sure of it. All she could do was hope that end came later rather than sooner.

"And you think she's okay with it? Me staying over?"

"She loves you, Ellie." He turned her in his arms, staring down at her with those brilliant green eyes. "Have to say, I'm pretty fond of you myself."

Fond didn't even begin to describe what she felt for Sullivan. If she were being brave, she'd admit that she'd fallen head over heels in love with the man. But bravery had never been big in Ellie's life. That was more her best friend's thing. Cam was outgoing and willing to lay everything out there. Ellie had trouble with even simple human interaction, let alone busting her heart open and revealing all her imitate feelings for someone to stomp all over.

Not that she'd believe Sullivan would do something so cruel, but he said he would never marry again. Did that also take love off the table?

Love? Ha! Her dark voice scoffed at her. *Why would she even think he could love her?*

She knew dealing with her…rituals and habits could grate on a person. She'd been told so, repeatedly. How long before Sullivan tired of them? Found her annoying? What if she confessed her love only to have it thrown back in her face when he couldn't handle her being…her?

"Hey."

His soft voice interrupted the dark thoughts swirling around in her brain. Whispering that this thing between them would be over before it could really get started.

"What happened? Where'd you go just now?"

"Huh?"

Placing a finger on the end of her chin, he tipped her face up until she couldn't look anywhere but into those brilliant, blindingly green eyes. Eyes filled with concern and, dare she say, caring?

"You were worried a moment ago about Charlotte, but then you went somewhere…dark."

He had that right.

"Um, sometimes I…"

Could she do this? Could she explain to Sullivan what went on in her mind? They'd talked a bit about her rituals, compulsions, her anxiety, but they hadn't discussed what caused them. Her dark thoughts. The insidious whispers in her mind. The obsessions that caused her compulsions.

He would understand, right? The man was a doctor, after all. She assumed he knew all about mental health and neuro-diversity. But would he understand in a non-clinical way? A relationship way?

"Ellie, you can tell me anything. You know that, right? It won't change the way I feel about you."

How did he feel about her?

Too afraid to ask that question, she tried to be brave like Cam.

"It's just that sometimes my brain goes to…dark places. Like a little voice inside my head whispering all the bad things that could happen and how, if they happen, it will be all my fault."

His eye lit with understanding. "You're talking about your OCD?"

She nodded, relieved he could understand that much, at least. "Yes. It's not about being clean or anal like the TV and movies depict. It's not quirky or fun. It's terrifying and even though I have a better handle on it than I used to, sometimes I can't stop myself from going to the dark places."

He pulled her into his arms, pressing her head against his chest. The beat of his heart was steady and strong, calming her nerves, soothing away the fear. But what really burst through the darkness were the words he spoke next.

"I practice internal medicine, not psychiatry, so I don't know in-depth what you have to deal with, but I do know you are the strongest, bravest, most astounding person I have ever met."

"You think I'm brave?" Her words were muffled against his chest, and she clung to him, reveling in the praise he gave.

His hand grasped the back of her neck, tipping her head back so he could stare into her eyes. "You fight a battle every day against an invisible force living inside you. Damn right I think you're brave."

Then his lips came crashing down on hers. This kiss was heated, passionate, but there was something else there. Reverence. Sullivan spoke only the truth. No placating or pity. He didn't tell her what she wanted to hear because he thought it would make things better. He believed the words, believed in her. This man not only understood her, but he admired her.

Now she had to admit she loved him. But only to herself. She wasn't brave enough yet to risk speaking the words out loud. Maybe someday, but not right now.

"Daddy and Ellie sitting in a tree. K-I-S-S-I-N-G."

They broke apart. Turning to face a smiling Charlotte, skipping into the kitchen. Ellie felt flames dance along her cheeks, and not from the scorching kiss Sullivan had just planted on her. For his part, Sullivan looked less embarrassed, but he did take a step away from her. It stung, but she tried not to let it show. She knew he didn't want to be too affectionate in front of Charlotte. No need to give the child any ideas about the future. Ellie was fighting enough of those, as it was.

CHAPTER 26

"Charlotte, would you like to help me make the pancakes?"

"Yes! Can Ellie help too?"

She wasn't a chef by any means, but Ellie supposed she could follow instructions. "Sure, what do I do?"

They spent the next twenty minutes making a massive pile of pancakes and an absolute disaster in the kitchen. By the time they all sat down to eat there was flour scattered about the countertops and floor. Drops of spilled batter and dirty dishes piled in the sink, and a slight stench of burning filled the air thanks to the Greens' deciding she should be in charge of pancake flipping. After the first three burnt pancakes, Sullivan had switched her to batter pourer. Which was why they currently sat eating inkblot-cakes.

How did someone mess up pouring batter into a circle? She didn't know, but somehow, she'd managed. Luckily, everything tasted delicious.

"Now that you and Daddy are special friends, does that mean I can come to the zoo whenever I want?"

Ellie choked on the bite of fluffy, cooked dough she'd just put in her mouth. Sullivan passed her a glass of milk with a small smile.

"No, Angel. You can't go to the zoo every day just because Ellie works there."

The big smile fell, green eyes filling with tears. Something sharp struck Ellie in the chest at the sight of that sweet little smile disappearing. When Charlotte's tiny bottom lip poked out, the words rushed out of her without thought.

"You can come today if you'd like. I have the day off so I can show you around to some of the places normal visitors don't get to go."

The young girl's face lit up again. "Really?"

"Of course, if it's okay with your daddy." She thought to add the second part, remembering she wasn't Charlotte's parent.

"Oh please, please, please, Daddy?"

Sullivan glanced from his daughter—holding her hands together like a prayer, big green puppy dog eyes to her father —to Ellie.

"I don't see why not."

"Yay!"

Leaning in close, his words were soft. "You are such a sucker."

She scowled, but then noticed not a single tear had fallen from Charlotte's eyes. The lip thing had been exaggerated too now that she thought about it. That little sneak. Smothering a grin, she whispered back, "Maybe, but you said yes, so that makes you as big a sucker as me."

"Touché."

A humorous sparkle lit his eyes. When his hand reached out to grab hers, she didn't even think. She just fused her fingers with his, like it was the most natural thing in the world. Sitting here, with Sullivan and Charlotte enjoying a Saturday morning pancake breakfast. Why did it feel so…right?

"Knock, knock. Anybody home?"

Sullivan rolled his eyes, grimacing at his brother as Gavin strode into the kitchen.

"You know, most people actually knock before barging into other people's homes."

"I did."

"No, you shouted *knock knock* as you burst in."

Gavin waved his complaint away. "It's Saturday. AKA pancake day. I didn't want to make you get up. Besides, I have a key, so it was entering. Not barging." His gaze fell upon Ellie. "Oh, hey, Ellie. You're here early."

Hazel eyes, flecked with a touch of brown, fell to where her hand was joined with his brother's. A knowing grin spread his wide lips. His gaze came back up, brows bobbing.

"Or are you here late?"

"Ellie stayed the night." Charlotte said with a big grin on her sticky face.

His amused glance shifted to Charlotte. "Did she now?"

"Yup. And we're going to the zoo today." Her face lit up like she had the most brilliant idea. "Uncle Gavin, you could come too!"

"Sure, Cheeky Monkey," he chuckled. "That is, if your daddy and Ellie don't mind."

"The more the merrier." Ellie tried to smile through the embarrassment at getting caught not only by Sullivan's daughter, but by his brother as well. Might as well tattoo it on her forehead. *I'm sleeping with Sullivan Green.*

"Hooray! Zoo day, zoo day, zoo day!"

Charlotte jumped up from her chair to perform an adorable little shimmy dance around the kitchen table. Ellie laughed at the small girl's enthusiasm, noticing the matching looks of love and indulgence on the faces of the Green brothers. Charlotte might not have a mother in her life, but it was clear the rest of her family adored her.

"We should probably clean up, and then I have to go home and change before we head to the zoo."

She'd also need to call Tammy and get approval for an unscheduled behind-the-scenes tour. Not that she had any doubt her boss would give her the go ahead. Since Ellie had saved Charlotte, she'd become the zoo darling. She could do no wrong. And she was pretty sure anything Sullivan asked for, the zoo director would bend over backwards to give him. Public image was very important when you were a non-profit. The zoo needed funding and bad press could kill the donations they needed to keep the animals fed and the doors open. Sullivan already assured her he would not sue—he knew the zoo wasn't responsible for what happened, and he wasn't that kind of person anyway—but Tammy still would be more than happy to allow Ellie to give the Greens a private tour.

"Don't worry about cleaning up, Ellie." Sullivan nodded his head to his brother. "We got an extra set of hands now."

"Oh, no. I couldn't. I helped make the mess."

"And now my brother is here to clean it up."

"I come over to brighten up your boring day and you put me to work doing dishes?" Gavin shook his head. "You cut me deep, brother."

"It's not a boring day, Uncle Gavin." Charlotte stared at him incredulously. "We're going to the zoo."

Gavin nodded his head with a smile. "Of course, you're right."

"Really, I don't mind helping—"

Sullivan cut her off with a quick kiss. The way she chased his lips when he pulled away would embarrass her, but he was a fantastic kisser. Anyone with half a pulse would go after more.

"We're fine. Go do what you need and meet us at the zoo in...say, an hour?"

Knowing she wouldn't win this argument, she nodded. "Okay, an hour. Bye Charlotte, see you soon."

"Bye, Ellie. I love you!"

Still unused to the freedom with which the young girl expressed affection, Ellie dabbed at her misty eyes.

"Love you too, sweetie."

As she stood up to leave, she noticed Gavin staring at her, a strange expression on his face.

"Come on, Gavin." Sullivan said, rising from the table. "You have wash duty."

"In a minute," he spoke to his brother, but his gaze still burned on her. "I forgot something in my car. I'll walk Ellie out and grab it real quick."

Well, that didn't sound ominous at all.

Charlotte grabbed all the plates and walked to the sink with the precarious pile. Sullivan waved them off, distracted by saving his daughter from dropping the wobbly tower and shattering the ceramic all over the floor.

Ellie tried to calm her breathing as she walked out the front door, extremely conscious of the man walking just a few feet behind her. She resisted the urge to tug on her ear, but just barely. Once she got to her car, she turned, staring Gavin straight in the eye.

"Okay, let's have it."

"It?" he questioned, a half-smile tilting the corner of his mouth.

"I know you didn't forget anything in your car." She wasn't naïve. "You wanted to talk to me about something without your brother present. So out with it."

Sullivan had called her brave, so that's what she was

trying to be. But her heart took a nosedive when the smile left Gavin's face. Somber reflection replacing the usual jovial humor she'd come to know Sullivan's brother for.

"Sullivan doesn't date. At all. Ever since Claire left, he's been focused on two things. Work and Charlotte."

She'd believe that. The man had a designated puzzle night on Fridays. She assumed he hadn't been out hitting the club scene. Then again, she was thrilled with Friday puzzles nights, so what did that say about her social life?

"I've never heard him talk about another woman, let alone bring one around Charlotte. Not until you."

That statement would have made her heart soar if it wasn't for the grim expression still affixed to Gavin's face.

"Is this the part where you warn me off?" She lifted her chin. "Because there's no need. Sullivan and I agreed this wasn't anything serious. He doesn't want to get remarried."

Gavin arched one eyebrow. "And what do you want?"

It didn't matter. He'd made his line in the sand clear, and she wouldn't cross it. No matter how much her heart screamed for her to race right over it.

"I want Sullivan and Charlotte to be happy," she said truthfully.

"And what if what my brother thinks makes him happy actually makes him miserable?"

What? The man was talking in circles, and she couldn't follow.

She frowned, brow furrowing as she tried to catch the hidden meaning in Gavin's words. Why couldn't people just say what they meant? Why all the double-speak and inference? "I don't understand what you mean."

Gavin shook his head, the hint of a smile returning. "Look, my brother can be pigheaded sometimes. All I'm saying is, I think you're pretty damn perfect for my brother."

Taken aback by his declaration, her mouth dropped open and it took her a moment to find her voice. "You do?"

"Yup. And you and Charlotte obviously have a special bond."

"We do." She loved that little girl. She'd never been much for connecting with others, but dang if that sweet child hadn't wormed her way past all Ellie's defenses and right into her heart.

"That's great. Charlotte needs some positive female influence with only me and my knucklehead brother around."

She chuckled softly, Gavin joining in, but then he turned serious again. Her heart kicked up, body tensing, bracing herself for whatever warning he had to give. Because no matter what the man said, she sensed a warning in this little chat.

"I love my brother and my niece. Very much."

She nodded. She did too. Not that she'd share with Gavin how she felt about his brother. First, she needed to gather the courage to tell the man himself.

"Sullivan has always looked out for everyone. He came home to look after me after our parents died. Left the ER, switching to private practice when Claire left so he could be there more for Charlotte. Sully always puts others before himself."

She knew that. The man did everything in his power to make sure she was comfortable and at ease. He'd even been happy to forgo the Ferris wheel when he noticed her panic attack. Which was why she made herself go on the damn thing. Sullivan sacrificed for people. Anyone who spent more than two minutes with the man would realize that.

"He's so use to ignoring his own needs, I'm not sure if he can stop." Gavin sighed. "He hides his fear behind protecting his daughter, so just…don't let him push you away, because I can tell he cares."

With that, Gavin turned and headed back into the house, leaving Ellie standing there wondering if the man was right about his brother. If she should let this tiny flame of hope for a future with Sullivan grow. Could she do that? Could she take risk knowing it could either spark a bright future...or burn down her entire world.

CHAPTER 27

he zoo had a perpetual smell of animal feces. Who knew? Not Sullivan, that was for damn sure.

"Sorry," Ellie winced as she noticed him wrinkle his nose. "It gets kind of smelly around here toward the end of the day. Especially when it's hot. The sun kind of *accentuates* the animal's enclosures."

He brought their joined hands up to place a soft kiss on her knuckles, enjoying the slight blush that rose on her cheeks. "No need to apologize. I grew up with Gavin. From age eight to eleven, he refused to take a shower. Had some vendetta against soap or something. Our mom had to douse his clothing in air freshener just so he wouldn't get sent home from school for smelling so bad."

"It was one week in eighth grade," Gavin called over his shoulder from a few feet in front of them. "And I didn't have an aversion to soap. I had a massive sunburn made even more painful by pounding water on my skin."

His head turned, and Gavin aimed a death glare directly his way. "A sunburn I received because my big brother said he put sunscreen on me, but in fact, only wrote the word *dork* on my back."

"Sullivan, you did not!" Ellie gave him a light smack on the arms, her face aghast. But there was a hint of a smile at the corner of her mouth.

He shrugged. "What can I say? He ate the last peanut butter cup, and I had already called dibs."

"I hope you don't also enjoy chocolate and peanut butter goodness, Ellie. Because my pig of a brother does not share his candy well."

"I'll share my chocolate with you as long as I get to eat my share off your sexy, naked, body." He whispered the words in her ear in a low, sultry voice, causing a shiver to vibrate her body.

Since the temperature was currently seventy-five degrees out, he knew it had nothing to do with the weather and everything to do with the mental image he'd suggested. Seemed Ellie liked the idea. Good, because just suggesting it had him half hard. Since they were in a very public place and his daughter was currently a few feet in front of them, swinging the hand she had clasped in his brother's, he needed to stop this line of thinking. They could experiment with all kinds of delicious, naughty desserts later. Right now, was family time. Smelly, wonderful family time.

They'd already explored half the zoo and were now headed to the aviary exhibit. His heart stuttered a beat when he caught sight of the penguin enclosure. The deep pool of clear liquid was scattered with bits of leaves and flowers floating on its surface. A few penguins were sunning themselves on the rocks, only one racing through the water. The tiny animal suddenly shot out of the water onto the ground, creating a ripple of small waves in the formerly still water.

His mind flew back to that day. He swore he caught a glimpse of a soaking wet Charlotte being held in Ellie's arms.

It still terrified him to think about it. What would have happened if Ellie hadn't been there? Hadn't dived in to save his daughter? He'd lost so many people in his life. He didn't think he would have survived losing his daughter.

"Hey."

Ellie's soft voice broke through the dark fog he found himself in. She squeezed his hand gently.

"Are you okay?"

He turned his head, focusing on her. He pushed out all the fear of what *could* have happened, and concentrated on what *did*. Charlotte was fine because the amazing woman in front of him—holding his hand, sharing his bed—had saved her. Saved his daughter without knowing her, without a thought to her own safety.

"Yeah. I'm fine. It's just…"

Her gaze flicked to the enclosure and back to him. "I understand. We don't have to go in if you don't want t—"

"Penguins! Daddy, the penguins!"

He chuckled. "Pretty sure we do."

At least the event hadn't traumatized Charlotte. Kids were resilient. Charlotte dropped Gavin's hand, running over to grab his free one and tug it up and down with childlike glee.

"Daddy, can we see the penguins?"

"Sure, Angel. But let's not get too close, okay?" Irrational as it may be, he still held a small bit of fear standing at the scene of her accident. He knew it wouldn't happen again, but protective dad brain had taken over.

"I have an even better idea," Ellie suggested, kneeling to get in Charlotte's direct eye line. "How would you like to go inside and meet some penguins?"

"Really?"

"Yup. I bet there are even some treats in there you could give them."

His daughter's eyes lit up with excitement and she practically dragged him toward the aviary building. Ellie laughed, being dragged along as well since she still clutched his hand. His brother—never one to be left out—hurried after them.

Once inside the building, Ellie quickly took control, guiding them all to a dark grey door marked *Employees Only.* She slipped a card out of her back pocket, sliding it over the smart lock on the door. There was a soft beep, then she turned the handle and ushered them all into a large grey room lined with a big, chrome sink and countertop on one wall and a large industrial sized silver refrigerator against the back wall. A very tall woman with red, curly hair, khaki shorts and a shirt emblazoned with *Sunlight Zoo Staff* on the front looked up from her position in front of the sink when they came in. Her face broke into an enormous smile, and she lifted her arms out of the sink to reveal a pudgy penguin.

"Hey, Ellie! I didn't know you were going to be here today."

"Cam. What are you doing here?"

Right, Cam. The other woman he'd met the day of Charlotte's accident and also Ellie's best friend. He hadn't spent any time with the woman, but Ellie had spoken of her fondly many times. Any friend of Ellie's had to be good people.

"Gus called in sick." The tall woman rolled bright blue eyes. "Sick my as—as if I believe that." She corrected as her eyes fell on Charlotte and spoke in a hushed voice. "I know he went to Red Rocks last night for a concert. He's sick, all right, but it isn't from illness."

"Why didn't I get called in?"

Cam laughed. "They only needed one body to cover the shift, Doll-face. Besides, I knew you'd be..." The woman's eyes shifted from Ellie to Sullivan and then down to their joined hands. A knowing grin ticked up the corner of ruby red lips. "Busy. And anyway, it seems you *are* here today. And with Miss Charlotte! How are you doing, sweetie?"

"Is that a real, live penguin?"

He looked over at his daughter's awed tone to see her eyes, wide as saucers. She was frozen in place, like the time he gave her his grandmother's gold necklace and told her it was a family heirloom and to be careful when wearing it.

"Sure is." Cam smiled wide, crouching down with the black and white bird who seemed totally content in the keeper's arms. "Charlotte, meet Bingo. He's very old and very sweet. You want to pet him?"

"Oh, can I? Can I?"

"Of course, real gentle now. Remember, he's still a wild animal and sometimes animals get scared."

He watched as his daughter crept ever so slowly toward the tiny bird, her little hand stretching out with the care of a movie thief, avoiding glowing alarm lasers.

"Here, sweetie."

Ellie released his hand, crouching down herself to scoot closer to Charlotte and Cam. She placed her palm loosely on top of Charlotte's hand, guiding his daughter to the animal's back.

"See? He likes it when you stroke him like that."

"Most men do," Cam snorted.

Ellie glared at the other woman. "Cam!"

"What? It's true."

He chuckled, knowing Ellie was worried about her friend's word choice in front of Charlotte. But he also knew his daughter wouldn't get the innuendo.

"You got that right, Red," his brother said, gaze zeroed in on the woman holding the penguin preening under Charlotte's touch.

Oh fantastic, Gavin was putting the moves on his girlfriend's best friend. Not good. His playboy of a brother would show her a good time and never call her again, and then Ellie would be upset for her friend—rightly so. He would not allow Gavin to screw up the best thing he'd had in a while just because his brother's dick decided it needed a new conquest.

He opened his mouth to tell Gavin to knock it off, but before he could get one syllable out, Cam narrowed her eyes and addressed him.

"Hello, I don't think we've met. I'm Camilla. Cam to my friends, but *you* can call me Camilla. Not Red, or Carrots, or Firecracker, or Hot Potato—"

"Hot Potato?" Gavin raised his brows.

Cam shrugged. "Some men like to think they're clever."

She sent a pointed look his way and Sullivan had to cover his mouth to contain the laughter. He didn't need to worry about protecting Ellie's friend from his brother. In fact, he might need to get some ice for all the burn the woman was putting on poor Gavin.

"And you are…let me guess, Jolly Green?" Cam said with a smirk.

Gavin glared. "Is that a height reference? Because I could say that right back at you."

True. Sullivan had noticed Ellie's friend was as tall as Ellie was short. He liked Ellie's height. It made it easy for him to wrap his arms around her and snuggle her to his chest.

"Try it and see what happens. Stretch."

Oh, he really, *really*, liked Cam. He had to smother another laugh as Gavin stood, open jawed. Finally, his brother found enough footing to mutter.

"I'm Gavin. Sullivan's brother."

"Ahhhh! He's pooping!"

Charlotte's shriek interrupted the verbal back and forth between his brother and Ellie's best friend. Everyone took a healthy step back as Bingo was indeed squirting a stream of white liquid out of his backside. He glanced at his brother to see a horrified expression he knew matched the one on his face. Charlotte had curled into Ellie's chest as much as humanly possible. Ellie and Cam, however, simply laughed.

"Okay, Bingo," Cam said to the pooping bird in a soothing voice. "I get it. You want to go back out with your lady."

The woman rose to her feet. Sullivan thought he heard Gavin mutter under his breath.

"See, she's almost as tall as me. Jolly Green, my ass."

Sullivan grinned. Anyone who could get under his baby brother's unflappable skin was someone he wanted around. A lot.

"Well folks, enjoy your day. I gotta take this little guy back out to bask in the sunshine. See ya Ellie, Sullivan, Charlotte." Her gaze focused on his brother, a smartass sparkle in her eyes. "Sasquatch."

Gavin opened his mouth, a dark scowl on his face. Sullivan feared he may have to intervene, but then his brother's expression smoothed. A knowing gleam lit his own gaze, and he curled his lips in a weird smile Sullivan had never seen him give before.

"Nice meeting you, Ginger Snaps."

Cam raised one dark cinnamon eyebrow but said nothing. She tucked the bird in her arms, turned and headed out a door he assumed led to the outside enclosure.

"What the heck was that all about?" Ellie whispered to him as she stood by his side again.

"I think my brother just met his match and I gotta say, I'm going to enjoy your friend taking him down a peg or two."

Ellie scoffed. "Cam wouldn't do that. She's the sweetest person ever."

To Ellie maybe, and he'd throw her a parade for that fact alone, but to horndogs like his brother, the woman obviously gave no quarter. He loved Gavin. The guy was a great brother and a fantastic uncle, but he'd always been lacking in the relationship department. It'd be nice to see a woman get the upper hand on his little brother for once. Let the man know he wasn't God's gift to all women the way he assumed.

"Awww, I didn't get to feed him."

Charlotte's pouty voice caused Sullivan to look down into the disappointed face of his daughter. He was just about to give her a speech on being thankful for what she had—come on, how many people got private tours with actual animal interaction—when Ellie wrapped an arm around her shoulders.

"I know, sweetie. But don't worry. I have a big surprise for you."

"A surprise?" Her tiny, round face lit up. "Really?"

"Really." Ellie nodded.

"When do I get it?"

Ellie laughed. The sound did strange things to Sullivan's chest. Warm, squishy things he wasn't sure he was prepared for.

"How about right now?"

"Yes!"

He had no idea what was coming next, but between the enthusiasm in his daughter's steps and the joy in Ellie's eyes, he'd follow these two anywhere. The thought made him pause, but he soon found himself being dragged along and out the door.

They headed out of the aviary through a back door leading to another door that took them into a very large, very smelly building.

"Stinky!" Charlotte complained, wrinkling her tiny nose.

"Yes, I know. But I think the smell will be worth it once you see—"

An extremely loud trumpeting sound interrupted Ellie. Sullivan turned his head to see far into the large space, at the back end, what looked like the entire side of the wall had opened and an enormous, grey elephant was currently making its way inside.

They were all currently standing behind a mid-height concrete wall so they could see the animal but had a modicum of safety. One glance down to his daughter's face and he saw the wall meant nothing. Charlotte's eyes sparkled like emerald gems, shiny with overwhelming elation.

"Is that a real live elephant?"

Ellie crouched down, placing her hands on his daughter's shoulders. "It sure is, sweetie."

"Can I ride him?"

"Her," Ellie corrected. "And they don't really like to be ridden, but I have some special branches here, and I bet we can get Tia to come over for a snack. Would you like to feed her?"

"Yes, please."

The words were whispered out in a hush of awe. He knew his daughter hadn't expected a moment like this. He didn't even know how to repay Ellie for this once in a lifetime memory he knew she was giving his daughter. This was a dream, Charlotte's dream, and Ellie had somehow managed to secure it.

I love her.

The words whispered in his head, but he dismissed them. No. He was just in awe of her. Grateful for the unique and astounding opportunity she'd provided for his daughter. He was grateful to her, enjoyed her company, liked her immensely. But he couldn't love her. He'd lost too many people he loved. It was hard enough worrying about something happening to Charlotte or Gavin. He couldn't add another person into the mix. The worry would kill him before he was fifty. He couldn't survive another loss, and he damn well wouldn't do that to Charlotte.

"Holy crap, Ellie," Gavin exclaimed. "This is amazing."

It was. So amazing that no one corrected the man for swearing in front of an eight-year-old.

"Hey, Chris," Ellie called to the Black man with a shiny bald head standing a few feet away from the massive animal, guiding it into the building. "Can you bring Tia over here? I've got a friend for her to meet and some yummy treats."

The man waved in acknowledgement. Soon, Chris and the huge pachyderm were lumbering over to where they all stood.

"Here." Ellie handed Charlotte a palm frond. "Hold this out like this to Tia. That's right, way out far so she can grab it with her trunk, and the minute she does, you let go. Elephants are very strong."

"Elephants can carry over six-hundred pounds," Charlotte announced proudly.

"That's right, sweetie. They can. Now hold it out. Here she comes."

He watched as his daughter held out the palm and the woman he cared for held onto her waist, talking her through it, guiding her as the large animal reached out with its trunk to snuff over Charlotte's hair—eliciting an adorable giggle—before grabbing the green leafy branch and depositing it in its mouth.

"I fed a real live elephant! I can't wait to tell everyone at school!"

He glanced over to his brother who had his cell phone out, camera recording. Damn, he was glad Gavin had the sense of mind to record such a momentous occasion. He'd completely forgotten. So wrapped up in the stupid shit going on inside his head, he'd totally spaced on the memory preserving moments.

"Send me that, would ya?"

His brother nodded, thumbs flicking over the phone

screen. His cell dinged a moment later, but he left it in his pocket. It would save. He'd watch it later, at Charlotte's insistence, he was certain. For now, he was content to stand there and gaze at the daughter he loved with the biggest, happiest smile he'd ever seen plastered on her face. And at the woman who'd put it there. The woman who'd also made him the happiest he could ever remember. The woman he feared was making herself indispensable to him in every aspect of his life.

CHAPTER 28

*E*llie sat on the couch in the Greens' living room, Sullivan on one side of her, Charlotte curled up against the other as they watched the movie with the princess and the magic shoes, for the fourth time in a month. She didn't mind though, not really. These past few months with Sullivan and Charlotte had been a dream. Ellie never knew she could be so…content.

A soft ping sounded from her pocket. Shifting without trying to disturb anyone too much, Ellie reached into the pocket of her pants and pulled out her phone. She smiled when she saw the text message.

Cam: Show this to the squirt

Followed by a picture of Bingo with a sardine in his beak. Cam had been sending her funny pictures of the penguins and other zoo animals to show Charlotte. She had also been making fast friends with the charming girl, as Charlotte had finagled a few more weekend visits to the zoo. The last one she'd asked if Cam could come along. Gavin had joined them, too. The verbal sparring between her best friend and Sullivan's brother seemed odd to her. The two acted like they hated each other, passing barbs back and forth, but there was always a weird smile on her friend's face when she sent veiled insults Gavin's way. Weirder still, the man grinned as each affront landed.

She had no idea what was going on with those two, but as long as it didn't upset Charlotte or Sullivan, she didn't really care. She was happy and in love. A fact she still hadn't revealed to Sullivan. As much as she wanted to shout the words from the mountain tops, she couldn't. Fear had a chokehold on her. Plus, there was the matter of them promising to keep this thing light and fun. But with each passing day, she fell deeper and deeper. It didn't feel light anymore. There were times when she looked into Sullivan's eyes and swore she saw love shining back at her in those green depths.

Or maybe she was just projecting what she wanted to see. For now, she told herself to just enjoy their time together, whether it be puzzle night, movie night, or the date nights they'd managed to sneak in thanks to Gavin's babysitting.

Life was good.

Not wanting to disturb the movie—even though it was the millionth time Charlotte had seen it according to her father—she slipped the phone back into her pocket. The photo could wait until after the show, during brownie time.

Brownie Time. Movie night. Puzzle night. Date night.

All her free time recently seemed to be categorized by activities. Activities involving actual people, not simply her and the nature channel. If someone had told her three months ago, she'd be spending most of her nights and week-ends with a handsome single dad and his daughter, she would have laughed in their face. Ellie didn't connect with other people very well. But it appeared she connected with

Sullivan and Charlotte just fine. The knowledge warmed her heart. Maybe she'd finally found her place to fit.

"Anything important?" Sullivan asked, his lips gently brushing the shell of her ear.

"Nope. Just, Cam sending more Bingo pics."

He chuckled, and the vibrations from his lips against her skin sent a thrill of anticipation through her. Over the past few weeks, she'd been staying over most weekends. Once they put Charlotte to bed, Sullivan would whisk her off to the bedroom and do the most inventive, delicious things. Her thighs squeezed together in anticipation just thinking about it.

"I'm growing fond of that old bird."

"Bingo has that effect on people. I think it only took a day for him to charm Cam and less than an hour where I was concerned."

He bopped her softly on the nose with his index finger. "That doesn't count. You're a softie for all animals. You wouldn't even squash a spider if it landed on your nose."

Now there he was wrong. Spiders had their place in the animal kingdom, but if a creepy, crawly eight-legged arachnid fell on her face without warning she would probably freak out a bit and smack the thing away, inadvertently crushing the poor creature and causing flies everywhere to celebrate.

"You guuuuuys!" Charlotte gave them both a disgruntled glare. "I'm trying to watch the moooooovieeeee!"

"Sorry, Angel."

"Sorry, Charlotte."

She glanced at Sullivan, sharing an amused expression. They'd seen this movie so often the little girl could recite it—and currently was, silently, her lips moving along with the talking animal currently on screen telling the princess to be her best and good things would follow.

They sat in silence, enjoying the movie. Well, Charlotte enjoyed it. Ellie tolerated it because the little girl loved it so much and it made her happy to see Charlotte happy. Besides, Ellie would get her happy later. A few happies if she was lucky.

Suddenly the sounds of ringing filled the air. Since Ellie had her incoming calls set to the sound of an elephant trumpeting—yes, she let Charlotte set it—she knew it had to be coming from Sullivan's phone.

"Daaaaaaaddyyyyyyyy!" Charlotte complained. "My favorite song is coming up. You promised to turn the ringer off."

True. Sullivan usually silenced his phone during movie night.

"Sorry, Angel, I forgot." He pulled the phone from his pocket, scowling at the screen. "California? Hold on, I gotta take this."

Rising from the couch, Sullivan headed out of the living room. Charlotte—content now that all distractions had been silenced—turned back to the television. Ellie snuggled the girl in close, preparing herself for the titular *who am I* song of the movie. It wasn't so bad, but the dang thing got stuck in her head after every viewing and the last thing she wanted was to be humming the bars during tonight's *activities*.

Near the end of the song, a loud crash came from the kitchen, followed by the harsh sounds of Sullivan swearing. Ellie jumped, feeling Charlotte tense in her arms.

"What happened?" Charlotte whispered.

Movie momentarily forgotten, Ellie glanced down into worried, emerald eyes. "I don't know."

"Is Daddy okay?"

Hard to tell, but she heard more muted swearing, so she assumed he wasn't lying dead on the floor. Pasting on what she hoped was a convincing smile, she hugged the girl tightly. "I'm sure he's fine, sweetie. Why don't you finish watching the movie while I go and check? Okay?"

Charlotte glanced worriedly toward the kitchen, but then the prince arrived on screen to save the princess who had already saved herself and the child's attention was diverted again.

"Okay."

Quickly slipping away, Ellie hurried to the kitchen. The sight she saw made her breath stop. Sullivan stood hunched over the counter, bowls and dishes from their earlier dinner scattered across the floor, some of the ceramic broken. It didn't appear to be an accident, either. From the heaving tenseness of his shoulders, it seemed Sullivan swept them all off the counter in a fit of rage. That would explain the loud noise, but not the reason for the outburst.

In all her time with Sullivan, she'd never seen him livid. Scared, upset, even angry, but never this raw fury that currently poured off him like lava from an exploding volcano.

"Sullivan?" She approached him cautiously. She wasn't afraid of him. Never that. Sullivan would never hurt anyone. Not only had he taken an oath as a doctor to do no harm, but inflicting pain on anyone just wasn't in the guy's DNA. She knew that. She knew him. "Are you okay?"

"She's dead."

He spoke the words so softly she didn't think she heard right at first.

"What?"

"She's dead. Claire is dead."

He lifted his head, and the sight broke her heart. Pain, raw and unchecked, blasted out of his gaze as tears leaked out of the corner of his eyes. There was anger and confusion as well, but it was the pain that was the strongest.

"Oh...I'm sorry."

That's what you were supposed to say, right? When someone died. Give your sympathies even if the deceased wasn't particularly close to the person anymore. He had been married to the woman for two years. There must have been some happy memories. Some love shared that would create pain at the loss.

"How did she—"

"Car accident." He scoffed. "Random, freak car accident. She got T-boned at an intersection by a guy who ran a red light. No alcohol or drugs involved."

Oh no! A car accident. Just the way his parents had died.

"She was totally sober," he continued, his voice becoming harsh and scratchy. "In fact, she'd been sober for the past two years, apparently."

"What?"

"Yeah."

He pushed off the counter to pace the hardwood floor. The emotions surrounding him were like a dark cloud, permeating the room, warning of the impending storm. She wanted to run to him, wrap her arms around him and tell him everything would be all right. But she wouldn't discount his feelings right now. With a blow this big, she knew it would take a lot to process. So she stayed where she was, tugging on her ear, watching the man she loved suffer and hurt.

"That was her sponsor who called me. Her *sponsor!*" He spat the word out like it was rotten milk and left a foul taste in his mouth.

"She'd been going to NA for a few years, had a few back slides, but according to this woman she'd been clean for twenty-two months."

But she hadn't called Sullivan to let him know. Hadn't contacted Charlotte to see how her daughter was. Ellie had zero experience with addiction or family abandonment, but she knew his ex's decision not to reach out in her sobriety had to hurt.

"How?" He shook his head.

Sullivan stopped pacing, coming to stand inches from her. His face was a tormented mask of agony and confusion. She wanted to reach out and touch him, offer some form of comfort, but she could read the signals his body was putting off. He didn't want comfort. He wanted answers. It ripped her to shreds that she didn't have any for him. The only person who did was gone forever.

"How could she have been sober for almost two fucking years and not contact her daughter? How could she not call or text or, hell, send a goddamn letter to check in on the child she created?"

"I-I don't know, Sullivan. I'm sorry." Such ineffectual words, but she didn't know what else to say. What else to do? What did someone do when the person they loved was breaking apart right in front of them? How did you fix that?

"What can I do to help?"

He turned away, pacing back to the counter again. "Nothing."

The word hit like a slap in the face. "Nothing?"

His head shook as he gave her his back once more. "This is a family matter. I need to talk to Charlotte. Explain... things to her. You should go."

She knew he had a lot to deal with right now. His ex-wife was dead, the mother of his child. A child he now had to break the awful news to. He was dealing with grief and anger and a fair bit of confusion at Claire's decision to not contact her daughter when she achieved sobriety. He had to be overwhelmed. But it didn't stop the lance of pain piercing her heart, the reminder that she wasn't family. They'd been playing house, some might say, but she wasn't Sullivan's wife or Ellie's mother. She was just the girlfriend, easily tossed aside.

She didn't fit into this part of their puzzle.

"O-of course. I'll just say goodbye to Charlotte and head home." As much as it hurt her to leave, she knew Sullivan was hurting far worse. Placing a gentle hand on his back, she rubbed slightly. Normally he'd reach over and take her hand whenever she touched him, kiss her knuckles, but tonight he did none of those things. He simply stood there like a statue. All stone and cold. "You'll let me know if there's anything I can do? Anything at all?"

He nodded, just the barest movement of his head. The tingles of warmth and elation she usually got from touching Sullivan were absent. Only worry and fear coursed through her veins as she lifted her hand from his back and set out of the kitchen. She found Charlotte still engrossed in the movie. Choking down her swirling emotions, she made her way to the couch, bending down to give the girl a warm embrace.

"Bye, Charlotte."

"You're leaving?"

Apparently, the child hadn't been as absorbed as Ellie thought. Her small head turned, light blonde hair slapping against her cheeks with the abruptness of the movement.

"Aren't you staying the night? It's pancake day tomorrow."

"Oh, I'm sorry, sweetie. I…I…"

What the hell did she say? She didn't want to lie to the girl, but she also didn't want to admit the child's father had all but kicked her out. Charlotte was about to get some of the worst news of her life. Ellie had no idea what to do. She knew what she wanted to do. Clutch Charlotte to her chest and promise nothing would hurt the little girl ever again, but that wasn't realistic. That wasn't life. And as Sullivan pointed out moments ago, this was a family matter and Ellie wasn't family.

"I promise we'll have another pancake day again real soon, okay?"

But would they? She didn't know what would happen next. Did Sullivan mean for her to leave only for tonight or forever? She couldn't very well ask the man. Not now.

"Okay, I love you, Ellie."

Charlotte threw her arms around Ellie's neck, as she always did anytime Ellie left. Tears clogged her throat, and she had to sniff to keep them from falling from her eyes. She wrapped her arms around the young girl, squeezing all the love she could into the hug. Wishing it could be a shield for the pain the child was about to receive.

"I love you too, Charlotte."

"Arrrrgh, too tight."

She let out a watery laugh. "Sorry."

Releasing Charlotte, she stood, glancing once more toward the kitchen. She couldn't see anything but the suffering coming from the room hung in the air around her like a suffocating blanket of agony. She headed to the front door, realizing for the first time since they'd started seeing each other, Sullivan hadn't walked her out to her car at night.

Get over it. He has a lot on his plate right now. He can't be concerned with you and your selfish feelings. The man just suffered a loss and all you can think about is yourself. No wonder he doesn't want you around. This is probably all your fault, anyway. This is why no one loves you and no one ever will. You ruin everything.

She shook her head, trying to dispel the dark voice whispering ugly lies in her head. But as she got into her car and drove toward her apartment, she wondered if the voice was right this time? People often said life was a rollercoaster full of ups and downs. What if she'd given Sullivan such an up that life had to crash him down?

It sounded ridiculous, even as she thought it, but that didn't stop the insidious idea from working its way into her head. Maybe she'd call Dr. Mitchell in the morning and get her opinion. Whatever was going on in her head didn't matter now. The dark voice and thoughts couldn't hold a candle to the pain encircling her heart, shooting out to every inch of her body, reminding her that once again she'd been found lacking by the one she loved.

CHAPTER 29

*H*e hurt her.

He didn't have to look in her eyes to know. Sullivan heard the pain in her voice when he told her to go. Felt the small cracking of her voice pierce his heart like an ice pick. His dismissal had hurt her, but fuck, he was hurting too. His daughter was about to hurt. One of the worst betrayals he could imagine had been thrust upon him along with a loss he hadn't imagined he would feel this deeply.

It'd been years since he loved Claire. Years since he wondered where she was and if she was ever coming back. He didn't have any romantic feelings for his ex-wife, but that didn't mean he had zero feelings for the deceased woman. She had been the mother of his child, someone he thought he would spend forever with. Stood to reason he'd have an emotional response to her death. He'd never imagined it would be anger, but he was angry. Fucking furious.

"Why, Claire?" He whispered into the empty room, knowing he wouldn't get a response. She was dead and dead people didn't speak, no matter how much you might wish they would. "Why didn't you come back to see her? Why didn't you love her?"

He wasn't upset for himself. The anger burning in his gut called him a liar. Okay, maybe he was a little upset. After years together, the woman up and left without a word. It had taken him a while to get over the loss, the abandonment. He never got a chance to ask her why, to get closure. Up until this moment, he hadn't even been fully aware it was something he still held onto. The hope that he could look Claire in the eyes one day and ask her how she could to this to him, to them. Now he'd never have the chance.

Their relationship had been over a long time ago. He'd just have to accept he'd never get the answers to his questions. Once again, life had taken someone from him in the blink of an eye. No chance for goodbyes. Anger and despair rose within, a raging tornado in his chest threatening to obliterate everything. The majority of the swirling pit of resentment and agony in his chest was reserved for his daughter, the sweet, wonderful child who had done nothing, *absolutely nothing*, to deserve her mother's abandonment.

Over the years, he'd explained to Charlotte that her mommy had been sick and needed to go away to get better. How did he look his daughter, the light of his life, in the eye and explain that mommy got better, but still didn't want to see her?

He couldn't. Even if it were true, he could never tell Charlotte that. Never let her know her mother didn't care. Whatever Claire's reasons were for staying away, even after she received treatment, he would never give his daughter any reason to think her mother hadn't wanted and loved her as much as he did.

Fuck, how the hell was he going to do this?

He had no idea, but he damn sure would figure it out.

Charlotte needed her parent—her only parent now—to be strong and help her through this.

"Charlotte," he coughed, his voice rough with emotion. No time for any of that now. He had to lock it up. For his daughter. Clearing his throat, he tried again. "Charlotte, can you come in here, please?"

He heard the movie pausing and tiny feet shuffling across the hardwood floors. In mere moments his daughter came into view, light blonde hair flying back with her hurried shuffle—because she knew she wasn't allowed to run in the house but liked to push her limits.

"Are you okay, Daddy?"

Her worried little eyes darted around the kitchen, falling on the scattered and broken dishes. *Shit!* He should have picked up before he called her in. She didn't need to see the aftereffects of her father losing control. He had to be better than this. He had to keep it together.

"I'm fine. I just had a little accident."

"Accidents are okay. I spilled the glue at school, but I told the teacher and said sorry even though it wasn't by purpose."

"On purpose, Angel. It wasn't *on* purpose."

Why the hell was he correcting her grammar at a time like this? Dammit, he was screwing everything up already.

"Sit down at the table, Charlotte. I have something very important to talk to you about."

Going to the freezer, he grabbed the chocolate ice cream, putting three heaping scoops into two bowls and heading to where Charlotte sat at the kitchen table. Cowardly of him to offer his child the distraction of sugar? Maybe, but all he could see in his mind right now was Claire sitting in that hospital bed right after she had Charlotte. Holding the sweet bundle to her chest, her eyes wide with all the emotions he'd been feeling in that moment: love, wonder, fear. She had loved Charlotte. She'd loved him. What happened to that? What happened to them?

Shaking off the questions he knew would never be answered, he focused on his daughter as she was now. A sweet, kind, happy child who had never known her mother and now never would.

He slid one of the bowls over to her. Never one to refuse sugar in any form, his daughter dug into the cold, creamy treat with glee.

"Yay, ice cream!"

"So, Angel, I want to talk to you about…mommy."

Except for the slightest decrease of velocity in which she consumed her ice cream, Charlotte showed no reaction.

"I know you don't really remember her."

How could she? Claire had left before their daughter even had the chance to turn one. Children didn't start developing permanent memory until age three at the earliest. He had given Charlotte a picture of her mother. One she kept in her room on her bookshelf. He never wanted to erase Claire from their lives, but he also hadn't wanted to give his daughter false hope of her returning. He would have never denied Claire access to their daughter. But they would never have whatever picture-perfect family life society still claimed to be normal.

Who got to say what was normal? Or perfect? Didn't the differences between people, the mish-mash of joining to create a loving family, whether by blood or choice, make the world a more interesting place? Wasn't happiness more important than one person's ideal of what a "family" should be?

"She had blonde hair like me, but her eyes are blue, not green."

True. Claire had gifted their daughter with her blonde wavy curls. Sullivan's hair held a bit of rusty tan to it. Not fully blond like his daughter. But she had inherited his eyes. Eyes he's gotten from his own mother. His mother always laughed about that, joking that she married their father because his last name matched her eyes, proving they were meant to be together. He didn't know if that held even an ounce of truth, but he knew his parents had loved each other very much and passed that love on to their sons. Too bad he and Claire hadn't found the same thing.

But they had made Charlotte together, and for that, he would be forever grateful.

"Yes, Angel. That's right." He put his spoon down—he hadn't eaten a bite anyway—and reached across the table to lightly grasp her hand, the one not currently shoveling a scoop of ice cream into her mouth. "You remember how I told you she had to go away because she was sick?"

Her little chin dipped up and down as she nodded. "Yes. You said she needed a special doctor because you couldn't fix her with your medicine."

Truth. He hadn't been the kind of doctor his ex-wife had needed. Or the kind of husband. No matter how angry he was at Claire, he had to admit some of the fault lay with him. If he'd been there for her more or noticed her struggles sooner... but none of that mattered anymore. There was no way to go back and change the past, and even if he could, he knew now that no matter what, he and Claire never would have lasted. They'd both been too stubborn to ask for help. How could you make a lasting life with a person if you didn't trust them with your vulnerabilities?

"Yes, Angel. She needed a special doctor." One she'd found, it seemed.

"So," Charlotte put down her spoon, fiddling with the napkin left on the table from dinner. "Does that mean she's coming back?"

Fuck! The air squeezed out of his lungs. It felt like a trash compactor was pressing on his chest, wringing the very essence of life from his body. He closed his eyes against the moisture gathering in them.

"No, Charlotte. She's not coming home."

"Oh good."

Good? What the hell? He opened his eyes to see Charlotte smiling up at him.

"Maddie Johnson's daddy went away, but then he came back, and her mommy had to stop seeing her boyfriend." She grimaced, tilting her head the way she did when she was thinking through her big spelling words. "It'd be okay if mommy came home, but I don't want Ellie to go away."

That's what she was worried about? That if her mother came home, he'd stop seeing Ellie? If only it was something as simple as that. Something he could assure her would never happen. Rising from his chair, he came over to kneel in front of her, still clasping her hand in his.

"Charlotte, mommy isn't ever going to come home."

Her smile fell, understanding sinking in. "The doctors couldn't fix her?"

They could, they did, apparently. But death still decided to take its pound of flesh.

"She had an accident. A car accident. She…she didn't make it, Angel."

Charlotte was the daughter of a doctor. While he never discussed his work or patients' problems at home, she knew he treated sick people and sometimes they died.

"Is…is she still my mommy?"

"She'll always be your mommy, no matter what."

He crouched there as still as he could, watching his daughter. Seeing the thoughts and emotions process over her young face. He didn't move a muscle, but inside he was being ripped apart by anger, guilt, and sorrow. A churning mess destroying everything in his mind's path. He locked it all away, refusing to let it show, knowing he needed to be strong for Charlotte. To take care of her.

She nodded her head, looking far too grown up for her eight years. "That's good."

She was taking this far better than he expected. Then again, his daughter had never really known her mother. Hard to miss someone you never knew. He assumed there would probably be issues later in life as Charlotte grew up. Things to process and discuss. He should probably call the school on Monday and inform her teachers and the school counselor just in case she needed to talk to a licensed professional. He knew a few excellent child psychologists himself. Perhaps he'd email a few and get their take on the situation.

All he wanted was to make sure his baby was going to be okay. That's all Sullivan ever wanted. To take care of the ones he loved. Yeah, he might overdo it. The phrase "Mother Hen" had been muttered under Gavin's breath a few times. Also "asshole" but that had been when he was his brother's guardian, enforcing strict curfew and homework rules.

"Are you okay?" He wanted to make one hundred percent sure his daughter was handling this news well, processing it as much as an eight-year-old could.

Charlotte nodded, her little nose scrunching up as she squinted her eyes. "I'm fine, Daddy. Are you okay? Your face looks funny."

Funny? If clenching his jaw to the point of cracking a crown just to hold everything in was funny, then he supposed he did look funny.

"I'm okay."

She tilted her head, staring harder. Sullivan tried to scrounge up a smile, to prove he was just fine and dandy when nothing could be further from the truth. Suddenly Charlotte jumped off her chair and ran from the room, exclaiming,

"Be right back!"

He rose from his crouched position, confused by the sudden move, wondering where his daughter had taken off to. The sounds of heavy footsteps pounding up the stairs, followed by the crash of her bedroom door hitting the wall, carried down to him. He winced but tried to remember he'd just laid a lot on her and shouldn't reprimand her for slamming doors. She was eight. They were working on it and frankly, tonight, he could give her a pass.

The thumping footsteps sounded once again, and he wondered how a tiny child could make such a racket. And then she was there, standing in front of him again, hands holding something behind her back, a sweet smile on her face.

"Here, Daddy." She brought the object out from behind her back, thrusting it toward him. "You can sleep with El tonight. Whenever I get sad or scared, El makes me feel better. She's great at snuggles."

He reached down, taking the soft, stuffed elephant from his daughter's generous, caring hands. Her gesture struck him like an arrow to the heart. She was worried about him? That wasn't how this was supposed to go. Parents worried over their kids, not the other way around. As he cuddled the fuzzy animal with the ridiculously big googly eyes, he felt his heart pound with so many emotions: anger, grief, fear, love.

"Thank you, angel. I'm sure El will make me feel much better. You sure you don't need her tonight?"

"No. I can cuddle CC."

CC. The stuffed penguin Cam had given to Charlotte on their last zoo visit. At this rate, his daughter could open her own stuffed zoo in no time.

"Okay, time for bed then."

They headed up the stairs—quietly this time—and went

through Charlotte's nightly routine. He tucked her into bed, kissing her softly on the forehead.

"Goodnight, Charlotte. I love you."

"Night, Daddy. Love you too." She gave a jaw-cracking yawn, tired little eyes closing as she muttered sleepily. "I like it when Ellie tucks me into bed. Why did she leave, Daddy? Tomorrow is pancake day. I like the funny shapes Ellie makes."

Sad little eyes glanced up at him, sleep creeping into their depths as she waited for his answer. A low burn started in his chest. He rubbed at the spot, recognizing the pain for what it was.

Guilt.

Ellie left because he told her to. Because he all but pushed her out the door. His brain had been about to explode, and he couldn't contain all the rage and despair inside as she stood there offering to help. Sullivan had been the head of his family for so long, the one everyone came to when they needed help. He'd forgotten how to ask for it himself. He didn't think he would even know what to do with the help that someone offered. The help Ellie offered. So he'd pushed her away. Hurt her.

Nice going, dickhead.

He'd been so consumed with how this news affected him and Charlotte, he'd completely disregarded Ellie. Treated her like she didn't matter, like she wasn't a part of their lives, when that couldn't be further from the truth.

"Maybe since mommy is gone, Ellie can be my new mommy." Charlotte said, her eyes drooping closed.

The words trailed off as she slipped off to sleep, but he heard them loud and clear. He had no idea what to do with them. He cared for the woman deeply. Might even say he was inching off the cliff into full-blown love. But after what he'd dealt with tonight, what he learned about his ex, the bottom of that cliff was filled with razor sharp rocks, just waiting for him to fall, and be impaled.

How could he trust in love when his own ex-wife not only abandoned her child—the one human a person is supposed to love unconditionally—but also never made contact once she gained sobriety? Could he take that leap, knowing Ellie might eventually leave? Her leaving would affect Charlotte on a deeper psychological level, considering she would be old enough to remember it. How could he risk his daughter's happiness?

Liar. It's not about Charlotte.

The words echoed in his head. Telling him he was full of shit. It wasn't his daughter he was worried about, not entirely anyway. He was worried about himself. Sullivan was afraid of putting his heart on the line again. Afraid of opening up, confessing his love and devotion only to have it thrown in his face, tossed to the side of the road like trash. It hurt when Claire left. More than he let anyone know. He'd sucked it up because he had to, because he had to be there for Charlotte. If he let himself love Ellie and she left him or she died….

An icy cold chill skated up his spine.

He couldn't handle that. It would break him, and he couldn't afford to be broken. Not when the people in his life depended on him. Gavin and Charlotte. That's why he pushed Ellie away tonight. He knew if he let her comfort him, their relationship would take a turn, one they couldn't come back from, and he couldn't handle that right now. Perhaps ever.

He clutched El to his chest, knowing the kind, caring woman who gave this to his daughter deserved better than a man like him. A man who, for all intents and purposes, appeared to have his life together. But he didn't. Deep down, he was broken. His jagged edges would only end up hurting Ellie in the end. She deserved more than him, better.

But I don't want to give her up.

It was a no-win situation. He should sleep on it, decide what to do in a few days. He needed to apologize, that much he knew for certain, but beyond that…He had no fucking clue what to do.

CHAPTER 30

"*A*ll right, Doll-face. Spill it."

Ellie looked up from the bottom of the tawny mouth owl enclosure she was currently cleaning into Cam's worried face.

"Spill what?"

"The reason you've been moping around ever since you got here today." Cam sighed. "For the past few weeks, you've been Mary-freakin'-Sunshine around here. I swear once I even heard you giggle!"

Giggle? Ellie didn't giggle. Snorted when she laughed too hard, wheezed if she tried to hold it in, but never giggled.

"It's been wonderful seeing you so happy, but today it's like you have your own personal rain cloud following you around. So fess up. What happened? Do I need to go kick Dr. Sexy's ass?"

"No. You don't need to do anything to *Sullivan*. Nothing is wrong."

One dark red eyebrow arched. "Really? Then why haven't I seen you look at your phone once today?"

She shrugged, using the scraper in her hand to pick up

some dried feces on one of the tree branches and drop it in the bucket by her feet. "I'm at work. We're not supposed to look at our phones while we're on shift."

Her friend choked out a strange sound, a mix between a laugh and a groan. "Yeah, we're not *supposed* to, but that doesn't stop most of us. You included, recently. You and your boyfriend send ridiculous animal puns back and forth all day."

Her jaw dropped as she stared at her nosy friend. "Have you been reading my text messages?"

Cam curled her lip in insult. "What? No! You talk to yourself, and not quietly, I might add, laughing very loudly at every silly text. It's cute, on the verge of annoying."

"Oh…well, I'm just…trying to be more professional lately."

Cam gave her a hard look. "Or you and Dr. Soon-to-have-my-foot-up-his-ass broke up."

She sighed heavily. "We didn't break up."

Right?

They hadn't. Sullivan never said anything about breaking up. He'd just asked her to leave after receiving bad news. Devastating news. News he needed to share with his family, with Charlotte. Not her, because she wasn't family. She was just his girlfriend…she was still his girlfriend, right?

I wouldn't be too sure about that. He obviously doesn't care that much about you if he doesn't want comfort from you in a time of crisis. That's what loved ones are for. To lean on when times are tough. Sullivan doesn't want or need to lean on you. Ergo, he doesn't love you. You're just a body to warm his bed. He doesn't care. No one does. Why would anyone care about you when you ruin everything? His ex-wife's death was probably karma for you barging in on his life and trying to take over the role of wife and mother. You wished her dead. You know you did. This is your fault.

No, it wasn't!

She never wished Claire any harm. How could she when she didn't even know the woman? And she hadn't barged in on anything. Sullivan had invited her to dinner that first time. Charlotte invited her to her birthday party. They wanted her there. They wanted her in their lives.

Then why doesn't he want you there now?

She didn't know, but it wasn't her fault. She'd done nothing wrong. The dark voice in her head could say whatever it wanted, but she knew the truth. Whatever reason Sullivan had for asking her to leave the other night had nothing to do with her.

"Hey, Ellie." Cam's warm hands cupped her face, pulling her in close. "Breathe, sweetie, just breathe."

It was then she realized she'd been holding her breath. Spots danced before her eyes, her vision fading in and out. She opened her mouth and gulped in a huge breath of air, the darkness receding, her friend's face coming into focus, concern etched on every flawless, contoured inch of it.

"That's it, in and out."

Cam breathed with her, taking slow breaths, which Ellie mimicked, until she finally found her voice.

"I'm okay now."

"You sure?" Cam stared hard. "You want me to call Dr. Mitchell?"

Her friend knew what her panic attacks looked like, having witnessed several over the years. Most people freaked out or didn't understand and thought she was being rude when she froze up like that, but not Cam. At least if her relationship with Sullivan crashed and burned, she'd always have Cam. She did not deserve such a wonderful friend, but she wasn't giving her up either.

"No. Really, I'm fine now."

Blue eyes narrowed, but after a minute of searching her face for any sign of deception, Cam nodded and released her.

"Okay, so no psychologist call, but do I need to call a certain PCP and chew his ass out for breaking my bestie's heart?"

"He didn't break my heart." Not yet anyway. "He just got some bad news over the weekend. I guess it's affecting me, too."

"Oh, sweetie."

Her friend opened her arms wide, and she wasn't too proud to step into her embrace and accept the hug she so desperately needed.

"I'm sorry," Cam said, pulling away. "Is there anything I can do to help?"

"I don't think so." Considering he wouldn't even let Ellie help she doubted Sullivan would welcome anyone else's. "He just needs time and space."

"Ugh! Men and their macho attitudes. It wouldn't kill them to cry on someone's shoulder every now and then or lean on someone else. But do they? No, because society brainwashes them from birth to be 'strong.' Ha!" Cam pointed a finger. "Show me one person who doesn't feel better after a good hard cry, and I'll show you the fountain of youth."

Anxiously wanting to change the subject, she spouted off the first thing that came to mind.

"So why do you hate Gavin?"

Cam's brow rose. "Hate Gavin? Why would you think I hate Gavin?"

She shrugged, getting the last of the mess off the tree branch and making her way out of the enclosure with Cam following. "You two are always fighting whenever you're together."

Her friend barked out a laugh. "Oh, sweetie, that's not fighting. That's verbal foreplay."

"Huh?"

Cam bent down to the large cage where Bert and Ernie—

the two tawny mouths from the exhibit—were happily resting. She opened the cage, reaching in to grab Bert, who opened one bright yellow eye and snapped at her hand in irritation at being disturbed.

"We do this every week, big guy. Do you want your home to smell like poop and rotten grasshoppers?"

"We really need to stop feeding those to them." Ellie mused as she put the rest of the cleaning supplies in the bucket by her feet. "They prefer beetles."

"Rob said the last beetle supply made them sick, so he wants us to hold off for a month. Sorry, guys."

She watched as Cam slipped a big fat earthworm out of her front pocket and held it out to the bird. Bert tipped his beak, pecking at the gift before opening and swallowing the thing whole quicker than a blink. After devouring the peace offering the cranky bird was much more acquiescent to being jostled from his slumber.

"Why did you have a worm in your pocket?"

Her friend glanced at her in disbelief. "Oh, like you don't have a sardine for Bingo hidden in your bra."

She didn't. It was in her shirt pocket. As if she could hold anything in her bra. She didn't even need the thing to hold her boobs. Sullivan didn't seem to mind the size of her breasts. In fact, the man commented on their perfection repeatedly. He had, that is. Would he ever do so again?

Her thoughts turned morose thinking of Sullivan and their whole situation once again, so she focused on what Cam had said a few moments ago.

"What do you mean, verbal foreplay?"

Cam—who had safely deposited Bert on a high branch and was now moving Ernie, who wouldn't wake even if the building were coming down around him—gave her a sassy wink.

"It means Gavin Green thinks he's the universe's gift to

women and I enjoy taking him down a peg or two. The man needs it."

Really? She'd always thought Gavin was very nice.

"So insulting each other is...sexy?"

Cam placed Ernie up next to Bert, standing on her toes to reach the branch. Ellie would have had to use a ladder. That's why she cleaned this exhibit, and Cam handled the animal removal and replacement. Dragging a ladder everywhere was cumbersome and annoying. But her height worked to her advantage in other ways. Like how she fit perfectly into the crook of Sullivan's arm as they fell asleep.

Stop thinking about him, it's only making you sad.

"It's not insulting so much as," Cam paused, scrunching up her nose in thought. "Baiting."

"Baiting?"

Her friend nodded. "Yeah, like in fishing, when you dangle the worm out there for the trout, luring it in with pretty bait and a sharp hook, but then, after you catch it, you take a picture for bragging rights and throw it back."

"Sooooo, you want to hook Gavin for bragging rights and throw him back?"

Cam laughed, her dark red ponytail bouncing as she threw her head back. "Oh no, Doll-face. He wants to hook me and throw me back. That's the playboy MO. But this player is about to realize he's not in the regular game. These are my rules, and this fish is the biting kind."

Her head was so dizzy she didn't even know which way was up anymore. "Okay, there were too many metaphors in that for me to follow. Do you want to sleep with Gavin or not?"

Cam shrugged. "Sure. He's hot and funny and while he seems like a bed-hopper, I don't think he's cruel about it. He's pretty straightforward in acknowledging his one-and-done policy."

"So why not just go for it?"

"Because then it'd be over. You know I live for the anti-ci..." Cam put her hands on her hips and did her best Tim Curry. "Pation!"

She couldn't help but laugh. She loved her friend and had no idea why dragging out something that was essentially going to be a one-night stand would be fun, but hey, whatever floated her boat. As long as Cam was happy, Ellie could understand that much.

The rest of the day flew by because of a burst pipe in the rainforest exhibit. They had to call maintenance to come fix it, and while that was being done, they closed the aviary and moved all the birds in the affected exhibits into the back room. All the cages they used to house the animals during cleaning times were full. The large gray room was a cacophony of angry and terrified squawking, chirps, and whistles. The poor creatures were upset and frightened. She and Cam did their best to calm them, but animals didn't understand they were being moved because their home was unsafe at the moment.

Finally, after a very long and noisy two hours, the problem was fixed, and all the birds returned to their homes. Ellie drove home from the zoo tired, stressed, and still sad. But the second she arrived home, the sight at her front door caused her heart to stop in her chest.

CHAPTER 31

*S*ullivan.

Leaning against her door, head down, dirty blonde hair slightly rumbled. A day's worth of stubble on his narrow jaw, stood Sullivan Green. He looked good. Okay, he didn't look *good*. He looked like he hadn't slept well the past few nights, but he was here. To see her presumably, and that made him a sight for sore eyes.

"Hi."

His head snapped up at her soft greeting.

"Hi, Ellie. How are you?"

She felt like she should ask him that question, but not sure of his response, she went with, "I'm good."

"Good, good, that's good."

He wasn't better. There was no smile on his face, no sparkle in his eyes. He seemed distracted and anxious. Not at all like the confident, sweet, funny Sullivan Green she knew and loved. She wished he would open up to her, share his pain so she could help him through this. It didn't matter how long it took. He didn't have to suffer through this alone.

Maybe that was why he was here. To lean on her. Talk things out. She hoped so.

"Do you—would you like to come in?" Gah, she was so nervous. Why was she so nervous?

"Yeah, that'd be great."

Relief rushed out of her on a deep breath. She pulled her keys from her purse and opened her front door, motioning for him to follow her in. She turned the lock three times and then three more. Her compulsions had increased since their...it wasn't really a fight, but she didn't know what else to call it. Troubles?

Sullivan's eyes followed her movement, his frown deepening at the repetition of her locking ritual. She had no idea what he was thinking right now, and she was too afraid to ask. It wasn't his fault her anxiety was going into overdrive right now. Well, it kind of was. It was the entire situation, not Sullivan specifically. But she could handle it.

She released the door and clenched her hands into fists to stop herself from checking a third time.

She would handle it.

"Would you like a drink?" she asked as they entered her small living room.

Sullivan shook his head. "No. I can't stay long."

Her heart sank.

"School night."

"Oh, yes, of course."

"But I needed to come and see you. I needed to...apologize."

"Apologize?"

They stood less than a foot apart, but to Ellie it felt like hundreds of miles.

"Yes. I didn't handle the news of Claire's death very well the other night and I wanted to say I'm sorry if I upset you or made you feel scared or bad in any way."

"Oh Sullivan." Unable to stand the distance, she took a step, placing her hand on his arm. The muscles were tense, like the strings of a bow before it snapped. "I don't think there's a rule-book on how to handle the death of someone you loved. No matter how many years you were separated, it still hurts."

When he said nothing, she pressed. "How's Charlotte doing with all this?"

He laughed, but there was no humor in it. "Fine. Better than me, that's for damn sure."

That was good. At least the sweet girl wasn't traumatized by her mother's death.

"I'm just..." He threw his head back, glaring at the ceiling as his eyes shone bright with unshed tears. "Shit, I'm just so fucking mad at her. I mean, how could she be sober for two years and not contact Charlotte once?"

His pain was tearing her apart. If she could, she would reach into his chest and rip it all out, toss it away so he never had to hurt again.

"Maybe she had a reason for staying away?"

His head snapped down, green eyes locking with hers. "What reason is there to abandon your daughter when you're fully capable of interacting with her?"

She had no idea. Crap, she always said the wrong things.

"I mean, I get why she stayed away when she was on drugs. I wouldn't have let her see Charlotte like that. But I told her when she sent the divorce papers that if she ever got clean, she could come see her daughter. Try to foster a rela-tionship with her. Now...Charlotte can never have that—she will never know her mother."

A tear slipped down her cheek, the warm wetness chilling in the coolness of her apartment, reminding her this wasn't her tragedy to bear, but she felt the pain all the same, because it affected those she loved. Sullivan. Charlotte.

His hand reached out, thumb brushing the fallen tear away. She turned her head, kissing his palm, putting all the love and support she could into the gentle graze of her lips against his skin.

"Do you need anything?"

He'd already refused her help, but she thought she'd ask again. Let him know he wasn't alone in this. She was here for him and Charlotte. If only he'd let her be. But her hopes were crushed again as Sullivan shook his head.

"No. I need...I think I need some time."

Time? Oh no, please no.

She cleared her throat of the sob threatening to break free. "Time?"

Pulling his hand back to his side, he took the slightest step backwards. One tiny step that may as well have been a thousand miles.

"Yeah. There are some legal matters to attend to and I need to focus on Charlotte right now..."

"I understand." She did. She really did. His daughter was the most important person in his life, as she should be, but she'd hoped Sullivan had room for her, too. "Will you call me? When you get everything settled?"

Desperate of her to ask? Maybe, but she was feeling desperate right now. And terrified, sad, lonely, a host of emotions she wanted to rip out of her chest and throw as far away as she possibly could.

Sullivan hesitated, his gaze darting to the door and back to her. His usually bright green eyes dulled, concern and regret filling them. "I...don't know if that's a good idea."

Her throat closed, heart racing in her chest. She swallowed past the fear and found enough of her voice to ask, "What do you mean?"

"This whole situation is," Sullivan ran a frustrated hand

over his hair, ruffling the unkempt style even further. "It's complicated and stressful."

Death was always complicated and stressful. It wasn't like people she loved hadn't died before. She might never have lost someone as significant as a former spouse, but she'd lost loved ones. She knew the devastating impact it had on a person.

"I don't want my issue to affect your…" he trailed off, the unspoken message loud and clear.

He thought she couldn't handle helping him through this loss because of OCD.

Bit by bit, anger replaced the fear. How dare he use her OCD as an excuse to shut her out of his life. Out of Charlotte's life. He said he understood. Was that all just a lie?

"I'm fine, Sullivan."

His brow rose, hand reaching out to grasp the fingers she hadn't realized were tugging on her ear.

"Really?"

She pulled her hand from his hold.

He shook his head. "Ellie, can you honestly say that this situation hasn't had a negative effect on your OCD?"

No. She wasn't saying that at all, but that didn't mean he could use it to shove her out of his life. She was so damn tired of letting people do that. She wouldn't allow it with Sullivan. Not when he and Charlotte were so important to her.

"I'll admit, lately, things have been a bit…difficult on that front, but managing my OCD is my business, Sullivan."

"And my ex-wife's death is mine!"

She winced at his shout. His eyes closed. When they opened again, she saw a world of pain in them. Her heart clenched. She could feel his emotions like a physical blow to the gut.

"I'm sorry, Ellie." Green eyes glossed over as he blinked

back tears. "But look what I did to Claire. I couldn't even help my own wife."

So how could he help her? She knew that's what he was thinking. But he didn't need to help her. Didn't he see?

"You don't have to fix every person around you, Sullivan." She placed a gentle hand on his arm, encouraged when he didn't pull away. "Everyone has their own problems, their own issues to deal with. All you can do is offer to help and accept help when it's offered to you."

He focused on the hand she placed on his arm. Her heart in her throat, she waited, hopeful wishes crushed when he shook his head and took a step away from her touch.

"I'm sorry, Ellie. But I just…I can't do this." He swallowed hard, voice cracking as he admitted, "I can't be the man you need me to be."

With those parting words he turned and headed out of her apartment door, leaving her standing there, her body as hard and frozen as a statue while her heart broke into a thousand jagged pieces. A broken puzzle she feared she'd never be able to put back together.

CHAPTER 32

"Charlotte, please come back here and hang up your backpack properly."

Sullivan sighed as his daughter skidded to a halt in the hallway. Her sneakers would leave scuff marks on the hardwood. Sometimes he wished he'd gone for a carpeted house instead, but his real estate agent had insisted hardwood had better resale value.

"Sorry, Daddy."

She flashed a bright smile at him as she hurried back to grab her discarded bag and hang it on the short hook his brother had installed for her the day she'd started preschool —dang, had it really been four years ago? Where did the time go? Some days, it felt like it stretched on forever, especially in those early years of midnight feedings and constant diaper changes. Yet here they were, Charlotte, a smart, sweet, independent little girl and Sullivan...

Lonely.

Yeah, he could admit he missed Ellie. It'd been four days since he'd gone by her place to give his piss-poor apology and ended up breaking things off. When he saw her compulsions had increased, knowing he caused it, it hit him like a punch to the gut. There he was, hurting the person he cared for, again. He couldn't do that to her. He couldn't be the one to make her backslide when she'd been doing so well. How many people did he have to fail before he realized he just wasn't meant to be with anyone?

He'd seen the pain in Ellie's eyes when he said they were over and called himself every foul name in the books—and a few he was sure he'd invented—because he knew she was hurting, but he also knew he was the wrong man for her. If they continued their relationship, he'd just end up failing her.

Like he'd failed Claire.

He'd taken the week off work to sort out all the legal issues, arranging for Claire's funeral, processing the death certificate, speaking to her lawyer about her last will and testament. Claire had been an only child and her parents died before he'd ever met her, so as her ex-husband, it listed him as her next of kin. All the paperwork had kept him busy, but there'd been a lot of moments the past few days where his thoughts had drifted to Ellie.

It was strange not to see her, talk to her, text her. In such a short time, she'd become such an important part of his daily life. It felt like he was missing an organ. That's how integral the woman had become to him. But he was trying to do the right thing. For Ellie. Even if it was slowly ripping his damn soul to shreds every day he went without her.

"Daddy, I'm hungry."

Blinking, he glanced down as his daughter's statement pulled him out of his thoughts.

"Okay, go wash up and I'll start making dinner."

She skipped off to the bathroom. He headed toward the kitchen, shifting through the pile of mail he'd grabbed from the mailbox on their way inside the house. Bills, junk mail, flyers, nothing of note. Until he came to a large manila envelope with his name and Claire's attorney's name in the upper left-hand corner.

He'd been receiving correspondence from the agency since receiving the news of his ex's passing. Legal stuff mostly, things he needed to sign. When he opened the envelope, he expected more documents, but what he pulled out was another, smaller envelope with his name scrawled on it in Claire's handwriting. There was also a slip of paper from the attorney.

He clutched the letter from his former wife in his hand tightly as he read the attorney's letter first.

Dear Mr. Green,

Again, I would like to extend my deepest sympathies for your loss. Your former spouse left this letter in our care to be delivered to you in the event of her demise.

Sincerely,

Aaron Stedman

Stedman, Bernstein, and Rhodes

She'd written him a letter to be delivered in the event of her death? What the hell did that mean? Only one way to find out. Taking a deep breath, he steeled his nerves and ripped open the envelope. It shocked him again to find yet another envelope in this one, along with a sheet of paper. This envelope was standard letter size, from Claire—judging by the identical handwriting—but addressed to Charlotte.

His heart pounded. She'd written a letter to their daughter. What could she have said? Did this mean she cared? Thought about Charlotte? If she had, why hadn't she visited? He wanted to rip open the envelope and scan the note for answers, but he wouldn't do that. It was addressed to his daughter from her mother. He wouldn't take that away from her.

Besides—he glanced at the handwritten page still sitting

in the middle envelope—it appeared he had his own letter to read. Hopefully, it would contain some damn answers.

He carefully set his daughter's letter on the counter and unfolded the slip of paper, presumably meant for him. When he saw the neatly rounded letters of his ex-wife's handwriting, a flood of memories filled his mind. Their first meeting in the university's library, first date at mini golf, first kiss...it hadn't always been bad between them. They'd loved each other once. Their time together hadn't been a waste, not when it created Charlotte.

Letting out a painful breath, he focused on the words on the paper.

Sullivan,

If you're reading this, I'm dead.

Too "spy movie" cliché?

Claire had always had a darker sense of humor.

I hope you never receive this letter because if you do, it means I really am gone, and I never got the chance to apologize.

His heart flipped in his chest, reading the last word.

I've done a lot of horrible things in my life. I cheated on my finals in AP Chem. I stole my roommate's blue sweater and told her it got lost in the laundry. I might have faked it that first time we were together (nothing against you, I was just too nervous and didn't want you to feel bad). But the worst thing I ever did, the most selfish, was abandoning you and Charlotte.

His vision blurred, but he blinked away the tears, determined to get through this.

I was in a bad place for a long time. I know you think it was having Charlotte, the pain and medication they prescribed me after, that made me fall into my addiction, but it wasn't. Those were just excuses, symptoms to blame on a bigger problem I'd been hiding for years. I've always struggled, but I was taught to hide my problems. Brush them under a rug and put on a happy face. In my house you didn't foist your problems on other people. You handled them yourself.

An uncomfortable ache burned in the center of his chest. Her words were hitting a little too close to home for him right now. How had he not seen his ex-wife was just like him? Hiding her pain, her needs, because it was what she thought she was supposed to do. Looked like they had more in common than he thought.

But after I had Charlotte, I don't know what happened. I couldn't put on a happy face anymore. The drugs they gave me made me feel content at first, but then I came to discover I needed more and more to get back to that place of bliss. The place where nothing mattered but the light, fluffy feeling I got whenever I shook that bottle, knowing oblivion was on its way.

I knew I was using the pills as a cover—a temporary solution that eventually turned into an even bigger problem. I'm so sorry I never talked to you or told you how I was really feeling. I shut you out. I thought I could handle everything on my own and that was wrong. I left because I thought you and Charlotte would be better off without me.

At first, I just figured I'd say fuck the world and stay in my drug-induced euphoria forever, but then I realized that wasn't what I truly wanted. I wanted to be happy. I wanted a relationship with my daughter. I knew I already screwed up too badly for you to take me back, but I wanted Charlotte in my life. Even if it was only part time.

He didn't know if he would have given Claire a second chance had she sobered up and come back. Honestly, by the end of their marriage they were so distant, so broken, he didn't know if it could have been repaired. Now he never would.

I tried to get better. Had a few slips up. But I've been doing well for the past year and a half. I promised myself if I made it to three years without falling off the wagon, I'd come back and ask for forgiveness. Maybe try to be the mother Charlotte deserves.

Of course, if you're reading this, it means I failed. Again. Big time.

She hadn't failed. Claire had experienced a common accident that could have happened to anyone, sober or not. One more year. She could have made it one more year. He didn't know how he knew that, but deep in his soul, he believed she would have succeeded in her sobriety.

I wrote a letter to Charlotte explaining things as best as I could. If you could give it to her when she'd ready, I would appreciate it. And please tell her mommy loved her and thought of her every single day. I never stopped being her mother, even when I wasn't there. I hope you can both come to forgive me, and I hope you find someone who makes you happy. Someone who you can be open and honest with, who loves without fear and will be a wonderful mother to Charlotte.

See you on the other side,

Claire

The edge of the paper crumpled slightly in his tight grip. A million thoughts raced through his mind at everything Claire had revealed. It took a moment for him to realize the warmth on his face was tears pouring down his cheeks. He sniffed, wiping away the moisture with the back of his hand. Claire had dropped a lot on him, including a very real, heartfelt apology. The anger he'd held for so many years for abandoning their daughter was still there, but muted, fading with the realization that she'd only done what she thought was best.

No one was perfect. He certainly wasn't. Eerie discovering how similarly they dealt with their problems, but then again, maybe that's why they got together. Like attracted like, but sometimes you didn't need a person who was your exact match. You couldn't fit two of the same pieces together. You needed to find someone who would complement your puzzle piece. Someone whose strengths compensated for your weaknesses, someone who smoothed out your rough edges, someone who filled in your holes with their love.

Someone like Ellie.

Yes. He loved Ellie. Loved her with a deep-seated fierceness he never imagined possible. He'd been afraid to reveal his weakness to her, afraid to ask for her help because he was too accustomed to being the fixer. Afraid he was bad for her would fail her like he failed Claire. But it turned out he and Claire failed each other. They hadn't even tried to be better. They'd just run away from their problems instead of opening up and facing them. Helping each other.

He didn't want to make that same mistake again.

"Daddy? What's wrong?"

He turned to see Charlotte had come back into the room, the sleeves of her shirt drenching wet because she'd most likely played in the sink again as she washed up. A small laugh escaped him, seeing the joy in her playful exploration instead of the annoyance he usually felt at her mess.

"Nothing, Angel. I just…I'm a little happy and a little sad."

Her tiny nose scrunched up in confusion. "How can you be happy and sad at the same time?"

Knowing he'd have to answer that, and a lot of other tricky questions throughout her life, he crouched down in front of her, giving her a big smile.

"Hey, how would you like to help me with a surprise for Ellie tomorrow?"

Green eyes lit up. "Oh yes! I can help. We haven't seen Ellie in like forever."

Felt that way to him, too.

"Okay, good. Let's have dinner and talk about the super-secret surprise for Ellie."

An idea was slowly coming together in his head. An apology, a real one this time, an honest explanation, and a promise. He had so many promises he wanted to give Ellie. The woman saved his daughter. She'd created a place in his heart and their lives for her. An Ellie place. He just hoped there was a Sullivan and Charlotte place in hers.

CHAPTER 33

*S*o this is what heartbreak feels like.

Ellie stood by the large sink in the back room of the aviary building, scrubbing out the end of day feed buckets. She was alone in the room, except for Bill, the parrot who had a nasty cold and was currently quarantined in a nice cage for his and the other birds' safety. Since the sweet, sick bird wasn't much of a conversationalist, it gave Ellie plenty of time to think. Unfortunately, all her thoughts lately revolved around Sullivan and how he was doing and how desperately she wanted to call and check up on him and Charlotte.

But she couldn't do that because the insufferable man broke up with her, claiming he was doing what was best for her. Why did people always say they were doing something for others when the truth of the matter was, they were just scared. She knew Sullivan was scared, terrified even. She'd seen it in his eyes. He'd had to deal with a lot lately. Things she would never understand, but dammit, she could help him if he'd just let her. That's what people in relationships do.

But you're not in a relationship. Not anymore. Because you ruined it.

She clenched her jaw, closing her eyes to take a few deep calming breaths and block out the dark voice.

She'd scheduled an emergency session with Dr. Mitchell because her anxiety had worsened. Her OCD reacting to the stress. Her rituals were getting longer, more involved. Monday, she was ten minutes late to work because she'd had to check every appliance in her apartment and unplug them, so nothing caught fire and burned her place down while she was away. That was the moment she knew it was time to get professional help.

Dr. Mitchell let her talk through everything that had been going on lately. They'd discussed her feelings around Sullivan's refusal of help, his declaration that he was wrong for her and how it hurt her, how it made her dark voice cry out in glee. Telling her it was right. She ruined everything. All the bad things in life were her fault.

But it wasn't true. She knew it deep down. They'd discussed how his actions made her feel and the reality of the situation. After a two-hour session, she left feeling much better, stronger, able to cope. She'd be eating instant noodles for a month just to cover the cost of the session, but it was a sacrifice she had to make. Hopefully, one day, mental healthcare would be more accessible and affordable. For now, she was just grateful her employer covered partial costs.

She'd been trying to keep busy this past week without the company of Sullivan and Charlotte. A quick call to her landlord revealed the apartment next door was indeed available for rent. She'd called her brother and given him all the information. In two weeks, she'd be living next door to her big brother. They hadn't been this close since he left home after high school, and she couldn't wait. It was a small bit of happiness in the dreariness that was her life at the moment.

"Awwwrk! Hello, Doll-face."

Bill squawked just as the employee door opened.

"Hey yourself, Bill. Ugh! I am so glad it's Friday," Cam said, as she came into the back room carrying a trash bag filled with droppings from the toucan enclosure she'd been cleaning. "This week has just draaaaaagged by. Ya know?"

"Yeah."

Did she ever. Since Sullivan left her apartment without so much as a backward glance Monday night, the minutes had felt like hours. Normally the week went by in a flash—caring for animals was busy work—but the past few nights Ellie had come home to her apartment, scrounged up some dinner and sat in front of her television catching up on nature documentaries. Just a short time ago, that would have been her norm. But the past few months had been packed with date nights, movie nights, puzzle nights. Wonderful, amazing nights filled with laughter, company, and love.

Her life before had been nice, but lonely. With Sullivan, she'd found that missing thing, the boom that made every day—even the bad ones—brighter. How long before she got that again? If ever?

"Hey, I have an idea." Cam came over to help her put the clean buckets on their shelf. "How about we go out tonight? Toppers started doing karaoke on Friday nights. We can belt out some old school Gloria Gaynor. I think *I Will Survive* is a requirement in situations like this."

This being Sullivan breaking up with her. She understood what her friend was doing, trying to get her out to the local bar for a night of drinks and fun. The crowds and karaoke sounded awful—Ellie had the voice of a shrieking barn owl— but spending time with her friend instead of another lonely night sitting in her empty apartment sounded like just what she needed.

"I'll go, but I'm not singing."

Cam stuck one ruby lip out in a pout.

She pointed a finger at her bestie. "I'm pretty sure every DJ ever has banned that song from their book. It's way overdone."

Cam shrugged. "Okay, we'll go emo then. My Chemical Romance?"

Chuckling, she shook her head. "I'll need a lot of vodka before I go anywhere near a mic."

"That can totally be arranged."

She hoped not. For the sake of everyone's ears at the bar tonight.

"Awwwwk, hello Doll-face!"

Ellie turned her head at Bill's greeting to see the employee door opening again. The bird would make a great alarm system. A smile curled her lips as Naya, one of Sunlight Zoo's chief security personnel, popped her head in. The cheerful woman with a light brown complexion and glossy dark hair —pulled back into a tight bun per security regulations— smiled as she glanced around the room.

"Hi Bill. Hey Cam, Ellie. Uh, Ellie, you have a couple of visitors. I told them I'd check to see if you were busy or not. I know it's close to quitting time, so I wasn't sure."

Wondering who would come to visit her since everyone she hung out with was either here or not currently speaking to her, she held her hands up and shrugged.

"We're pretty much done for the day. Show them on back."

Naya's smile widened. She glanced over her shoulder, motioning someone into the room.

"Ellie!"

Her heart stopped as the sweetest little angel with bouncing blonde pigtails ran into the room, arms stretched out wide. Reaching down, she grasped Charlotte as the girl collided into her. Tears filled her eyes as tiny arms squeezed tightly around her neck. It became slightly difficult to breathe, but she didn't care. She'd gladly give all the air in her lungs just to hold Charlotte again. She'd missed the little girl so much.

"Charlotte, what are you doing here?"

"We came to see you."

At the deep, familiar voice, Ellie glanced up to see Sullivan standing a few feet away, a blue gift bag clutched tightly in his left hand. Right, Naya had said a *couple* of people meaning more than one. Charlotte *and* Sullivan. The two people she'd wanted to see most in the world. The two people she'd been afraid she'd never get to see again. Why were they here? What was going on? More bad news? Oh, she hoped not. She hoped it was something good.

"Sullivan...hi."

"Hi."

"What, um, what are you doing here?"

He shifted on his feet nervously. "I wanted to talk to you."

"And give you a present!"

She looked down at the child in her arms and smiled at the excitement on her face.

"A present?" She gave an exaggerated gasp. "I love presents."

"Me too and you're really, really gonna like this one, Ellie. I helped pick it out. We had to go all the way to Denver to the mall, and we went to a bunch of stores, but they didn't have any anim—"

"Charlotte," Sullivan interrupted, waving his hand in the air. "You don't want to ruin the surprise."

Tiny hands covered her mouth as the girl bunched her shoulders sheepishly. "Oh, right."

"Remember what we talked about, Angel? Do you think you could wait with Naya for a minute while I talk to Ellie?"

"I was just about to do my final walkthrough of the building," Cam said. "She can come with me if she likes."

"That'd be great, Cam. Thank you."

"No problemo. Come on, sweetie. Let's go say goodnight to all the birds."

Her friend held a hand out to Charlotte, who wiggled out of her arms and rushed to grab it.

"Yay! Birdies!"

"Thank you, Naya. And thank you, too, Cam," Sullivan said.

Naya gave a simple nod and smile, but her bestie narrowed her gaze, taking two fingers and pointing first to her eyes, then to Sullivan. Once everyone left, the room fell quiet. Only Sullivan and her, and Bill of course, but for once the noisy bird was being silent.

"I can see I've made an enemy." Sullivan grimaced. "Does she know about—"

"I didn't tell her anything," she quickly interrupted. "But Cam is my best friend. She noticed I was being mopey lately and she kind of...guessed."

"She's smart."

Yes, her best friend was very smart and fiercely protective of those she loved. Ellie was glad to count herself in that group.

"I got a letter from Claire."

Stunned, Ellie didn't know what to say. Thankfully, she didn't have to say anything, as Sullivan continued.

"She wrote one for me and another for Charlotte to open when she's ready. She wrote them in the case of her...well, you know."

Her death. Something that no one planned on happening, but came for everyone in the end.

"She said a lot in the letter. A lot of things she needed to say. A lot of things I needed to hear. There were apologies and explanations, but none of that is why I came here to talk to you today." He sucked in a deep breath. Bright green eyes focused on her, shining with glossy tears. "I'm so sorry for hurting you, Ellie. For making you feel like you don't matter to me, to us. You are so important to Charlotte and me for so many reasons. You saved my daughter's life, but you also saved mine. Before you I was just going through life so focused, I didn't realize how lonely I was, how empty parts of my life were. I thought all I needed was Charlotte and work. As long as I concentrated on those two things, everything would be fine. But it wasn't fine. I wasn't fine."

A tear slipped from the corner of his eye. He did nothing to hide it, nothing to brush it away.

"I was so intent on taking care of everything and everyone else, I forgot to take care of myself, allow someone else to care for me every once in a while. Then you came into my life and changed all that. You became someone I could lean on. Someone I could call for help with an elephant birthday party on less than a week's noticed."

She gave a watery laugh, her own eyes filled with moisture.

"You brought laughter into our house. Fun. Animal puns. So, so many animal puns."

"Well, I do have the necessary *koala*-fications for those."

He laughed along with her, reaching out his right hand. When she extended her own hand, he grasped it, pulling her to him. Her arms automatically went around his neck.

"Ellie, you give us laughter, friendship, love. You fit into our life perfectly."

She shook her head. "I'm not perfect. You know that."

He nodded. "No one is perfect. Me especially."

He grimaced, brow furrowing as she watched him concentrate hard on what he wanted to say next. She stayed silent, waiting with hopeful anticipation and a fair amount of caution.

"I thought I failed Claire, but it turns out we failed each other."

She squeezed him gently, encouraging him to continue.

"I didn't want to make your life worse, make it harder for you, but I realize now I can't be responsible for other people's happiness. We each take the love we think we deserve and until you...I guess I thought I didn't deserve love at all."

She shook her head, a warm tear slipping down her cheek. If anyone deserved love in this world, it was the wonderful man standing in front of her.

"But then I met you and I started to question everything I ever thought. We're all a bit damaged. No one gets through life without a few nicks and bruises along the way. But you are perfect for us. You fit. Like puzzle night. We need all of us. All the pieces to come together as one to make the picture. I wouldn't change one thing about you. Not one. Because when you find the person you love, you love everything about them because it's what makes them *them*. And I love you, Eleanor Clark."

The tears were flowing now. Big fat drops rolling down both cheeks. When her lips parted in a smile, she could taste the salty warmth sliding into her mouth. She was an ugly crier. She knew it, but Sullivan didn't care. He simply stood there, holding her, gazing at her as if she was the most beautiful thing he'd ever seen. She knew he certainly was to her.

"You love me?"

"With all my heart."

"I-I love you too." She could barely get the words out past the emotions choking her. Sullivan loved her! He wanted to lean on her, share with her. He needed her in his life! Never had she felt so awed, so accepted.

"Kiss me, Ellie. Please."

He didn't need to beg. She'd gladly do it. She'd been aching to kiss the man for days.

Going up on her toes, Ellie crashed her lips against his. No slow and gentle right now. She couldn't do it. There was too much stored-up need, too much happiness bursting from her body to be anything but demanding. Sullivan seemed fine with that if his eager participation was any indication. He cupped her face with one hand, tilting her head to better fit their mouths, deepening the angle of the kiss.

"Awwwwk, hello Doll-face!"

Bill's squawk pulled her out of a lust filled fog. She pulled back from Sullivan just as Cam and Charlotte came back into the room.

"Did you give it to her? Did you give it to her?" Charlotte asked, skipping into the room.

Give what to her? Oh, right. The present. Sullivan still clutched the blue gift bag in his left hand.

"Not yet, Angel. I was waiting for you to get back."

And too busy kissing her senseless to give her anything, but she wasn't complaining.

"I take it you made amends?" Cam arched one perfectly sculpted eyebrow.

"Cam." She grimaced at her friend, but Sullivan just smiled.

"I did indeed."

"Good."

"Daddddddyyyyy," Charlotte gave an exasperated eye roll. "Give her the present."

He smiled down at his daughter, handing over the blue gift bag. Ellie took it, not even caring what was inside. Sullivan loved her! What more did she need? Opening the bag, she reached in and pulled out a soft blue piece of material. It fell open to reveal a T-shirt with a picture of two large cartoon elephants with a baby elephant between them. Over the elephants were the words *We Love You A Ton!*

"Do you like it?" Charlotte asked, bouncing up and down with excitement.

She smiled down at the sweet girl. "I love it and I love you."

"I love you too, Ellie."

"And I love both of you," Sullivan said, pulling both of them into his arms.

A flash blinded her for a moment, and she glanced over to see Cam, phone in hand, tears shining in her eyes.

"Now that's a picture-perfect moment."

No. There were no perfect moments, no perfect people, but if you were really, *really* lucky, then you could find the other imperfect people in your life to help make it beautiful. And Ellie was very lucky because she'd found two.

EPILOGUE

*E*llie woke with a smile. It could have been because for the past three months she and Sullivan had been spending as much free time as they could together, with the bonus of her getting to hang with Charlotte loads. Maybe it was because Cam and Gavin had started dating and Ellie was finding she adored couple dates. Or because her brother had moved next door and started working for the Sunlight Fire Department and she got to see him regularly now. Her mother had been slowly coming around to accept her daughter as she was—she had a sneaking suspicion Sullivan had something to do with that development.

But if she had to put her finger on it, she'd say it was the hard, thick morning erection currently pressing against her backside. She thanked her lucky stars Charlotte was gone at a sleepover this weekend. Instead of going home to her apartment after their date last night, Sullivan had invited her to stay the night. The man had begged, on his knees, with his tongue in interesting places. Judging by the hardness pressing against her, he was ready for a repeat performance.

"Good morning."

The deep rumble vibrated against her back, sending a wake-up call to all her good places.

"How did you know I was awake?"

The arm around her waist tightened as his hand slipped up to cup her breasts. She let out a low, loud moan. No one was home but them. They could be as noisy as they wanted.

"You make this adorable little sigh the moment you wake up."

She snorted. "I do not."

"Do too."

She opened her mouth to argue, but his lips found that sweet spot on the back of her neck, the one that made her eyes cross, and she lost all train of thought. Since they'd fallen asleep after a marathon bout of lovemaking, they hadn't had the energy or desire to put on any pajamas. A fact for which she was now grateful, as Sullivan's hand slipped down between her bare legs to rub her just where she needed it. He worked her into a frenzy with his hand and mouth until she couldn't stand it anymore.

"Now, Sullivan. I need you now."

He shifted, rising above her to place himself at her entrance. For the millionth time, she reveled in her decision to get on the pill three months ago. Being a doctor, Sullivan was all about safety. They'd both gotten physicals, discussed health, and decided together that relying on one form of birth control was the best option for them.

Bright green eyes gazed into hers. "I love you, Ellie."

Her heart skipped a beat, as it always did when he said those words. And he said them often. During sex, in the morning, at night, when they said goodbye and hello. Any chance he got, really. And she loved saying them back.

"I love you too."

Then he pressed inside. Filling her, making her feel whole and complete. An astounding sensation she knew she'd never tire of. They moved as one, setting a familiar pace that both excited and comforted. It wasn't long before her breath quickened. Sullivan's muscles tensed above her. The sharp ball of pressure begging to be released coiled low in her belly.

"Sullivan!"

He knew exactly what to do at her cry. His hand reached down between their bodies, finding her clit, stroking, rubbing in small circles. In less than a minute, she was crying out with her release as it crashed over her like a waterfall of pure heavenly bliss. Sullivan followed soon after, shouting out her name as his body tensed, muscles pulling tight against her.

He collapsed, falling to the side of the bed so as not to land on top of her. His arm reached over to pull her onto his chest, where he played with her hair.

"Good morning indeed."

He chuckled. "I miss Charlotte when she's away, but I gotta say, it's nice not having to shout my release into a pillow."

She laughed along with him. Sullivan could be...noisy with their nighttime activities. But she didn't care if they had to be quiet. Honestly, they rarely engaged in anything when Charlotte was in the house. She still had her apartment, where they spent most of their intimate moments. One day she might give it up. If she and Sullivan decided to make a real go at this family thing, that was. She was game—was she ever! Ellie had no idea if she'd make a good mother for Charlotte, but she loved the little girl and her father. Wanted what was best for both of them. Wasn't that all you needed to be a good parent?

"Let's get ready for the day," he murmured against her brow. "The Cheeky Monkey will be home in a few hours."

More laughter escaped her. Sullivan had finally accepted that his brother would never give up the nickname and decided to follow the old moniker "if you can't beat 'em, join 'em."

They got out of bed and showered together—to conserve water, of course—then dressed for the day and headed down to the kitchen for breakfast. She made the coffee while Sullivan prepared eggs and bacon. They'd promised Charlotte not to make pancakes until she got home from her sleepover. Ellie couldn't believe how happy she was. Even her dark voice had quieted. It was still there, taunting her from time to time, whispering horrible things in her mind. OCD didn't go away simply because you fell in love.

But she could cope with it like she always had and even better, she now had someone by her side to fight with her whenever times got too dark. Sullivan didn't expect her to be "normal" or scoff whenever she performed her rituals to calm her anxiety. He patiently waited with a smile on his face, allowing her to do what she needed, checking in to make sure she was all right. They communicated with each other, leaned on each other. Problems seemed far less scary when you had someone by your side to help fight your battles.

It's going to end, eventually. You'll screw it up.

She tensed at the cruel thought in her head, but then a pair of warm, strong arms embraced her from behind and a low voice whispered in her ear, "I love you, Ellie. Nothing will ever change that."

She didn't deserve this man, but no way was she ever letting him get away. A smile curled her lips as she asked, "How do you always seem to know when I need reassurance?"

"Because I know you and you know me."

True. In the past few months, Sullivan had opened up, sharing his anger and guilt over his failed marriage and Claire's passing. They'd talked about the future and what they wanted in life. It wasn't always easy, but communicating openly and honestly, being vulnerable with each other, had bonded them in a way she'd never experienced before.

Once breakfast was ready, they sat down to eat, chatting about their upcoming week. The zoo was eagerly expecting the birth of a new giraffe, so her work had been hectic. Stephan and Rob pretty much lived at work these days and she and Cam had taken turns bringing the veterinarians meals. Sullivan's practice had been steadily gaining new patients. One of his longtime patients recently passed away in hospice care. Ellie had held him as he cried.

It humbled her he trusted her enough to do that. Allowed her to comfort him in such a time of pain, see his grief. Sullivan cared about all his patients. It absolutely destroyed him when he lost one. Every day she didn't think she could love him more and every day she found she did. She could only hope that love would grow forever.

"So," he said as he grabbed their plates and placed them in the dishwasher. "Charlotte has informed me of what she's going to ask Santa for Christmas this year."

"Christmas? It's not even Halloween yet."

He smiled, shaking his head slightly. "It wouldn't matter if it was the fourth of July. In kid world, any time is a good time to think about what you want for Christmas."

She supposed that was true. After all, she knew what she was going to ask Santa for this year. It involved four little words and was a cheery little tune sung by the late great Eartha Kitt.

"Okay, I'll bite. What does Charlotte want for Christmas?"

She hoped the girl didn't want to take Mimi—the baby elephant, at the zoo—home again. Much as they tried to explain that Mimi would soon be as big as her parents and therefore could not stay in the backyard, Charlotte still wanted her very own personal pet elephant.

"She wants a baby brother."

Ellie had chosen that unfortunate moment to take a sip of her coffee. Light tan liquid spewed out of her mouth as the shock of the request hit her. She coughed, having inhaled some of the caffeinated beverage down the wrong pipe. Sullivan hurried over with a napkin, gently rubbing her back until she could get herself under control again.

"A baby brother?" The words squeaked out, her throat still raw from the coughing.

He chuckled, gazing at her with a smile on his face and love in his eyes. "Yup."

"Considering Christmas is about three months away, that might be a little impossible."

"True, but she had a second present request and I think this one I can give to her. As long as you're willing to help, that is."

Help make Charlotte happy, was that a trick question? She'd do almost anything to see the sweet smile on that little girl's face.

"What?"

Sullivan reaching into his pocket, pulling out a small black box and went down on one knee. Ellie sucked in a sharp breath, eyes immediately filling with tears of joy. Her lungs seized, refusing to work, but she somehow forced oxygen into them. She'd be damned if she passed out and missed one of the greatest moments of her life.

"Eleanor Clark, you saved my daughter and my heart. Before you, I never imagined finding love again. I didn't trust it. I was scared. I failed before and feared I would fail again. I thought all I needed to do in life was make sure my daughter was cared for and happy. But then you came along and opened my eyes. I saw that life wasn't just about taking care of the ones I loved, because if I wasn't taking care of myself, as well, how could I ever properly care for them?"

She placed a hand over her heart, feeling the fast and furious pounding of the muscle ready to burst right out of her chest.

"I didn't have faith in love, but it had faith in me. *You* had faith in me. You gave me everything I needed, even when it hurt you to do so. I can't promise our life will always be perfect, but I can promise you that if you agree to spend yours with me, I will try every day to show you how much I love you. I'll work hard to share every up and down, every success and failure with you, and I hope you'll share yours with me. Charlotte's other Christmas wish was to be a flower girl in Daddy and Mama's wedding."

The precious girl had called Ellie mama a time or two when she had been tucking the girl in at night. Each time had stolen her breath and filled her heart.

Sullivan opened the box to reveal a beautiful silver ring with three stones set in it. Each one representing her, his, and Charlotte's birthstone. "Would you do me the honor of marrying me, completing our little family and hopefully adding more to it in the future?"

Somehow, she managed to speak past the tears, and thrill, and pure, rapturous love clogging her throat to utter, "Yes!"

He slid the ring on her finger, standing and pulling her up into his arms for a toe-curling kiss. When he pulled back, he let out a breath of relief.

She laughed. "Oh, like you were ever worried I'd say no."

He shrugged. "Hey, you could have just been after me for my sweet animal pun T-shirt collection."

She glanced down at today's shirt, which had a large manatee on it in rainbow colors with the words *Oh The Hue-Manatee* printed above it. She gently smacked him on the arm.

"You only have that collection because you keep buying

me shirts and they're two-for-one, so you get yourself one as well."

Sexy, sweet, and he shared her love of puntastic humor? Yeah, he was a keeper.

"Maybe." He nuzzled her nose with his own, a big goofy grin on his face. "I'd buy you the world if I could, Ellie."

"I don't need the world. All I need is you and Charlotte."

"You have us, sweetheart. For as long as you want us."

Forever sounded good to her. Yeah, forever sounded like the best word ever.

The End

ACKNOWLEDGMENTS

I want to thank Ashley for answering all my questions about zoos and zookeepers. Any zoo mistakes in this book are my own. As always, a big thank you to my kids and spouse for supporting me and always being there when I need encouragement. Thank you to P.K. for all the wonderful suggestions on making this book the best it could be. A huge thank you to Eva for pushing me to include more on page OCD compulsions and believing in this book.

When I had the idea of writing a heroine with OCD, I was terrified. Sometimes depictions of compulsions can make my own OCD worse. It was difficult to see those rituals on the page, to know it might trigger others, but I knew it was an important story to tell. Too often, OCD is depicted as a quirky trait or a need for symmetry and cleanliness. Like most things in life, OCD varies from person to person. There are different types of OCD (like harm based, which I shared with Ellie). It's not fun or quirky and not all who live with OCD are neat and clean (just look at my house and you'll see that's not true, lol).

I wrote this book because I was tired of seeing it being used inaccurately. OCD is something many people struggle with, but it doesn't make us broken or quirky. It's simply another aspect of what makes us who we are. Neurodiversity and mental health are important issues that need proper representation in our media. If you'd like more information on OCD or you're struggling with mental health, you can visit: https://www.nami.org/Home

ABOUT THE AUTHOR

Bestselling author Mariah Ankenman lives in the beautiful Rocky Mountains with her two rambunctious children and loving spouse who is her own personal spell checker when her dyslexia gets the best of her. Mariah loves to lose herself in a world of words. Her favorite thing about writing is when she can make someone's day a little brighter with one of her books. To learn more about Mariah and her books, visit her website or follow her on social media, or sign up for her newsletter.

http://mariahankenman.com/

ALSO BY MARIAH ANKENMAN